PENGUIN CLASSICS

TROILUS AND CRISEYDE

ADVISORY EDITOR: BETTY RADICE

GEOFFREY CHAUCER was born in London, the son of a vintner, in about 1342. He is known to have been a page to the Countess of Ulster in 1357, and Edward III valued him highly enough to pay a part of his ransom in 1360, after he had been captured fighting in France.

It was probably in France that Chaucer's interest in poetry was aroused. Certainly he soon began to translate the long allegorical poem of courtly love, the *Roman de la Rose*. His literary experience was further increased by visits to the Italy of Boccaccio on the King's business, and he was well-read in several languages and on many topics, such as astronomy, medicine, physics and alchemy.

Chaucer rose in royal employment, and became a knight of the shire for Kent (1385–6) and a Justice of the Peace. A lapse of favour during the temporary absence of his steady patron, John of Gaunt (to whom he was connected by his marriage), gave him time to begin organizing his unfinished *Canterbury Tales*. Later his fortunes revived, and at his death in 1400 he was buried in Westminster Abbey.

The order of his works is uncertain, but they include *The Book of the Duchess*, *The House of Fame*, *The Parliament of Fowls*, *Troilus and Criseyde* and a translation of Boethius' *De Consolatione Philosophiae*.

·

PROFESSOR NEVILL COGHILL held many appointments at Oxford University, where he was Merton Professor of English Literature from 1957 to 1966, and later became Emeritus Fellow of Exeter and Merton Colleges. He was born in 1899 and educated at Haileybury and Exeter College, Oxford, and served in the Great War after 1917. He wrote several books on English Literature, and had a keen interest in drama, particularly Shakespearean. His translation of Chaucer's *The Canterbury Tales* is also published in Penguin Classics. Professor Coghill, who died in November 1980, will perhaps be best remembered for this famous translation which has become an endearing bestseller.

GEOFFREY CHAUCER

Troilus and Criseyde

TRANSLATED
INTO MODERN ENGLISH
BY NEVILL COGHILL

PENGUIN BOOKS

Penguin Books Ltd, Harmondsworth, Middlesex, England
Viking Penguin Inc., 40 West 23rd Street, New York, New York 10010, U.S.A.
Penguin Books Australia Ltd, Ringwood, Victoria, Australia
Penguin Books Canada Ltd, 2801 John Street, Markham, Ontario, Canada L3R 1B4
Penguin Books (N.Z.) Ltd, 182–190 Wairau Road, Auckland 10, New Zealand

—

This translation first published 1971
Reprinted 1971, 1972, 1974, 1977, 1979, 1980, 1982, 1984, 1985, 1987

—

Copyright © Nevill Coghill, 1971
All rights reserved

—

Made and printed in Great Britain by
Richard Clay Ltd, Bungay, Suffolk
Set in Monotype Plantin

But how although I kan nat tellen al,
As kan myn auctor of his excellence,
Yit have I seyd, and god toforn, and shal,
In every thing the gret of his sentence;
And if that I at loves reverence,
Have any thing in eched for the beste,
Doth therwithal right as youre selven leste.

Troilus and Criseyde, III. 201.

CONTENTS

INTRODUCTION

GEOFFREY CHAUCER

GEOFFREY CHAUCER was in his early forties when he began *Troilus and Criseyde*, and it seems to have taken some four or five years to complete. There are reasons, as will be seen, for dating it between 1382 and 1386 or 7. He wrote it in the spare time of a busy professional life in the King's service, for Geoffrey, by profession, was a courtier. It is his greatest poem; *The Canterbury Tales*, which he wrote later, is unfinished, and so remains a splendid assembly of poems of a widely ranging nature, their unity, in terms of the pilgrimage, suggested rather than achieved. But *Troilus and Criseyde* is complete, and, to the last Amen, in perfect unity with itself. It also has a concentration and a depth never reached in *The Canterbury Tales*. It is, in my opinion, the most beautiful long poem in the English language; but, to test the full truth of that, and for other reasons too, it is best to read it in the original.

In those years he was reaching the first crest of his career in the royal world of the Plantagenets, into whose service, by astonishing good fortune, he had been enlisted as a page many years before; his name first appears in the household accounts of the Countess of Ulster (daughter-in-law to Edward III) in the year 1357. He must then have been in his early teens, for by 1359 he was thought old enough to be sent on active service to France; the Hundred Years War was, like a wounded snake, dragging its slow length along, and it swallowed young Geoffrey for some four months. He was taken prisoner almost at once, and ransomed in March of the following year. King Edward contributed sixteen pounds to redeem him. We must multiply this by at least fifty to get his approximate value at the time, in terms of our own currency.

He was, however, of humble bourgeois origin, a Londoner. His father was a wine-seller in Thames Street, not far from the Tower of London, and had once risen to the position of Deputy

Butler to the King. The Court connexion had somehow been
maintained, and so his son was elevated to the position of a
royal page. Pages in royal households were often themselves
young noblemen; they were given an excellent and useful
education there, especially in manners, languages and horse-
mastership, and they did useful menial jobs like making beds,
and, when they rose to Squire, reading aloud to their betters,
for their entertainment and instruction, especially from martial
chronicles (according to the *Liber Niger* of Edward IV). Chaucer
was, later, to do still better and read them his poetry.

After his brief and inglorious campaign as a soldier, he was
taken on by Edward III as a valet ('*dilectus vallectus noster*'); by
1368 he was an Esquire, one of the thirty-seven in the royal
household, and he began to be sent abroad from time to time
as a kind of King's Messenger, with letters, and later, as an
assistant negotiator in matters of trade and the King's busi-
ness.

At home – or, rather, at Court – he presently met with a
domicella – that is, a young lady – in the service of Queen
Philippa. Her name was Philippa too, Philippa de Roet. By
1366 she had become Philippa Chaucer. Nothing is known of
their courtship or of their married life; if he ever wrote a poem
to her, which is unlikely, it has not come down to us. She lived
long enough to have heard her husband read his *Troilus and
Criseyde* to the Court, for she was still alive in 1387; but that
was the last year in which her pension was paid her; from which
it is safe to infer that she was dead.

Of Chaucer's journeys abroad, those most important to us
were his mission to Genoa and Florence in 1372–3, and to
Lombardy in 1378. Until then he had only made contact with
French culture and poetry, which is everywhere reflected in
his earliest, most dawn-like work as a poet; especially in his
translation of the *Roman de la Rose*, a poem in which *Troilus
and Criseyde* is deeply drenched, though it is not its main source.
In the same French manner is his own first large-scale poem,
The Book of the Duchess, a dream-elegy for the Duchess of
Lancaster, who died in 1369.

But his contact with Italy broke him out of the dreamlands of poetry, and gave him new and increasing power as a writer about the waking world. It put him in touch with the *Divine Comedy* of Dante (1265-1321), with the sonnets (and other work) of Petrarch (1304-74), one of which he took and turned into a love-song for Troilus; but his most exciting discoveries were in the works of Giovanni Boccaccio (1313-75) whose *Teseida* was the source of Chaucer's grandest short story, *The Knight's Tale*, and whose *Il Filostrato*, under Chaucer's hand, became *Troilus and Criseyde*.

As he rose to power in his poetry, so, on a smaller scale, he rose to position as a courtier; his main official work was as a Customs Officer at the Port of London. In 1374 he had been appointed Comptroller of the Customs and Subsidies of Wools, Skins and Tanned Hides; he had to keep the books in his own hand and do his duties in person. In 1382 he was promoted to the office of Comptroller of Petty Customs, and was allowed a deputy. In 1385 he became a Justice of the Peace for Kent and in 1386 he sat as a member of Parliament for that County (one of two) probably nominated as a member of the King's party (Richard II). It was a stormy session and, so far as is known, Chaucer kept his mouth shut. The scene may have come back to him as he was writing of the stormy scene in the Trojan Parliament in the Fourth Book of his poem.

This success story of the steady rise of a young nobody to a position of authority at the elbow of majesty, seems due to three certain, and one probable cause: the luck or cunning by which his parents got him into a royal household at an early age; his native intelligence, diligence and efficiency (which is well attested) in the royal service; and the unfaltering support of John of Gaunt, Duke of Lancaster (whose mistress and, later, third wife was Katherine Swynford, *née* de Roet, and sister of Philippa Chaucer). The Duke was the most powerful and cultivated of the uncles of Richard II, and the father of his deposer, Henry Bolingbroke, later Henry IV. It was to him that Chaucer addressed what is probably his last poem, an ironical complaint to his empty purse. In addition to these reasons for Chaucer's success as a courtier we may probably count his work as a poet. So far as we know, he was never paid for any of it, but the fact that he read much of it aloud to the Court (and often composed it, as is manifest from his occasional asides, for that purpose) must have contributed enormously to his standing there; but it did not prevent him from losing all his jobs between 1386 and 1389, during which John of Gaunt was out of the country, battling in Spain. However, on the Duke's return, Chaucer was restored to even greater office as Clerk of the King's Works.

Notwithstanding his busy public life and his life as a writer, he found time for his life as a reader, and a man of science. He was perhaps the best-read layman of his day and what he read he remembered tenaciously and used in his own poetry. Fluent in French and Latin, he became fluent enough in Italian too. He was also a distinguished amateur mathematician, astronomer and astrologer (astrology counted then as a science) and wrote a learned work on the astrolabe for the instruction of 'lyte Lowys my sone'. He was very well informed in medicine and psychology; psychology was already, then, an abstruse and elaborate quasi-medical subject, much concerned with the nature of dreams and their interpretation; there are two significant (prophetic) dreams in *Troilus and Criseyde*. There is also an important astrological passage, as we shall see.

In philosophy he made his mark by translating *The Consolation of Philosophy* by Boethius (A.D. 470(?)–525), one of the most regarded authorities of the Middle Ages, and he made impressive use of his Boethian understanding of the universe, and of Tragedy, in *Troilus and Criseyde*.

In a stormy age of war, plague, revolution, schism, and regicide, he led a quiet life at the centre of things in London, in the Aldgate, in Greenwich and in Westminster; but he was really a citizen of the world, or at least of Western Christendom, at home in its culture and languages. His last high appointment was to be Clerk of the King's Works (1389–91). This put him in close personal touch with the other towering genius in the arts of his Age, Henry Yevele, who built the naves of Westminster Abbey and Canterbury Cathedral. It is pleasing to think of these two working together in their old age, quietude and fame, chief among the builders of our first civilization. They died in the same year, 1400.

John H. Harvey, Yevele's biographer, rightly says of him: 'He did for our architecture what Chaucer did for our language, giving to it a special character which was altogether national, even though it was a part of a common European heritage.'

TROILUS AND CRISEYDE: THE DATE (1382–6 OR 7)

Two intriguing passages have helped to fix the date of our poem; the first was noted in a flash of insight by the late J. L. Lowes, who drew attention to a passage in the early part of the work:

> Among thise othere folk was Criseyda
> In widewes habit blak, but natheles,
> Right as oure firste lettre is now an A,
> In beaute first so stood she makeles.

(I. 169–72)

Criseyde, the passage says, stood first in beauty just as, nowadays, A is the first letter of our alphabet. We all know that A is the first letter of the alphabet, but Lowes reminded us that A was also the first letter of Anne – Queen Anne of Bohemia, beloved wife of Richard II. They had married in 1382; they were both rising sixteen and of great personal beauty. It was a charming, ephemeral compliment to her; but it has survived to show that the poem cannot have been written before 1382.

The second passage, much later in the poem, runs:

> The bente moone with hire hornes pale,
> Saturne, and Jove in Cancro joyned were,
> That swych a reyn from hevene gan avale,
> That every maner womman that was there
> Hadde of that smoky reyn a verray feere.

(III. 624–8)

This is the astrological passage I have already referred to. This conjunction of the new moon with Saturn and Jupiter in the sign of Cancer, as R. K. Root and H. N. Russell have pointed out, is of great rarity, astronomically speaking. Its last occurrence before the birth of Chaucer was in the year A.D. 769. But it occurred again in the Spring of 1385. It was noted as a portent in contemporary chronicles; Chaucer, as an astronomer and astrologer, could not but have been very well aware of it. We may certainly infer that he was still at work on the poem when he wrote of it; it must have been in 1385 or 6, for his next poem, *The Legend of Good Women*, which cannot be later than 1386 or at latest 1387, mentions *Troilus and Criseyde* as one of his completed works – one indeed for which he ought to be ashamed of himself (says the *Legend*) for having dared to suggest in it that a woman could be false in love; here we must again suspect a glance at Queen Anne, who is said to have imposed the writing of the *Legend* on him, as a penance for this heresy. From all this we may date *Troilus and Criseyde* with some certainty (1382–6 or 7).

THE SOURCES OF TROILUS AND CRISEYDE

The Troy story was a part of our national myth in the Middle Ages; it derived from Geoffrey of Monmouth (1100(?)–54), who declared on what he believed to be good authority that our island, originally called Albion and inhabited by giants, was invaded by Felix Brutus, a Trojan Prince, and great-grandson to Aeneas (Virgil's hero), in the year 1116 B.C. Brutus landed at Totnes, defeated the giants and renamed the country after himself. In Chaucer's day this was so flourishing a tradition that there was a movement during his lifetime to rename London Troynovant – New Troy. All that concerned Troy and the Trojans was therefore of patriotic and poetic interest to us.

Homer, being Greek, was not known to Chaucer except by name; so far as Chaucer was concerned, the matter of Troy had descended (more or less directly) from two somewhat fabulous writers, Dares the Phrygian and Dictys the Cretan, supposed eye-witnesses of the Trojan War. What purported to be their accounts of it had survived in Latin prose translations of the fourth and sixth centuries A.D., respectively.

In the second half of the twelfth century, a vigorous but long-winded French poet, Benoît de St Maure, basing himself partly on Dares and Dictys, composed his tremendous *Roman de Troye*, 24,500 lines long, in which the seed of the story of Criseyde's faithlessness lies; he called her Briseida. In the thirteenth century this French poem was taken up by Guido delle Colonne, a Sicilian judge, who translated it in turn under the title *Historia Trojana*, and it was this work that led Boccaccio to his own poem; he fastened upon the episode of Briseida and elaborated it into a kind of novel-poem, which he named *Il Filostrato*, a title which it is supposed he intended to mean *The Man Struck down by Love*.

The affirmed purpose of this work was to show, through the sufferings of his Troilo, the sufferings he himself was undergoing at the hands of his own mistress, Maria d'Aquino, Fiametta, the Little Flame. This was the story Chaucer set himself to translate, helping out his knowledge of Italian with his knowledge of French, by using a translation of Boccaccio's poem, probably made by Beauveau, Seneschal of Anjou. Professor Pratt (*Studies in Philology*, Vol LIII, pp. 509 ff.) has shown that Chaucer had Boccaccio and Beauveau texts to work from, sometimes following them line for line and word for word (often choosing Beauveau's word rather than Boccaccio's) and sometimes soaring off into pure creations of his own, so entirely fresh as to change the whole tone and purpose of the poem.

The most beguiling, and, at first sight, the most apparent change is in Chaucer's handling of the character of Pandarus. In place of Boccaccio's fashionable young man, cousin of Criseyde, and in no sense a striking personality, he offers us her worldly-wise and witty uncle, of unstated age, a man of fond affections, not only for her and for an imaginary lady-love of his own, to whom he constantly refers as a sort of stock joke against himself, but who never appears in the poem in person, but also, and perhaps even more so, for Troilus, to whose love-affair he dedicates his whole imagination and effort. He is full of stratagems, proverbs, jokes and fibs, a character memorable in the ways in which a Shakespeare or a Dickens character is memorable. He is the first great study in idiosyncrasy and personality in modern English literature.

A still more important change is borne in upon the reader as he becomes aware of Chaucer's own presence in the poem. He does not appear as Boccaccio does, identified with Troilo and his anguish; he makes no personal application of the story to himself; on the contrary, he continually disclaims all knowledge of the experience of love; he is to be the spokesman of lovers, the servant of the servants of love, knowing nothing of it himself, but having, or seeming to claim, a particular vocation for expressing their blisses and their griefs.

By this ironic declaration Chaucer achieves a grave but smiling personal detachment from his story, identified with none of his characters, yet retaining a total sympathy in his understanding of them all, and, at the end, enabling him to beg our compassion for his heroine, because she was so unhappy for her betrayal of Troilus. He does not seem to sit in judgement over them, yet is perfectly and fascinatedly aware of their self-contradictions, self-deceptions, absurdities and attitudinizings, just as he is tenderly aware of their charm, beauty and idealisms, their romantic feelings, their eloquence, their moments of melodrama, the poetical plane of their adventures; through it all there bubbles his feeling for comedy. All this became possible for Chaucer by his exchanging personal detachment for the personal involvement of Boccaccio. With utmost modesty, not daring to be of their element, he watches the servants of Venus as they rise and fall on the wheel of Fortune.

THE WHEEL OF FORTUNE

Essentially in this poem, Chaucer is meditating the nature of Love, and mainly human love, as it enraptures and afflicts us in this sublunary world, which is under the government of Fortune. Fortune, good and bad, is common to all; each may be bound in his turn to her great wheel; as she turns it, he rises; he reaches the top; Fortune turns on; he begins to fall, he is cast off the wheel and falls to a miserable end; the following hexameter shows the pattern for her victims:

Regnabo; regno; regnavi; sum sine regno.

[I shall rule; I rule; I have ruled; I am without kingdom.]

A world governed according to this ticklish pattern is a brittle place for a world-without-end affection. For if, in the name of human love, an attempt for such an affection is adventured, it can, by a stroke of *mis*fortune lead to utter loss, as the world counts loss. A lover may lose his lady, as a king his kingdom; both may end wretchedly, and this wretchedness (says Boethius) is the work of Fortune, and is the true subject of tragedy:

> What other thyng bywaylen the cryinges of tragedyes
> but oonly the deedes of Fortune, that with unwar strook
> overturneth the realmes of greet nobleye?
>
> (Boethius, Book II, Prose ii)

Chaucer was so much impressed by this passage as he translated it that he added a footnote of his own:

> Tragedye is to seyn a dite of prosperite for a tyme
> that endith in wretchidnesse.

It was the first time the word Tragedy had ever been used in English. He fastened upon it to describe the poem he was at work on:

> Go, litel bok, go litel myn tragedye

In a world that knew neither Aeschylus, Sophocles, Euripides, nor Shakespeare, his claim could stand; his poem was tragic in form and substance, by Boethian definition, though not by the Aristotelian; for though it stirs pity, there is no terror in it. The *Poetics* of Aristotle, however, had not then been rediscovered, and the demand that Tragedy should terrify was unknown.

Still, at the heart of *Troilus and Criseyde* there lies the seed of tragic terror, in the notion of *fatality*; Fortune, in Chaucer's poem, is more than a personification of chance. She is 'executrice of wyerdes' (III, 617), the Power that puts into action the dooms of the Almighty; she is equivalent with the Fates or Parcae, who seem to take over from her in the last Book, that opens so majestically with:

> Approchen gan the fatal destyne
> The Joves hath in disposicioun,
> And to yow, angry Parcas, sustren thre,
> Committeth to don execucioun

These glimpses of a supernatural hierarchy ordering the lives of men and women must cast doubt on the existence of human

Free Will, which seems to be manifestly in conflict with Pre-destination. That this conflict intrigued Chaucer can be seen by his handling of it, in a comic vein, in *The Nun's Priest's Tale*; here, in our poem, it appears in full formality in Troilus' temple-soliloquy (IV, 953–1082), where he concludes

> Thus to be lorn, it is my destinee
>
> (IV, 959)

The argument uttered by Troilus is taken straight from the Fifth Book of Boethius, and he stops short at the point I have quoted, convinced that he has no Free Will and lives in a deter-minist world. This, of course, is not Boethius' opinion. Boethius takes the argument further, and would persuade us, if he could – persuaded himself at any rate – that the contradiction between Free Will and Predestination is resolved if we take the problem out of Time and contemplate it in Eternity, where God sees Past, Present and Future in one timeless, eternal act of aware-ness. But we are not shown Troilus nearing eternity until the very end of the poem, when he is taken up into it. A new per-spective then begins to dawn on him.

THE NATURE OF LOVE

Even Pandarus knew that human love was of two kinds – sacred and profane:

> 'Was nevere man nor womman yit bigete
> That was unapt to suffren loves hete
> Celestial, or elles love of kynde.'
>
> (I, 977–9)

[Never was man or woman yet begotten unapt to suffer the heat of celestial love, or else of natural love]: the contrast intended is that between a supernatural and a natural human love.

In an age when a normal alternative to matrimony was a monastery or a convent, this was a truism. Until the last mo-ments of the poem, *Troilus and Criseyde* is a poetical study of natural human love, fully romantic, fully sexual; but in the last moments, in what is called 'the palinode' this sexual human love is suddenly placed in the context of a higher love, the love of God. With this goes the rejection of the gods of the Ancients.

Human love is subject to fashion, as Chaucer was well

aware; its fashions changed just as language itself changed over a
period of a thousand years:

> Ye knowe ek, that in forme of speche is chaunge
> Withinne a thousand yeer, and wordes tho
> That hadden pris, now wonder nyce and straunge
> Us thinketh hem, and yit thei spake hem so,
> And spedde as wel in love as men now do;
> Ek for to wynnen love in sondry ages,
> In sondry londes, sondry ben usages.
>
> (II, 22–8)

Aware as he was, Chaucer nevertheless boldly attributed the
fashions in love current in fourteenth-century Christendom, to
his Trojan lovers, just as he pictured his fighting men as Knights
in coat-armour. He often also slips into the way of making his
characters speak of God as though they were Christians, with
souls to save and salvation to swear by. It gives a great four-
teenth-century naturalness to the dialogue of the poem; at the
same time they talk Christian only, as it were, in accidental
conversation; their formal religion is most carefully classical, and
is everywhere interwoven with their behaviour; for instance the
first thing Troilus does when he finds himself at last in
Criseyde's bed, with her in his arms, is to utter a rapturous and
beautiful prayer of gratitude to Venus, Cupid and Hymen.

The great advantage of the classical setting to his story was
that Christian ethics in sex did not apply; the only ethic that
applied was that of what is often called the code of 'Courtly
Love'. Another lucky feature of the story, from Chaucer's point
of view, was that Criseyde was a widow; this meant that the
story was not complicated by a husband, or by a reader's misgiv-
ings about adultery; also that it was not complicated by virginity
in her. Virginity had a mystical value in the fourteenth century
that would have made the seduction, or even the free self-gift
of Criseyde, a complication that must have clouded his central
theme, the free love of a man and woman outside mat-
rimony. The lovers retain and live by such religion as they
know, or could be supposed to know, in Pagan times; so there is
no offence here; they lived and loved according to their lights,
at least until Criseyde proved false; and this she did when

Fortune forced her out of Troy. Until then her love had been pure and constant some three years. But Fortune took her out of that security and put a demand upon her character which it could not meet. We are told '*she was the ferfulleste wight that myghte be*' (II, 450–51); she was frightened. She took another protector. She was false. She had not the strength which the code demanded of her. She was a part of the brittleness of this false world:

> Swych fyn hath false worldes brotelnesse!
>
> (V, 1832)

in which free human love cannot be safeguarded, whatever the conventions. Human love by itself is not strong enough.

The code by which we are invited to understand and judge this love, commonly called 'Courtly Love' has been much discussed, especially since the publication, in 1936, of the late C. S. Lewis's masterly book *The Allegory of Love*. This book sheds a flood of understanding on *Troilus and Criseyde*, as well as on many other works of medieval poetry and thought in this field; it has been followed by many further studies and the subject is so delicate, complex and extensive that it would be an impertinence to attempt even a brief summary of what has been thought about it in this introduction. I shall therefore confine myself to a few of the underlying notions of the code or cult, particularly those which are manifested in *Troilus and Criseyde*.

First must come the principle that in this way of love the lover is in total and voluntary submission to the lady he has chosen to serve, by an irrevocable choice. He is a worshipper, and he worships her with his body and soul; to worship is to do honour. What he demands of her is the privilege of being received into her grace, to be accepted as the man who has the unique privilege of serving her. That is all the return he dares demand. If he should fail her in any way (and she is the judge of failure) she may punish him, even to death. He must at all times and in all places obey her lightest word, or whim.

Next to service, *fidelity*. But this was binding both on lover and beloved, once the lover had been accepted. Suspicion of unfaithfulness was liable to provoke mad jealousy, but jealousy was often held to be a proof of love.

Next to fidelity, *secrecy*. Because in 'courtly love' an illicit or even adulterous relationship was so often envisaged, the need for secrecy was paramount; but apart from the more practical aspect of this need for secrecy, in that it was a protection against the risk of a husband's discovery, it was also a protection against gossip – 'wicked tongues'. To be talked about was shameful; no one must ever suspect that your mistress is your mistress; it must never get about. For the same reason, boasting of one's conquests, real or imaginary, is absolutely forbidden. Liar and braggart are one, for inasmuch as a lover brags of his success with a lady, he gives away a secret he has sworn to preserve.

Worship, service, fidelity, secrecy; these add up to a general ideal of personal integrity in love, called 'truth'. Shakespeare's Troilus has it, like Chaucer's before him; he is an absolute pattern of lover's truth:

> I am as true as truth's simplicity
> And simpler than the infancy of truth.

Truth may be called the lover's general virtue in the way that 'honour' is the lady's. To guard his lady's honour is the first duty of a 'servant'. Her honour is not an easy thing to define; she loses no honour in yielding herself bodily and spiritually to an accepted lover, provided it is kept secret; her honour is not the same as her chastity; but if the secret is let loose and she is talked about, that is loss of honour. But unfaithfulness in her is loss of honour too, and Criseyde is unfaithful; in the end she breaks her word to Troilus and gives her body to Diomede; Chaucer refuses to say she gave him her heart as well, for that would be a total, a virtually inexcusable loss of honour in her; but others say she did, he sadly tells us.

Although the lover, whatever his service, cannot demand anything as of right from his lady, some yielding of sexual favour may be expected of her; Criseyde kisses Troilus after she has accepted his first declaration; but it took Pandarus to get them into bed. When at last Troilus calls upon her, as she lies in his arms, to yield, she answers that had she not yielded long before she would not now be where she was.

The ground on which the code claimed to be morally defensible was that love created virtue in the lover. It made him brave, generous, dependable, courteous, friendly, noble and chaste. No other woman might he touch; as for nobility, only noble natures are capable of love or friendship. Love ennobles them, if they have the capacity for it. A man may be noble in this sense, even if he is a peasant, a villein. A nobleman, not noble in this sense, is spiritually his inferior. To be 'villein' is in any way to be dishonourable, boorish, mean, insensitive, bloody-minded, animal. Troilus, of course, is never less than princely in his behaviour, but we are told how startlingly he increased in virtue as soon as he began to have hopes of Criseyde:

> For he bicome the frendlieste wight,
> The gentileste, and ek the moste fre,
> The thriftieste, and oon the beste knyght
> That in his tyme was, or myghte be.

$$(I, 1079-82)$$

One exception was allowed to the rule of secrecy. A lover might reveal his love to a trusted friend who could be of service by passing their messages between them and arranging assignations; also, by talking to his friend about his lady, a lover increased his passion for her. This was a role for Pandarus.

There is one element in Chaucer's vision of romantic or courtly love that I have not found elsewhere in poems or treatises of the time, such as the romances of Chrestien de Troyes (c. 1175), the *Libri Tres De Amore* of Andreas Capellanus (c. 1185), in the *Roman de la Rose* (c. 1240–80) or elsewhere, and that is Chaucer's full awareness that a romantic hero is often ridiculous, especially at his most romantic; but he is not in the least the less sympathetic for being so. Infatuation is simply funny, because it takes itself so seriously; but it is very endearing; for instance when Chaucer gravely records how Troilus, having heard the shrieking of the owl 'Escaphilo', prepares for his own death and burial with tragic solemnity. In that he is like the Duke in *Zuleika Dobson*. It is remarkable too how often Chaucer refers to his hero as 'this Troilus', as though he were an exhibition piece; I have not dared in this translation to use this phrase as often as he does, for I think it is more noticeable now than it would have been to Chaucer's audiences. But Chaucer is making what I think is a modern point, in seeing the ridiculous *included* in the sublime. But the comedy is kindly, and like so many of Chaucer's ironical observations, is offered *au grand serieux*.

THE PALINODE

I consider the Palinode to be among the nearer approaches to sublimity in the secular literature of our language. If, as I fear, this is not apparent from the version here offered, I beg the reader, for his joy, to turn to the original, using my version (if he needs one) for a crib; it is close enough to the literal meaning for that.

The palinode occupies the last twelve stanzas of the poem, beginning (I would think) with Chaucer's formal Envoy; it is wonderfully surprising, yet inevitable. We are allowed to follow Troilus, after his 'tragedye' is over, out of this world, and to look down with his new awareness at those who are so busily weeping his death; Troilus laughs within himself to see them doing so, and condemns all that we do on earth in following blind desire, which cannot last; in which there is no 'full felicity'. Human love is thus suddenly lifted into the context of divine love, taken out of Vanity Fair; and the poet in his most splendid stanzas calls us home to the love of God, in a prayer with which the poem ends:

> O yonge fresshe folkes, he or she,
> In which that love up groweth with your age,
> Repeyreth hom fro worldly vanyte,
> And of youre herte up casteth the visage
> To thilke rod that after his ymage
> Yow made, and thynketh al nys but a faire
> This world, that passeth soone as floures faire.

> And loveth hym which that right for love
> Upon a cros, oure soules for to beye,
> First starf, and roos, and sit in hevene above
> For he nyl falsen no wight, dar I seye,
> That wol his herte al holly on hym leye.
> And syn he best to love is, and most meke,
> What nedeth feyned loves for to seke?

Thow Oone, and Two, and Thre, eterne on lyve,
That regnest ay in Thre, and Two, and Oon,
Uncircumscript, and al maist circumscrive,
Us from visible and invisible foon
Defende: and to thy mercy everichon,
So make us, Jesus, for thi mercy digne,
For love of mayde and moder thyn benigne!

Every reader will make what he can of this *volte-face* that is of
such astonishing poetic force and simplicity; for myself I cannot
see that Chaucer in any way un-says what he has so long and
understandingly been recounting – the feverish desires, the
tendernesses, the anguish, the ecstasy, the pledges, the false
hopes, the racks of doubt, the risks of Fortune – every human
experience of the affections from despair to bliss and back again
to despair, that arise in the story he has told us. They are all part
of the overwhelming experience of human love, and have their
own beauty, virtues and weaknesses, and suffer from their
tragic impermanence. Such is 'the love of kind'; but it has, as it
were, an elder sister in celestial love, compared with which
human love is a feigning; that is '*eterne on lyve*', and will '*falsen
no wight*'. Many will say this is no resolution of the paradox,
just to be advised to relinquish the vanities of the world, to
reach for the substance, not the shadow. But Chaucer seems to
say that these are his conclusions, and I do not see that he says
more; the love of Troilus is never condemned outright, never
condemned by him as *sin*; but as sorrow, the *double sorwe* of
which the poem set out to tell us. We live in an insecure and
sorrowful world.

ACKNOWLEDGEMENTS

I owe much help from many friends who have kindly and carefully read my versions through at one time and another, and offered criticisms which I have often profited by; in particular I am grateful to Mr Christopher Scaife and Mr Francis Warner, both poets themselves, who have given me many helpful suggestions. I would also like to record my gratitude to the late Stephen Potter, who directed the first version I made of the poem in 1948, on the Third Programme, and to Mr Raymond Raikes, who directed my second version, on the Third Programme, in 1969; their help, advice and interpretation were most stimulating. The present version here published is a blend of the 1948 and the 1969 versions.

Book I

1

Before we part my purpose is to tell
Of Troilus, son of the King of Troy,
And how his love-adventure rose and fell
From grief to joy, and, after, out of joy,
In double sorrow; help me to employ
My pen, Tisiphone[1], and to endite
These woeful lines, that weep even as I write.

2

To thee I call, whose joy is to torment,
O cruel Fury, in thy drear domain!
Help me, that am the sorrowful instrument
Of help to lovers, for I sing their pain
As best I can; and it is true and plain
That a sad fellow suits a sorry mate,
And sorrowing looks a tale of sorrowful fate.

3

Serving the servants of the god of love,
Not daring love in my ungainliness,
Though I should die for it I look above,
And pray, far off in darkness, for success;
But if this bring delight or ease distress
For any lover that may read this story,
Mine be the labour and be love's the glory!

4

But all you lovers bathing in delight,
If any drop of pity in you be,
Remember the despair of some past night
You have endured, and the adversity
Of other folk; you too have bitterly
Complained when love has ventured to displease
You – or you won him with too great an ease.

5

And pray for those who now are in the case
Of Troilus, which you shall later hear,
That love may bring them to his heaven of grace;
And also pray for me to God so dear
That I may show, or at the least come near
To show the pain of lovers suffering thus,
In the unhappy tale of Troilus.

6

And also pray for those that have despaired
In love and look for no recovery;
Also for those maliciously ensnared
By wicked tell-tales, whether he or she;
Pray thus to God in His benignity
To grant them soon their passing from earth's face
That have despaired of love and of his grace,

7

Pray also for all those that are at ease,
That God may grant them long continuance
And perseverance in the will to please
Their ladies, for love's honour and romance;
And I will pray, the better to advance
My soul, for all love's servants that may be,
And write their woes and live in charity,

8

And have a true compassion for their pain,
As though I were their brother, close and dear;
Now listen to me in a friendly vein.
For I shall go straight on, as shall appear,
To my main matter now, and you shall hear
The double sorrow of Troilus and Criseyde,
And how that she forsook him ere she died.

★ ★ ★

9

It is well known the Greeks in all their strength
Of arms, and with a thousand ships, set out
For Troy and they besieged it at great length
– Ten years it was before they turned about –
With one design (by many means, no doubt)
To take revenge upon the ravishment
Of Helen by Paris; that was why they went.

10

Now it fell out that living in Troy town
There was a lord of great authority,
Calkas by name, a priest of high renown
And learned in the art of prophecy;
He, by the answer of his deity,
Phoebus Apollo, whom they also call
Apollo Delphicus, knew Troy must fall.

11

And so when Calkas knew by calculation,
And by the answer this Apollo made,
The Greeks would mount so great a preparation
That Troy must burn and be in ruin laid,
He sought to flee the city, to evade
The doom he knew she was to undergo,
To be destroyed whether she would or no.

12

And so this wise, foreknowledgeable man
Took purpose quietly to slip away,
And, to the Greek host, following his plan,
He stole in secret from the town, and they
Received him courteously, with great display
Of reverence; they trusted to the skill
Of his advice to ward off every ill.

13

When this was known, noise of it far and wide
Spread through the town and it was freely spoken
'Calkas has fled, the traitor, and allied
With those of Greece!' Their vengeance was awoken
Against a faith so treacherously broken.
'He and his family and all he owns
Ought to be burnt,' they shouted, 'skin and bones!'

14

Calkas had left behind, in these mischances,
One who knew nothing of his wicked deed,
A daughter, whose unhappy circumstances
Put her in terror for her life indeed,
Not knowing where to go or whom to heed,
For she was both a widow and alone,
Without a friend to whom she might make moan.

15

Criseyde this lady's name; and, as for me,
If I may judge of her, in all that place
There was not one so beautiful as she,
So like an angel in her native grace;
She seemed a thing immortal, out of space,
As if a heavenly, perfected creature
Had been sent down to earth, in scorn of nature.

16

This lady, having daily at her ear
Her father's shame and treason to the town,
Out of her mind, almost, with grief and fear,
Dressed in her widow's weeds of silken brown,
Sought Hector out and on her knees went down,
Tenderly weeping, and in piteous fashion
Excused herself and begged for his compassion.

[6]

17

This Hector was by nature full of pity
And saw she was in misery and dread,
One of the fairest, too, in all the city;
So, in his kindness cheering her, he said
'Your father's treason – put it from your head!
A curse upon it! You yourself in joy
Shall stay among us while you please, in Troy.

18

'All shall be done to honour and respect you,
As much as if you had your father here;
I'll see that there are people to protect you,
And I shall try to keep an open ear.'
She gave him humble thanks and, drawing near,
Began her thanks again, but he prevented her;
Then she went quietly home, he had contented her.

19

So in her house, with such in her employ
As it concerned her honour to uphold,
She stayed, and, long as she remained in Troy,
Held her high rank, was loved by young and old,
And was well spoken of; I am not told
Whether she had children; if she had or no
My author does not say. I let it go.

20

And things fell out, as often in a war,
With varying chance for Trojan and for Greek;
At times the men of Troy paid dearly for
Their city, but at others nothing weak
Their enemies found them; upwards to the peak
Then down and under Fortune whirled them fast
Upon her wheel, until their anger passed.

21

I don't want to digress not in control oh & on

But how this city came to its destruction
Is not my present purpose to relate,
For it would make too long an introduction
So to digress, and you would have to wait;
But, of the Trojan war and Trojan fate,
All those who can may study the vagaries
In Homer and in Dictys and in Dares.[2]

22

Though shut within their city by the might
Of the Greek host, which was encamped about,
The men of Troy gave up no ancient rite
Due to their gods; they were indeed devout,
And their most sacred relic, beyond doubt,
Highest in honour, was named, as I recall,
Palladion[3], which they trusted above all.

23

And so it happened when there came the time
Of April, when the meadows all are spread
In newest green, when Spring is at its prime
And sweetly smell the flowers, white and red,
In various ways the Trojans, it is said,
Did their observance, as they long had done,
To grace the feast of this Palladion.

24

And to the temple in their Sunday-best
They crowded generally, to hear the rite
Of their Palladion, and with the rest
There came, more prominently, many a knight
And many a lady fresh and maiden bright,
In fine array, the greatest and the least,
In honour of the season and the feast.

25

And among these, in widow's black, and yet
Unequalled in her beauty, came Criseyde;
Just as an A now heads our alphabet[4],
She stood unmatchable; she glorified
And gladdened all that crowded at her side;
Never was seen one to be praised so far,
Nor in so black a cloud, so bright a star

26

As was Criseyde; so all were glad to own
That saw her there, gowned in her widow's grace;
And yet she stood there, humble and alone
Behind the others in a little space
Close to the door, for modesty; her face
Was cheerful, and the dress that she was wearing
Simple; there was composure in her bearing.

27

This Troilus, whose custom was to guide
His younger knights, now led them up and down
Through the great temple, and from side to side;
He studied all the ladies in the town,
Bestowing here a smile and there a frown,
Servant to none – none troubled his repose,
And so he praised or slighted whom he chose.

28

And as he walked he was for ever glancing
To note if any squire of his or knight
Began to sigh, or let his eye go dancing
Towards some woman who had come in sight;
Then he would say 'God knows, it serves you right!
Softly she lies asleep for love of you,
Who turn in restless pain the whole night through!

29

'I've heard, God knows, of how you lovers live,
Your mad observances and superstitions,
The pains you take, the services you give
To win your love; when won, what dread suspicions!
And when your prey is lost, what exhibitions
Of woe, fools that you are – and blind, dear brothers!
Not one of you takes warning from the others.'

30

And with that word he puckered up his look,
As if to say 'Was that not wisely spoken?'
At which the god of love arose and shook
His angry head, revenge in him awoken,
And showed at once his bow was yet unbroken;
He smote him suddenly and with a will;
And he can pluck as proud a peacock still.

31

O blind-eyed world! O blindness of intention!
How often counter to the boasts we air
Fall the effects of arrogant invention!
Caught is the proud, and caught the debonair.
This Troilus has climbed a slippery stair
And little thinks he must come down again;
The expectations of a fool are vain.

32

As when proud Dobbin[5] starts to shy and skip
Across the road, pricked on by too much corn,
Until he feels the lash of the long whip,
And then he thinks 'Although I may be born
To lead the team, all fat and newly shorn,
Yet I am but a horse, and horse's law
I must endure as others do, and draw.'

33

So was it with this proud and fiery knight,
Son of a famous king though he might be;
He had supposed that nothing had the might
To steer his heart against a will as free
As his; yet, at a look, immediately,
He was on fire, and he, in pride above
All others, suddenly was slave to love.

34

And therefore take example, from this man,
You wise ones, proud ones, worthy ones and all;
Never scorn love, for love so quickly can
Put all the freedom of your heart in thrall;
It has been ever thus and ever shall,
For love can lay his bonds on every creature,
And no one can undo the law of Nature[6].

35

Now this has long proved true, and proves so still.
It is a thing that everybody knows;
None, we are told, has greater wit or skill
Than they whom love most powerfully throws;
The strongest men are overcome, and those
Most notable and highest in degree;
This was and is and yet again shall be.

36

And truly it is well it should be so;
In love the very wisest have delighted,
And they that most of all have felt its woe
Most have been comforted and most requited;
It softens hearts by cruelty excited,
And to the noble gives a nobler name,
And most it teaches fear of vice and shame.

37

Now since it is not easily withstood
And is a thing of virtue, in its kind,
Forbid love not to bind you as he would,
Since, as he pleases, he has power to bind.
The twig that bends is better, to my mind,
Than that which breaks; and so I would advise
You let love lead you, who is proved so wise.

38

But to proceed with what I have to say,
And more especially of this king's son,
Leaving collateral matters by the way,
It is of him I mean to speak or none,
Both in his joy, and his cold cares begun,
And all he did, as touching this affair;
Having begun, let me return to where

39

This Troilus and his knights were gallivanting
About the temple, quizzing and pointing out
This or that lady, all the while descanting
On where she lived, within town or without,
And it so fell that, looking through the rout,
His eye pierced deeply and at last it struck
Criseyde where she was standing, and there stuck.

40

And suddenly he felt himself astounded,
Gazing more keenly at her in surprise,
'Merciful god! O where' he said, confounded,
'Have you been hiding, lovely to my eyes?'
He felt his heart begin to spread and rise,
And he sighed softly, lest his friends should hear,
And he recaptured his accustomed sneer.

41

Now she was not among the least in stature,
But all her limbs so answerable were
To womanhood, there never was a creature
Less mannish in appearance standing there;
And when she moved, she did so with an air
Of ease and purity, so one could guess
Honour and rank in her, and nobleness.

42

To him her look and movements, all in all,
Were wonderfully pleasing, with her clear
Semblance of light disdain, when she let fall
A sidelong glance, as one who might appear
To put the question 'What! May I not stand here?'
And then her face unclouded and shone bright;
Never had he seen so beautiful a sight.

43

And as he looked at her his pulses thickened;
Such passion, such desire, began to race
That at the bottom of his heart there quickened
The deeply printed image of her face;
His insolent staring now had given place
To drawing in his horns, and gladly too!
Whether to look or not he hardly knew.

44

He who had thought his cleverness so telling
And lovers' anguish something to despise,
Was now aware that love had made his dwelling
Within the subtle currents of her eyes;
Now, suddenly, at a mere look, there dies
The spirit in his heart, all is laid low;
Blessed be love that can convert us so!

45

She in her black, so deeply to his liking,
Above all else he lingered to behold;
But why he stayed and what desire was striking
Upon his sense he neither showed nor told,
And, to maintain his manner as of old,
He looked at other things, or so pretended,
Then back at her, until the service ended.

46

And after that, not wholly in confusion,
Out of the temple casually he pressed,
Repenting every cynical allusion
That he had made to love, for fear the jest
Might turn against himself; he did his best
To hide his misery, lest the world should know it,
Dissimulating, so as not to show it.

47

When from the temple he had thus departed,
Back to his palace instantly he turned;
While through and through her image shot and darted
Within him; trying not to seem concerned,
He burnished up his looks, and gaily spurned
At all love's servants in his speech the while,
To cover up his feelings with a smile;

48

'Lord! What a happy life,' he said, 'how blest,
A lover leads! The cleverest of you, now,
Who serves love most attentively and best,
Comes to more harm than honour, you'll allow;
Your service is requited god knows how,
Not love for love, but scorn for service true;
There's a fine rule to bind an Order[7] to!

49

'All your observances are quite unsure
Of their result, save in a point or so;
No other Order claims so great, so pure
A servitude as yours, and that you know;
But you have worse than that to undergo.
Were I to tell you, though it made good sense,
What the worst is, you all would take offence.

50

'Yet notice this: what you refrain from doing,
Or indeed do, but with the best intention,
Your lady will be ever misconstruing,
Deem it an injury and start dissension;
If, for some reason of her own invention,
She's angry, you will get a scolding too;
Dear Lord! How lucky to be one of you!'

51

For all this, when he judged it time, he duly
Fell into silence; what was there to gain?
For love had limed his feathers, and so truly,
He scarce had strength enough in him to feign
That he had work to do, and would detain
His followers no longer; sunk in woe,
And at an utter loss he bid them go.

52

When he was in his chamber and alone,
At his bed's foot he sank in indecision;
At first he sighed, and then began to groan,
Till, thinking of her thus without remission
As there he sat, he had a waking vision;
His spirit dreamed he saw her, as before,
There in the temple, and he gazed once more.

53

And thus he made a mirror of his mind
In which he saw her image all entire,
And was well able in his heart to find
That it was high adventure to desire
One such as her; and if he did not tire
In serving her, he well might win to grace
Or be accepted in a servant's place.

54

In his imagination neither pain
Nor toil in service ever could be thrown
Away on one so beautiful; again
His passion was no shame, though it were known;
Rather, an honour, as lovers all would own,
Greater than all before; he argued so
In utter ignorance of his coming woe.

55

He settled then to learn the craft of lover,
And thought to work at it in secrecy;
First he must keep his passion under cover
From every living creature, utterly,
Unless there was some hope of remedy,
Remembering that a love too widely blown
About yields bitter fruit, though sweetly sown.

56

On, on he thought, and, over and above
All this, what he should speak and what keep in,
What he could do to kindle her to love,
And with a song decided to begin
At once, and so he sang aloud to win
Himself from grief, and gave his full assent
To love Criseyde and never to repent.

57

And not the gist alone of what was sung
By him, as says my author, Lollius [8] –
But also – bar the difference of tongue –
The very phrases used by Troilus
I shall repeat; they went exactly thus;
He who would hear them as the text rehearses
Will find them all set down in the next verses.

58

The Song of Troilus [9]

'If there's no love, O God! What am I feeling?
If there is love, who then, and what, is he?
If love be good, whence comes this sorrow stealing?
If evil, what a wonder it is to me
When every torment and adversity
That comes of him is savoury, to my thinking!
The more I thirst, the more I would be drinking.

59

And if so be I burn at my own pleasure,
Whence comes my wailing, whence my sad complaint?
Why do I weep, if suffering be my treasure?
I know not. Nothing weary, yet I faint!
O quickening death, sweet harm that leaves no taint,
How do I find thee measurelessly filling
My heart, unless it be that I am willing?

60

And yet, if I am willing, wrongfully
I make complaint! Buffeted to and fro,
I am a rudderless vessel in mid-sea,
Between the double-winded storms that blow
From ever-contrary shores; alas, for woe!
What is this wondrous malady that fills me
With fire of ice and ice of fire, and kills me?'

[17]

61

And after that 'O god of love,' said he
In piteous tones, 'dear lord, my spirit is
For ever yours, as yours it ought to be;
I thank you, lord, that I am brought to this.
If she be woman or goddess out of bliss
That you have made me serve, I know not, I;
But as her man I mean to live and die.

62

'You in her eyes are standing mightily,
As in a place worthy of your divine
Virtue; if I, or if my service be
Acceptable to you, be you benign!
And all my royalty I here resign
Into her hand, as humbly as I
As to my lady, and become her man.'

63

The fire of love – which God preserve me from –
Deigned not to spare in him his royal blood,
But held him like a thrall in martyrdom
And did not pay the high respect it should
Have paid his virtue or his soldierhood,
But burnt him in so many ways anew
That sixty times a day his face changed hue.

64

His thought of her so much began to mount
From day to day, to quicken and increase
In passion, that he held of no account
His other duties; often to release
Himself from torment and in hope of peace
He pressed for glimpses of her, but the flame
More fiercely burnt, the nearer that he came.

65

'The nearer to the flame, the hotter 'tis',
As everyone among you is aware;
But were he far or near, I can say this:
By night or day, in wisdom or despair,
His heart – the eye within his breast – was there,
Fixed upon her, more lovely in his view
Than was Polyxena,[10] and Helen too.

66

There never passed an hour of the day
But that at least a thousand times he cried
'Lovely and good, to thee, as best I may,
I give my service; would to God, Criseyde,
You would take pity on me before I died!
Dear heart, alas! my health, prosperity
And life are lost unless you pity me!'

67

So all his other troubles left his head,
Fears for the siege, his safety, they all went;
There were no other fawns of fancy bred
In him by passion: all his argument
Was for her pity, all his good intent
Was to be hers – her man – while life gave breath:
That would be life indeed, his cure from death.

68

The deadly showers that are the proof of arms,
Where Hector and his brothers showed their zest,
Never once moved him now, though these alarms
Still found him, as before, among the best
On horse or foot; and longer than the rest
He stayed where danger was, and, as to that,
He did such work as must be wondered at,

69

But not to show his hatred of the Greek,
Nor even for the rescue of the town;
What made him battle-mad was just to seek
A single end, namely to win renown
And please his lady better; up and down
And day by day in arms, he beat the life
Out of the Greeks, went through them like a knife.

70

And from then on love robbed him of his sleep
And made an enemy of his food; his sorrow
Increased and multiplied, he could not keep
His countenance and colour, eve or morrow,
Had anyone noticed it; he sought to borrow
The names of other illnesses, to cover
His hot fire, lest it showed him as a lover.

71

wasting away about love

He said he had a fever and was ill.
I cannot say whether his lady knew
And feigned an ignorance, or if she still
Knew nothing – one or other of the two;
But I am well assured that it is true
It did not seem that she so much as thought
About him, or his griefs, or what he sought.

Narrator loves Criseyde trying to justify what he did.

72

ideas get gendered

And knowing this, the fever in him ran
Almost to madness, for his fear was this,
That she already loved some other man
And had no care for any love of his.
His heart was bleeding into an abyss,
And yet, to win the world, in all his woe,
He could not bring himself to tell her so.

73

Yet he, in moments of release from care,
Scolded himself, and over and again
Would say 'O fool! now you are in the snare,
Who used to mock at lovers and their pain;
Now you are caught, go on and gnaw your chain!
You lectured lovers, saying they were senseless,
For just those things in which you are defenceless.

74

'And what will lovers say, do you suppose,
Should this be known? Ever, behind your back,
There will be scornful laughter: "There he goes,
Our man of wisdom, bold in his attack
And his irreverent scorn for us who lack
His judgement! Now, thank God, he'll join the dance
Of those whom love hastes slowly to advance!"

75

'But O thou woeful Troilus, would to God,
Since thou must love by force of destiny,
Thy heart were set on one that understood
Thy sorrow, though she lacked in sympathy!
But she, thy lady, is as cold to thee
As is the frost under a winter moon,
And thou art snow in fire, and lost as soon.

76

'Ah, would to God that I had reached the harbour
Of death, to which my miseries must lead!
Lord, what a comfort to me, what an arbour!
I should be quit of languishing indeed!
For if it's blown abroad how much I bleed
In secret, I'll be mocked a thousand times
Worse than the fools they pillory in rhymes.

77

'Ah, help me, God! And help me, sweetest heart!
Yes, I am caught – none ever caught so fast!
Dear love, have mercy on me, take my part,
Save me from death; and, until life is past,
More than myself I'll love you, to the last!
Gladden me, sweetheart, with a friendly glance,
Though I may never hope for better chance!'

78

These words and many another he let flow;
And all his lamentations would resound
With her dear name, to tell her of his woe,
Till in salt tears he very nearly drowned.
But all for nought, she never heard a sound;
And to reflect a little on that folly
A thousand times increased his melancholy.

79

Bewailing in his chamber thus alone,
To him there came a friend called Pandarus;
He slid in unperceived and heard him groan,
And, seeing his distress, addressed him thus:
'Good gracious! What's the reason for this fuss?
Merciful God, whatever can it mean?
Is it the Greeks have made you look so lean?

80

'Is it some fit of conscience or remorse
That now has brought you round to your devotions?
Ah, you are weeping for your sins, of course;
The dread of punishment has bred these oceans.
God save the Greeks if they and their commotions
Can wring our jolliest fellows in a mangle
And give the lustiest life a holy angle!'

81

These words he rattled off in the belief
They would convert his sorrows to vexation;
Anger, for once, might overmaster grief,
And rouse his heart to sudden indignation;
He knew of course, by common reputation,
There was no braver soldier in the war
Than he, or one who cherished honour more.

82

'What mischief brings you here, or has selected
This moment to intrude upon my care,'
Said Troilus, 'who am by all rejected?
For love of God, and at my earnest prayer,
Take yourself off; for how are you to bear
Seeing me die? And therefore go away,
For die I must; there is no more to say.

83

'But if you think me ill because of fear,
You may take back your scorn; for I am one
Whom other cares oppress and hold me here,
Greater than anything the Greeks have done,
Which it is death for me to think upon;
But though I will not tell you, or reveal it,
Do not be angry, for I must conceal it.'

84

Pandarus, almost melting with compassion,
Kept saying 'O alas! What can it be?
Dear friend, are love and friendship out of fashion?
If ever truth, as between you and me,
Existed, never show such cruelty
As not to share your miseries with candour!
Don't you know well that it is I? It's Pandar!

85

'Come, let me have a part in your despair,
And even if I cannot comfort you
One of the rights of friendship is to share
Not only in pleasure, but in sorrow too;
I have and ever shall, in false and true,
In right and wrong, backed you and loved you well,
So do not hide your grief from me, but tell.'

86

This sorrowful Troilus began to sigh
And said 'God grant it may be for the best
To tell you everything and satisfy
Your longing, though it burst my very breast;
And yet I know you cannot give me rest.
Still, lest you think I do not trust a friend,
Here's how it stands; now listen and attend.

87

'Love, against whom he who would most securely
Seek a defence will find it least availing,
So grievously assails me, that he surely
Is teaching me despair; my heart is sailing
Straight into death, so burning, so prevailing
Are my desires, and it were greater joy
To die than to be King of Greece or Troy.

88

'Dear Pandar, best of friends, I've said enough;
I've told you the whole secret of my woe.
For God's love, think my cares are dangerous stuff
And keep them hidden; only you must know,
For great would be the evils that could flow
From them if they were known; be happy, friend,
Leave me in grief unknown to meet my end.'

89

'What could be more unnatural or dafter
Than hiding this, you fool?' said Pandarus,
'Perhaps the very one you're pining after
Is placed where my advice could profit us.'
'A wonder that would be!' said Troilus,
'In your own love-affairs you seldom shine,
So how the devil can you help in mine?'

90

'Now listen, Troilus,' said Pandar, 'Yes,
Fool though I be, it happens every day
That one whose life is ruined by excess
Can save his friend from going the same way;
I saw a blind man go, the other day,
Where others tumbled down who had their eyes;
Besides, the fool may often guide the wise.

91

'A whetstone is no instrument for cutting,
Yet it can put an edge on cutting tools;
I may have lost my way when I went rutting,
But my mistakes should teach you all the rules.
The wise, I say, may take advice from fools;
If you'll take warning, you'll improve your wits.
Things are defined best by their opposites.

92

'How ever could one know what sweetness is
If one had never tasted bitterness?
For inward happiness was never his
Who never was in sorrow or distress.
Set white by black, and shame by worthiness,
Each seems the more so by its opposite;
So say the wise, and so we all admit.

93

'And, as this law of contraries will show,
I who have often striven with immense
Troubles in love, ought all the more to know
How to advise you and to talk good sense
About what staggers you; take no offence
If I should wish to help you, and to share
Your heavy load. So much the less to bear!

94

'I am well aware that things are much with me
As with Oenone, the fair shepherdess,
Who wrote to your good brother, Paris – she
Made a lament out of her wretchedness;
You saw the letter that she wrote, I guess?'
'No, not as yet, I think,' said Troilus.
'Indeed?' said Pandar, 'Listen, it went thus:

95

'"Phoebus, who was the first to find the art
Of medicine, knew, for everybody's care,
What herbs to give, he knew them all by heart;
But in his own case found his wits were bare,
For love had caught and bound him in a snare;
And it was all for King Admetus' daughter;
His potions did him no more good than water."

96

'It's just the same, unhappily, with me;
I love one best, and oh my heart is sore!
And yet perhaps I know the remedy
For you, if not for me; then say no more.
I have no cause – I know it well – to soar
Like a young falcon, up and off to play,
Still, to help you, there's something I can say.

97

'One thing there is of which you can be certain;
Though I should die in torture, for no pain
Would I betray you; I will draw the curtain
Upon your secret; nor will I restrain
You, were it Helen's love you would obtain,
Your brother's lady, were it known to me;
Love whom you like, whoever she may be!

98

'Tell me straight out what was the origin,
Since you must trust me fully as a friend –
The cause of all this fever you are in;
And have no fear to speak, I don't intend
Or not just now, to scold or reprehend;
No one can wean a lover from the cup
Of love, until he choose to give it up.

99

'Let me inform you there are these two vices,
Trusting in everyone, and trusting none.
But there's a happy mean, and that suffices;
For it's a proof, if you can trust to one,
Of constancy and truth; and therefore shun
Excess, and give your trust to somebody
And tell your grief; and, if you like, tell me.

100

' "Woe to the man", they say, "who is alone,
For when he falls there's none to help him rise."
But since you have a friend, tell him your moan!
The best way, certainly, to win the prize
Of love is not – according to the wise –
To wallow and weep like Niobe the Queen
Whose tears (in marble) still are to be seen.

101

'Let be your weeping and your dreariness
And let's have lighter topics for relief;
Your time of sorrow then will seem the less,
Do not delight in grief to seek more grief,
As do those fools, who, when they strike a reef,
Egg misery on with misery, resolved
To lend no ear or have their problem solved.

102

'People have said it is a consolation
To find a fellow-sufferer in woe;
A view that ought to have our approbation
Since we are both of us tormented so
By love; I feel so wretched, as you know,
That surely there could be no heavier doom
Upon my shoulders. Why? There isn't room!

103

'I hope to God you do not think me shady,
One who would trick you of her by a wile?
You know yourself I love a certain lady
As best I can – it's gone on a long while.
And since you know I do it for no guile,
And trust me better than to think me double,
Tell me a little; for you know my trouble.'

104

Yet, for all this, no word said Troilus,
But lay there long, like one upon a bier;
Then he broke out in sighing, and he thus
Turned round, and lent to Pandar's voice an ear.
His eyes rolled up, and Pandar was in fear
Some frenzy had taken him and he might fall
Into a fit and die, and end it all.

[28]

105

'Wake up!' cried Pandarus; his voice was sharp.
'Are you asleep? Is this a lethargy?
Or are you like some ass that hears a harp,
And gets the sound of strings in harmony,
But in his mind there sinks no melody,
He finds no pleasure to be had in it,
So dull and bestial is his donkey-wit?'

106

Pandarus stopped with that, and silence fell,
For still no answer came from Troilus,
Whose fixed intention was never to tell
A soul for whom it was he suffered thus;
The wise have told us it is dangerous
To cut a stick, for he who cuts it may
Live to be beaten with it, one fine day.

107

And this is specially true, they say, in love;
What touches love is secret, or should be.
Rumours of love spring out and spread enough,
Unless it's governed very carefully.
And there are times when one should seem to flee
The thing pursued; it is the hunter's art.
Troilus turned this over in his heart.

108

Nevertheless, on hearing Pandar's shrill
'Wake up!' he gave a sigh that seemed to come
With anguish, and he said 'Though I lie still,
Dear friend, I am not deaf; could you be dumb
A little? I have heard your rules of thumb;
So leave me to my wretchedness and grief;
Truly your proverbs bring me no relief.

109

'And they are all the cure you have for me;
I do not want a cure, I want to die.
What do I care about Queen Niobe?
Drop your old parallels, they don't apply.'
'No?' Pandarus retorted, 'That is why
I said just now it is a fool's delight
To hug his grief, rather than put things right.

110

'I see that you are losing hold on reason;
But answer me, if she you hold so dear
Were known to me, might not a word in season,
If you permit it, whispered in her ear
By me – the things you dare not speak, for fear –
Draw forth her pity for a certain youth?'
'Never, by God,' he said, 'and by my truth!'

111

'What, not if I went earnestly about it,
As if my life depended on the need?'
'No,' Troilus said, 'I'd rather die without it.'
'And why?' 'Because you never could succeed.'
'Are you so sure of that?' 'I am indeed,'
He said, 'however skilful you may be,
She'll ne'er be won by such a wretch as me.'

112

Said Pandarus: 'Alas! How can this be,
Despairing, without reason, of your case?
What! She's alive – your lady – isn't she?
How do you know that you are out of grace?
Such troubles, if you look them in the face,
Aren't without remedy; do not think your cure
Impossible! The future's never sure.

113

'I grant you're suffering from as sharp a pain
As Tityus[11] does – the fellow down in Hell,
Whose stomach birds tear out and tear again,
Vultures, they call them, so the old books tell;
But for all that I cannot have you dwell
In an opinion so ridiculous
As that there cannot be a cure for us.

114

'But just because you have a coward heart
And angry ways, and foolish, wilful scares
About not trusting me, you won't impart,
You will not stir to mend your own affairs
So much as to give reasons for your airs,
But lie there dumb for hours at a stretch;
What woman could feel love for such a wretch?

115

'What else will she suppose about your death,
If you should die, and she not know the cause,
Save that in fear you yielded up your breath
Because the Greeks besiege us. You should pause
And think what thanks she'll give you, what applause,
For that! She'll say, and so will all the town,
"The wretch is dead, the devil drag him down!"

116

'Here you may weep alone, cry out and kneel,
But, love a woman when she doesn't know it
And she'll requite in ways you cannot feel;
Unknown, unkissed; "unsought-for" means "forgo it".
Many a one who loved and did not show it
Has bought love dear, a twenty-winter drouth
Of knowing her, that never kissed her mouth.

117

'What! Should he therefore fall into despair,
Turn infidel in love – for grief, I mean?
Or kill himself although she still seems fair?
No, no! But ever constant, fresh and green,
To love and serve his lady, his heart's queen,
And think himself rewarded that he serves her,
More by a thousand times than he deserves her.'

118

And of these words young Troilus took heed,
And saw at once the folly he was in;
What Pandarus had said was true indeed;
To kill himself was not the way to win,
For it was both unmanly and a sin,
Nor would his lady ever know the fashion
Of his death, not knowing of his pain and passion.

119

And at the thought he sorrowfully sighed
And said 'Alas! What then is best to do?'
'If you are willing,' Pandarus replied,
'The best would be to tell, and tell me true;
And, on my honour, I will see you through;
If I seem slow, or find no remedy,
Drag me in pieces, hang me on a tree.'

120

'Yes, so you say,' said Troilus, plunged in care,
'God knows it will be none the better so;
Help will be hard indeed in this affair,
For – well I know it – Fortune is my foe;
Not one of all the men that come and go
On earth can set at naught her cruel wheel;
She plays with us and there is no appeal.'

121

Said Pandar, 'You blame Fortune for your fall
Because you're angry; yes, at last I see.
Don't you know Fortune is the same for all,
Common to everyone in some degree?
Yes, there's this comfort for you; goodness me,
Just as her joys pass over and are gone,
So come her tribulations, and pass on.

122

'For if her wheel should ever cease to turn
Fortune would then no longer Fortune be[12];
But since her wheel is always on the churn,
Perhaps her very mutability
May bring about what you desire to see;
She may be going to help you in this thing;
For all you know, you have good cause to sing.

123

'Accordingly I make it my petition,
Give up this grief, stop looking at the ground!
For he that seeks a cure from his physician
Will have to take the bandage off his wound.
May I be chained to Cerberus, Hell's Hound,
Though it be for my sister – your love-sorrow –
If, by my will, she is not yours tomorrow!

124

'Look up, I say, and tell me who she is
At once, that I may go about your need;
Come, do I know her? Can't you tell me this?
For if I do, there's hope I may succeed.'
A vein in Troilus began to bleed,
For he was hit, and reddened up in shame.
'Aha!' said Pandar, 'here we start the game!'

125

And on the word, he gave him a good shaking,
And said 'Her name, you thief! You've got to tell!'
And foolish Troilus then started quaking,
As if some fiend were taking him to Hell,
And said 'The fountain of my woe, my well
Of grief, my sweetest foe, is called Criseyde.'
He trembled at the word, he almost died.

126

When Pandar heard the name that he had given,
Lord, he was glad, and said 'My dearest friend,
I wish you joy, by Jupiter in Heaven!
Love has done well for you! O happy end!
Be cheerful; wisdom and good name attend
Upon her, she has gentle breeding too;
Whether she's beautiful I leave to you.

127

'I never have known one of her position
So generous, so happy in her mood,
So friendly in her speech and disposition,
Or one that had more grace in doing good,
And how to do it better understood;
And, to cap all, as far as honour stretches,
Compared to such as she is, kings are wretches.

128

'And so, take heart; the first point, certainly,
In noble natures, truly apprehended
And properly established, is to be
At peace within themselves, division ended;
So should you be, for what is there but splendid
In loving well and in a worthy place?
You should not call it Fortune; call it Grace.

129

'Then think of this, and let it gladden you;
Your lady has great virtues, as you know;
It follows that she has compassion too,
Where goodness is so general; and so
Be specially attentive to forgo
Any demand that injures her good name,
For virtue does not stretch itself to shame.

130

'Happy indeed the day that I was born,
To see you settled in so fair a place!
Upon my word I truly could have sworn
You never would have won to such a grace
In love! Do you know why? You used to chase
And chaff the god of love, and in your spite
Called him "Saint Idiot, Lord of Fools' Delight"!

131

'And many a sly, sophisticated prod
You gave, and said that people who were prone
To serve in love were very Apes of God;
And some, you said, would munch their meat alone,
Lying in bed and heaving up a groan;
"White-fevered ones", you called them, "shivering
    lovers".
"Pray god," you said, "not one of them recovers."

132

'And some of them took on about the cold[13]
Rather too much – so you asserted roundly –
And others were pretending when they told
Of sleepless nights, when they were sleeping soundly.
That's how they hoped to rise, but were profoundly
Mistaken, so you said, for they would fall;
That's how you went on jesting at them all.

133

'You also said that far the greater part
Of lovers spoke in general, and took care,
If they should fail with one, to learn the art
Of finding compensation otherwhere.
Now I could jest at you, if jest it were;
Nevertheless I'd stake my life, God knows,
And swear that you were never one of those.

134

'Now beat your breast, and say to him above
"Have mercy on me, Lord, for I repent,
If I said ill; I am myself in love."
Speak from your heart, let it be truly meant.'
Said Troilus, 'Lord Cupid, I consent;
Pardon my mockeries! If thou forgive,
I never more will mock thee while I live.'

135

'Well said, indeed,' said Pandar, 'that should stop
The god's displeasure; he should feel appeased.
And now that you have wept so many a drop,
And said those things whereby a god is pleased,
I hope to God your sorrow will be eased,
And think that she, the cause of all your grief,
Hereafter may be cause of its relief.

136

'A soil that nurtures weeds and poisonous stuff
Brings forth these herbs of healing just as oft.
Next to the foulest nettle, thick and rough,
Rises the rose in sweetness, smooth and soft;
And next the valleys rise the hills aloft,
And next the dark of night the glad tomorrow;
And joy is on the borderland of sorrow.

137

'So, lay a temperate hand upon the bridle;
Wait for the tide in patience, for the best,
Or otherwise our labour will be idle;
More haste, less speed; the faster for a rest.
Be diligent, true, secret, self-possessed,
But gay and open-hearted; persevere
In serving love, and then you need not fear.

138

'"The heart divided over many places
Is nowhere firm in any," say the wise.
Such hearts can never gain a lady's graces;
And some who love are like the man who tries
To plant a herb or tree, and then will rise
And pull it up, to see if it's alive
Next day; no wonder if it does not thrive.

139

'And since the god of lovers has bestowed
A worthy place upon you, stand you fast!
Into a happy harbour you have rowed,
And so I say, in spite of sorrows past,
Hope for the best; because unless you blast
Our work by over-haste, or by despair,
There's hope for a good end to your affair.

140

'Do you know why I feel the less dismay
In thinking how this matter might be tendered
In treating with my niece? The learned say
That never man or woman was engendered
Unapt to suffer love; we're all surrendered
To a celestial or a natural kind[14],
One or the other, and so I hope to find

141

'Some grace in her; and in regard to her,
In the young beauty of her womanhood,
It would not be becoming to prefer
A love celestial, even if she could.
Not yet at least; it's clearly for her good
To love and cherish some distinguished knight;
Not to would show a vicious appetite.

142

'So I am ready, and shall always be,
To go to work for you in this affair
– For both of you – I have a hope in me
To please you later; you're a sage young pair
And know how to keep counsel. Take good care
That no one is the wiser of it; thus
We shall be happy – all the three of us.

143

'And on my honour, at this moment too,
I have been struck by quite a happy thought;
And what it is I shall impart to you.
I think since Love, in goodness, has not brought
You out of all your wicked ways for nought;
He'll make you the best pillar, I suppose,
Of his whole cult, the more to grieve his foes!

144

'Example why: think of those learned men
Who most have erred against God's holy law,
And whom He has converted back again
From heresy, because He wished to draw
Them back to Him; and they stand most in awe
Of God, strongest in faith, it is confessed;
I understand they combat error best.'

145

When Troilus heard Pandarus consenting
To help him in the loving of Criseyde,
His grief, as one might say, was less tormenting,
But hotter grew his love, and he replied
With sobered look (although his heart inside
Was dancing), 'Blessed Venus from on high
Help me to earn your thanks before I die!

146

'Is there a means to make my suffering less
Till this be done, dear friend? Can you achieve it?
What will you say of me and my distress?
I dread her anger – how will she receive it?
Suppose she will not listen or believe it?
I dread it all; and then, that it should spring
From you, her uncle! She'll hear no such thing.'

147

And Pandarus retorted 'I should worry.
Afraid the Man will fall out of the Moon?
Lord, how I hate your foolishness and flurry!
Mind your own business! Let me beg a boon
Of you: leave everything to me, and soon
You'll find I've acted in your interest.'
'Well, friend,' he answered, 'do as you think best,

148

'But listen to me, Pandar, just a word!
I would not have you think me so demented
As to desire – in all that you have heard –
Anything shameful, or to be repented;
I'd rather die. So let her be contented,
I mean no villainy; make it understood
That every thought I have is for her good.'

149

Pandarus gave a laugh, and he replied
'With me for surety? That's what they all say.
I shouldn't care if she had stood beside
And heard it all! Farewell! I must away.
Adieu! Take heart! God speed us both today!
Give me this work, hand me this job to do;
Mine be the labour, and the sweets to you!'

150

This Troilus fell down upon his knees,
Seized Pandar in his arms and held him fast;
'Death to the Greeks! Down with our enemies!'
He cried, 'and God will help; the worst is past!
You may be sure, if life in me will last,
With God's good help, there's some of them will smart!
Pardon this boast; it comes from a full heart.

151

'Now, Pandarus, here's all that I can say:
O wise, O wonderful, O man of skill!
O all-in-all! My life and death I lay
In your good hands; help me!' 'Of course I will.'
'God bless you; whether it is cure or kill,
Commend me to her; say her lightest breath,'
He added, 'may command me to the death.'

152

This Pandarus, in eagerness to serve
This his full friend, smiled back and gave his views:
'Farewell, and think I'm trying to deserve
Your thanks;' he said, 'I promise you good news.'
He turned and off he wandered, in a muse,
Thinking how best to win to her good graces;
What were the proper times, the likely places?

153

For nobody who has a house to build
Goes dashing out to work and make a start
With a rash hand; he waits, if he is skilled,
And sends a line with caution from his heart
To win his purpose, first of all by art;
So Pandar inwardly prepared his plan
And wisely gave it shape ere he began.

154

Then Troilus no longer laid him down,
But sallied out at once upon his bay
And played the lion to defend the town;
Woe to the Greek who met with him that day!
From that time on so winning was his way
With everyone in Troy, he gained in grace;
They loved him that but looked upon his face.

155

For he became the friendliest of men,
The noblest, the most generous and free,
The sturdiest too, one of the best that then,
In his own times, there were, or that could be.
Dead were his jesting and his cruelty;
His loftiness, the arrogance that hurt you,
Yielded their place, exchanging with a virtue.

156

Of Troilus I now shall say no more
Awhile; he is like one that's gravely wounded,
Who finds the wound no longer is so sore,
But knows the corner has not yet been rounded;
An easy patient, with his faith well founded
On the physician's skill who is attending,
He faces the adventure now impending.

Book II

1

Out of these black waves, let us at last make sail;
O wind, O wind, the day begins to clear!
In such a sea my boat is like to fail,
It is in travail and I scarce can steer.
This sea is the tempestuous career
Of black despair that Troilus was in;
But now the calends of his hope begin.

2

O lady mine, Clio,[1] be thou the one
Henceforth to speed me; O be thou my Muse!
Rhyme this book well for me till I have done;
Here there's no other art for me to use.
And so I ask all lovers to excuse
My story, not of my own feeling sung,
But taken from Latin[2] into my own tongue.

3

Therefore I wish for neither thanks nor blame
In all this work; meekly, I beg you try
To overlook it if a word be lame,
For just as said my author, so say I.
And though I speak of love unfeelingly
That's nothing new; no wonder I am duller
Than he; a blind man is no judge of colour.

4

And then, you know, the forms of language change
Within a thousand years, and long ago
Some words were valued that will now seem strange,
Affected, even; yet they spoke them so,
And fared as well in love, for all I know,
As we do now; in various lands and ages
Various are the ways to win love's wages.

[45]

5

And therefore, should it happen by some chance
That one of you, some lover, listening here
To what I tell you of the slow advance
Troilus made to gain his lady's ear,
Thinks "I would never buy my love so dear!"
Or marvels at this phrase, or at that blunder,
I do not know; to me it is no wonder.

6

Not all who find their way to Rome will trace
The self-same path, or wear the self-same gear,
And in some lands they'd count it a disgrace
Were they to act in love as we do here,
With open doings, looks that make all clear,
Visits, formalities and tricks of phrase;
To every land its own peculiar ways.

7

For there are scarcely three among you all
Who have said alike in love, or done the same;
What pleases one of you (it may befall)
Won't suit another; but on goes the game.
Some choose a tree on which to carve a name,
And some a stone; and I, as I began,
Will follow on my author, if I can.

* * *

8

Now in that mother of happy months, in May,
When the fresh flowers, blue and white and red,
Quicken again and every meadow-way
Is full of balm, that winter left for dead,
When blazing Phoebus with his beams outspread
Stands in the milk-white Bull, it so occurred
– As I shall sing – I say, on May the third,

9

This Pandarus, for all his crafty speech,
Felt in himself the shafts of love so keenly
That, notwithstanding all his gift to preach,
His colour came and went a little greenly;
For love, that day, had treated him so meanly
He went in woe to bed, and there he lay
Tossing and turning till the break of day.

10

The swallow Progne[3], with her mournful song,
When morning came, began on that embittering
Tale of her change of shape, while Pandar long
Lay half asleep in bed. When dawn was glittering,
She, close beside him, started on her twittering
About her sister, Philomela, taken
And raped by Tereus; Pandar began to waken;

11

He called his servants and began to rise,
Remembering his errand and the boon
Promised to Troilus – his enterprise.
He made a calculation by the moon,
And found her favourable for journeys. Soon
He reached his niece's palace, close beside;
Now Janus, god of entry, be his guide!

12

When, as I say, he reached his niece's place,
He knocked: 'Where is her ladyship?' said he;
And when they told him, in he strode apace,
And found two ladies in her company.
They sat in a paved parlour, and all three
Were listening to a girl reading a measure
Out of *The Siege of Thebes*[4], to give them pleasure.

13

'Madam,' said Pandar, 'Blessings on your head,
And on the book, and all the company!'
'Ey, uncle, welcome! Welcome indeed!' she said,
And up she rose at once and cordially
Captured his hand; 'Three times last night,' said she,
'I dreamt of you; good fortune come of it!'
She showed him to a bench and made him sit.

14

'You'll be the better of it all this year,
Dear niece, if God is good,' said Pandarus,
'But I have interrupted you, I fear;
What book is it that you are praising thus?
For God's love, what does it say? Impart to us;
Is it of love? Give me good news, my dear!'
'Uncle!' she said, 'Your mistress isn't here.'

15

And they all laughed; and after that she said
'It is *The Siege of Thebes* that we are reading;
I think we just had left King Laius dead,
Murdered by Oedipus, that sad proceeding;
We stopped at the next chapter; it is leading
On to Amphiaräus[5], how he fell
– He was the Bishop – through the ground, to Hell.'

16

'I know all that' said Pandarus 'myself,
And all the siege of Thebes, unhappy place;
There are twelve books about it on my shelf,
But let's forget it. Let me see your face,
Come on, take off that wimple and uncase!
Down with that book, get up and let us dance
And give the month of May some countenance!'

[48]

17

'I? God forbid!' she answered, 'Are you mad?
Heavens! Is that how widows are behaving?
You frighten me! It really is too bad
To say such crazy things; you must be raving!
I should be sitting in a cave, and saving
My soul by reading holy martyrs' lives;
Let girls go out to dances, or young wives.'

18

'As ever I hope to thrive,' said Pandarus,
'I know a reason why you should be gay.'
'Now, uncle dear,' she answered, 'tell it us,
Is the siege over? Have they gone away?
Those Greeks! They frighten me to death, I say.'
'No, no,' said he, 'and I can tell you flat,
My secret is a thing worth five of that!'

19

'Heavenly gods!' said she, 'What can you have got?
Worth five of that? No, no, it can't be so.
But for the world I can't imagine what
It could be; it's some joke of yours, I know,
You'll have to tell us; we are all too slow;
And my poor wit in any case is lean,
For, by the Lord, I don't know what you mean.'

20

'And never shall,' he said, 'depend on that!
Secrets there are I may not bring to birth.'
'But why not, uncle? What are you hinting at?'
'By God, I'll tell you this, for what it's worth;
There'd be no prouder woman on the earth
If you but knew, or in the town of Troy;
No, I'm not joking, as I may have joy!'

21

And she began to wonder more than ever
A thousand times, and lowered her eyes a touch,
For since the day she had been born, she never
Had wanted to know anything so much;
She sighed and answered, 'If your news is such,
Dear Uncle, I will promise not to tease you,
And ask no more about it than will please you.'

22

So after that, with many happy rallies,
Gay looks and gossip, talk began to range;
They joked on this and that, and there were sallies
On many matters, pleasant, deep, and strange,
Such as good friends together will exchange,
When newly met; and then she asked of Hector,
Scourge of the Greeks, the town's wall and protector.

23

'He's very well, thank God,' said Pandarus,
'Save for a slight arm-wound – not to be reckoned
As serious; and then there's Troilus,
His fresh young brother, Hector, indeed, the Second;
There's one who has followed virtue where she beckoned,
A man all truth, as noble as his birth,
Wise, honoured, generous – a man of worth.'

24

'O I'm so glad! And Hector's better since?
God save them both and keep them from all harms!
How nice it is, how fitting to a Prince
To be so valiant in the field of arms!
And to be so well-natured! That's what charms
Me most; such goodness and such strength, I mean,
So royally combined are seldom seen.'

25

'That's true, that's very true,' said Pandarus,
'My word! The King has two such sons today
– Hector, I mean, of course, and Troilus –
And I would stake my life on it that they
Are free of vices, freer, I dare say,
Than any man alive under the sun;
Their strength and worth are known to everyone.

26

'Of Hector there is nothing need be said;
In all the world there is no better knight;
Indeed he is the very fountainhead
Of valour, and more in virtue than in might;
Experienced soldiers say so, and they're right.
I'll say the same of Troilus, but then
I don't know any two such fighting men.'

27

'By God,' she said, 'of Hector that is true,
And it is true of Troilus, I agree:
Everyone talks of what they've seen him do
In arms, day after day – so gallantly!
And then at home he is all courtesy
And gentleness, in fact he wins attention
From everyone whose praise is worth a mention.'

28

'You certainly are right in what you say,'
Said Pandar, 'anybody's heart would warm
To see him as I saw him yesterday!
Never fled bees in such a mighty swarm
As fled the Greeks; he was in fighting form,
And through the battlefield, in every ear,
There ran no cry but "Troilus is here!"

29

'Now here, now there, he hunted them and coursed
  them;
Nothing but Greek blood! There was Troilus
Dealing out doom; he wounded and unhorsed them
And everywhere he went it happened thus;
He was their death, but shield and life to us;
That was a day! Not one dared make a stand
Against him, with his bloody sword in hand.

30

'Added to that, he is the friendliest fellow,
Considering his rank, I ever knew,
And, if he chooses, can be warm and mellow
To anybody that he thinks will do.'
And then, abruptly, Pandarus withdrew,
Taking his leave and saying 'I must fly!'
'Uncle! I hope I'm not to blame, am I?

31

'What's wrong with you to weary of our chatter?
Especially a woman's! Must you go?
Now do sit down, I have a business matter
Which needs your wisdom, Uncle; don't say no.'
And those who were about her were not slow
To move away, so that she might discuss
The run of her affairs with Pandarus.

32

When they had finished all they had to say
About her household and its maintenance,
He said 'Well now I really must away;
But still I say stand up and let us dance,
Throw off your widow's habit, now's your chance!
Why make yourself look ugly? I'll prevent you
When such a glad adventure has been sent you.'

33

'Ah, well remembered! Now, for heaven's sake,
May I not know the meaning of all this?'
'No, for it asks some leisure; it would make
Me most unhappy, if some prejudice
Should lead you into taking it amiss;
It's better I should hold my tongue in patience
Than tell a truth against your inclinations.

34

'For, by divine Minerva, dearest niece,
And Jupiter who thunders from afar,
And blissful Venus – whom I never cease
To serve – you, of all earthly women, are
The one I love the best – I'll go so far,
(Not counting mistresses); I will not grieve you,
As well you know yourself; and so I leave you.'

35

'I know,' she said, 'dear Uncle, all my thanks!
You've always been a friend, I must admit.
And there is nobody I know who ranks
So high with me – and so ill-paid for it!
But by the grace of God and by my wit,
You shall be one I never will offend;
And if I did before, I will amend.

36

'But I beseech you, for the love of God,
You that I trust,' she said with emphasis,
'To drop your distant speech that sounds so odd,
And tell your niece whatever is amiss.'
On hearing that, her uncle, with a kiss,
Said to her 'Gladly, little niece, I will;
And what I say – try not to take it ill.'

37

She lowered her eyelids, ready to attend,
And Pandarus began to cough a bit
And said 'Well, dearest, always, in the end,
Though story-tellers like to show their wit
By adding on embellishments to fit,
Yet in reality they all intend,
For all their artifice, to reach an end.

38

'And since the end is every story's strength,
And this one so befitting, and so fine,
Why should I paint or draw it out in length
For you, who are so true a friend of mine?'
Speaking, he sought some answering inward sign,
And long beheld her, gazing in her face,
And said 'In such a mirror, be there grace!'

39

Thinking 'To make a business of my tale
And tease it out, will make it none the fresher;
She'd take no pleasure in it, and could not fail
To think it was my purpose to enmesh her;
Sensitive minds distrust a form of pressure
They do not understand; I'll have to sense
Some way of touching her intelligence.'

40

He went on staring in his busy way,
And she, aware that he beheld her so,
Said 'Did you never see me till today?
Lord, how you stare! Answer me, yes or no!'
'Yes, yes, I'm staring, and before I go
I shall stare more; I'm wondering,' said he
'If you are lucky; well, we soon shall see.

41

'For every creature there is shaped a time
Of high adventure, if he can receive it;
Should he be careless of it, then his crime
Is wilfulness, disdaining to achieve it;
It is not accident, you may believe it,
Nor fortune that's to blame, but his demerit,
His very sloth and wretchedness of spirit.

42

'A fair adventure into happiness,
My lovely niece, is yours if you can take it;
And for the love of God, for mine no less,
Catch hold of it at once, lest luck forsake it;
What need of a long speech? I will not make it;
Give me your hand; no one, if you but knew
– And if you cared – has had such luck as you!

43

'And since what I shall say you must put down
To good intentions, as I said before,
And since I love your honour and renown
As much as any one, and maybe more,
I swear by all the oaths I ever swore
That if it angers you, I tell you plain,
I never will set eyes on you again.

44

'Why, look! You're all a-tremble! Don't be frightened!
You've changed your colour; fear has made you pale!
The worst is over! There, the skies have brightened!
Of course it's a surprise; my little tale
Is new to you. But you won't find me fail.
Always trust me! Would I be one to shame you
With tales of anything that misbecame you?'

[55]

45

'Good Uncle, for the love of heaven, pray
Come off it, tell me what it's all about!
I'm terrified of what you're going to say,
And, at the same time, longing to find out.
O do say on! Don't leave me in this doubt,
Do tell me, whether it be good or ill!'
'Well, listen, then,' he said, 'for so I will.

46

'Now, little niece of mine, the King's dear son,
Good, wise, and open-hearted, fresh and true,
Who bears himself so well to everyone,
Prince Troilus, is so in love with you
That you must help; he'll die unless you do.
Well, there it is. What more am I to say?
Do what you like; but you can save or slay.

47

'But if you let him die, I'll take my life
– And that's the truth, I'm telling you no lies –
I'll cut my throat, ay with this very knife!'
At that the tears came bursting from his eyes;
'And when you've killed us both, you'll realize
Just what a fine day's fishing you've enjoyed;
What good is it to you if we're destroyed?

48

'Alas that he, who is my own dear lord,
That true man, ay, that gentle, noble knight,
Who asks for nothing but your friendly word . . .
I see him dying as he walks upright,
And hurrying desperately out to fight
Seeking his death, seeking his fate, on duty.
Alas that God has sent you so much beauty!

49

'But if indeed you prove yourself so cruel,
So careless of his death, that you would fetch
No deeper sigh in losing such a jewel
Of honour than a trickster or a wretch,
If you are such, your beauty cannot stretch
To justifying such a cruel deed;
So, with a choice before you, take good heed.

50

'Woe to the gem that has no native force![6]
Woe to the herb that has no healing shoot!
Woe to the beauty that knows no remorse
Or pity, but treads others underfoot!
And you, the crop of beauty and its root,
If, in such beauty, pity cannot thrive,
Then it is pity you should be alive.

51

'You may be sure this is no trick or fraud;
For I would rather you and I and he
Were hanged than I should live to be his bawd,
Hanged high enough for everyone to see;
I am your uncle; it were shame to me
As well as to yourself, if I should let him
Despoil you of your honour, or abet him!

52

'Now understand, my dear; I do not ask you
To bind yourself to him in any way;
No pledge is wanted, but I gently task you
To smile at him, to be more kind, more gay,
Friendlier than before; and so you may
To save his life, and that's my whole intent;
God help me, that is all I ever meant.

[57]

53

'Look, this request is purely reasonable,
There is no reason to distrust it, none.
And what you fear – the worst you would be able
To say against it – is that everyone
Would think his visits rather overdone;
But I reply none but a fool would find
More in it than pure friendship of the mind.

54

'Who would suppose, were he to see a man
Going to church, that he was on his way
To desecrate the images? He can
Govern himself; reflect, and you will say
He's wise and forgets nothing; every day
His praises mount; besides, he'll come so seldom,
What would it matter if all the town beheld him?

55

'Such friendly loves are quite the rule in Troy;
So wrap that cloak well round you; it's a cover.
And surely, as the Lord may give me joy,
It's best to do so, as you will discover.
And, niece, to ease the anguish of a lover,
Sugar your cold aloofness with a breath
Of kindness; don't be guilty of his death!'

56

Criseyde, who heard him broach this enterprise
Thought 'Well, I'll feel for what he's leading to.'
And said, 'Now, Uncle, what would you advise?
What would you think it best for me to do?'
'That is well said,' he answered; 'best for you
Would be to love him of your own accord,
Since love for love's a reasonable reward.

57

'Think that in each of you, from hour to hour,
There is some part of beauty laid to waste
By the advance of age; ere Time devour
You, *love!* When you are old, there's none will haste
To love you; there's a proverb to my taste:
"'*Aware too late,' said Beauty, as she passed*"
And age will cure disdain in you at last.

58

'The King's Fool has a trick, to cry aloud
On seeing a woman hold herself too high,
"May you live long enough, and all the proud,
To see the crow's foot walk about your eye;
Send for a mirror then, in which to pry
Into the face that you will bear tomorrow!
I cannot wish you any greater sorrow."'

59

With that he ceased to speak, and hung his head,
And she burst out in tears as she replied
'Alas, for grief! O why am I not dead,
Since all good faith on earth has surely died?
What would a stranger do to me,' she cried,
'When one I thought my friend, the best of them,
Bids me to seek a love he should condemn?

60

'I could have trusted you to play your part
If I had fallen, by some calamity,
In love with him, or Hector, lost my heart
To fierce Achilles, or some other he;
You would have shown no mercy then to me.
Imagine the rebukes you would have hurled!
But O, there's no believing this false world.

61

'What! Is this all the joy, is this the pleasure?
This your advice? And this my blissful case?
Is this the true reward and promised treasure?
Is all your painted argument in place?
Was this your object? Pallas, Queen of Grace,
Provide for me, protect me from on high!
For I am so astonished, I could die!'

62

She sighed in sorrow and she ceased to speak.
'Is that the best that you can do?' said he,
'By God, I shan't come here again this week,
Since I am so mistrusted; I can see
That you make light enough of him and me
And of our death, alas. O wretched pair!
If only he might live I would not care.

63

'O cruel god, O Mars the merciless!
O Furies Three of Hell, to you I call!
Let me not leave this house if I profess
The slightest villainy or harm at all!
But as I see my lord is doomed to fall,
And I with him, I wash my hands and say
Your wickedness has slain us both today.

64

'And since you would be glad to see me dead,
By Neptune, that is god of the salt sea,
From this time forth I never will eat bread
Until my own heart's blood flows out of me;
Certainly I can die as soon as he.'
And up he jumped and made as if to leave,
But she was quick, and caught him by the sleeve.

65

Criseyde indeed was almost dead with fear,
Being the timidest, most shrinking creature
That ever was; not only could she hear,
But see his earnestness in every feature;
And she sensed nothing evil in the nature
Of what he asked her for; there might be harm
If she refused; she melted in alarm.

66

She thought 'Misfortunes happen thick and fast
All the day long for love; in such a case
Men can be cruel, of a wicked cast,
And if this man, here, in this very place,
Should kill himself, it's more than I could face.
What would they say? Should I not be to blame?
I'll need to play a very subtle game.'

67

Three times she murmured with a sorrowful sigh
'O heaven, how unfortunate for me!
For my good name and my position lie
In danger – and my Uncle's life, maybe.
But, by God's guidance, I shall presently
Think how to keep my honour, and to keep
My Uncle too!' and then she ceased to weep.

68

'Well, of two evils one should choose the less;
I'd rather show him some encouragement
Than risk my Uncle's life, I must confess.
There's nothing more to which I must consent?'
'No, dearest niece.' 'O well, I am content;
I'll do my utmost in the situation,
And force my heart against my inclination.

69

'But do not think I mean to lead him on,
For love a man I neither can nor may
Against my will; be certain thereupon.
But pleasant I will be, from day to day;
"No" is a thing that I would never say
(My honour safe) – save from timidity.
But "kill the cause and cure the malady".

70

'And here I make a solemn protestation:
Go any deeper into this affair,
And certainly no thought of your salvation
– Though both of you should die in your despair,
And though the world should hate me then and there –
Will get him any pity out of me.'
'Of course, of course,' said Pandar, 'I agree,

71

'But may I really trust you on this head?
And to the promise you have given here,
That you will truly keep to what you said?'
'Why, certainly,' she answered 'Uncle dear.'
'And I shall have no reason – is this clear? –
To scold or lecture you on any score?'
'Why no indeed,' she promised, 'say no more.'

72

And then they fell to other pleasant chatter,
Till, at the last 'Good Uncle,' she said, wheeling
Back to his news, 'do tell me, in this matter,
How did you come to know what he was feeling?
Does anyone know of it?' 'No.' 'Is he appealing?
Can he speak well of love? As if he cared?
Do tell me that I may be well prepared.'

73

Pandar began to smile a little then
And answered 'Well, it happened, truth to tell,
The other day – I can't remember when –
Down in the palace garden, by a well,
We spent the day together, so it fell;
We met to talk about a stratagem
Against the Greeks, that should embarrass them.

74

'And not long after, we began to leap
About and try our javelins for a throw
Or two; at last he said he wished to sleep
And down he lay upon the grass; and so
I wandered off, and, roaming to and fro,
I overheard him, as I walked alone,
Give utterance to a miserable groan.

75

'And so I stalked him softly from behind,
And this, to tell you truly, was the main
– As far as I can call it now to mind –
Of what he said. He started to complain
To the god of love; "Have pity on my pain,
Lord, though I have rebelled in my intent
Against thee; *Mea culpa!* I repent!

76

'"O God, that leadest, at thy disposition,
Thy creatures, each to his appointed end,
Justly foreseen by thee, my true contrition
Accept with favour, and, as may please thee, send
My penance, Lord; yet shield me and defend
Me from despair, dividing me from thee;
Be thou my shield for thy benignity!

77

'"So sorely she that stood in black, apart,
Has wounded me – the beauty in her eye
Has sounded to the bottom of my heart;
By which I know that I must surely die
And, worst of all, I may tell no one why;
And hotter grow the embers when they're spread
With covering ashes that are pale and dead."

78

'With that he smote his head to earth and lay
Muttering there – I really don't know what.
And I, in turn, went tiptoeing away
From his distress, as if I knew it not;
Then I came back; "Wake up, you sleep a lot!"
I said, gazing upon him from above,
"It's obvious you cannot be in love,

79

'"If you can sleep so that there's no awaking
You! Was there ever such a dull young man?"
"Go on," he said, "enjoy your own head-aching
For love, and let me live as best I can."
And though his griefs had left him pale and wan,
He gave himself as fresh a countenance
As if he had been leading a new dance.

80

'Well, this passed over, till, the other day,
It happened that I wandered all alone
Into his bed-chamber; and there he lay
Flat on his bed; I never heard man groan
More sorrowfully; the reason for this moan
I did not know; as I came in, and went
Towards him, he abandoned his lament.

81

'As that gave rise in me to some suspicion,
I neared and found him in a flood of tears;
And, as the Lord may save me from perdition,
I felt more pity than I've felt for years;
My ingenuity, my tricks and fleers
Could barely keep him from his death! I vow
My heart is weeping for him even now.

82

'And never, heaven knows, since I was born
Have I so preached! I preached with might and main;
Never to secrecy have been so sworn
Before he told me who could cure his pain;
Don't ask me to rehearse his speech again,
His woeful words, his melancholy tune,
Or not unless you want to see me swoon.

83

'It is indeed to save his life – no less –
And do no harm to you, I am thus driven;
That we may live, show him some friendliness;
Be gentle with him, for the love of heaven!
Now I have told you flat; my heart is shriven;
And since you know that my intention's clean,
Take heed of it; no evil do I mean.

84

'And now good luck; dear God, that's all I care;
You who have caught your fish without a net,
(And such a fish!) be wise as you are fair;
The ruby in the ring will then be set.
Never were two so fortunately met
As you, when you are wholly his, will be;
Almighty God! May I be there to see!'

85

'No, I said nothing about that!' she cried,
'Aha! God help me, you will spoil it all!'
'Dear niece, forgive me,' he at once replied,
'I meant it well whatever I let fall
By Mars, his helmet and his battle-call!
Do not be angry, we are one blood, dear niece.'
'Well, all's forgiven,' she answered, 'and at peace.'

86

With that he took his leave and, well content,
Went home in high good humour on his own;
Criseyde arose and, never pausing, went
Straight to her private chamber, all alone,
And there she sat, as still as any stone,
And every word he had said began to wind
And echo up and down within her mind.

87

And there was some amazement in her thought,
At this new situation; but when she
Had taken stock, she did not find it fraught
With danger – not as far as she could see;
A man – it is a possibility –
May love a woman till his heart will crack;
But she is not obliged to love him back.

88

But as she sat and meditated thus,
The clamour of a skirmish rose without,
Men in the street were shouting 'Troilus!
He has just put a horde of Greeks to rout!'
At that her servants all began to shout
'Ha! Come and see! Open the lattice wide!
This is the street through which he'll have to ride

89

'To reach the palace – the only way, of course,
From Dardanus Gate, that's where the chain is down.'
With that he came, leading his little force
In file, at ease; and so they entered town.
It was his lucky day, without a frown
On Fortune's face; nothing, they say, can be
Hindered that happens by necessity.

90

This Troilus sat high on his bay steed,
Fully and richly armed, showing his face.
His horse, being wounded, had begun to bleed;
He rode him homeward at a gentle pace,
And truly such a sight of knightly grace,
As seen in him, was never seen before,
Even in Mars, who is the god of war.

91

So like a man of arms, so like a knight
He seemed, so full of high courageousness,
For he had both the body and the might
For gallantry, as well as hardiness;
And then to see him in his fighting dress,
So fresh, so young, so thoroughbred, so trim,
It was a very heaven to look at him.

92

His helmet, which was hewn in twenty places,
Hung by a tissue down behind his back;
His shield was battered in by swords and maces,
With arrows lodged in it in many a crack
That had pierced horn and rind and sinewy pack;
And still the shout went up 'Here comes our joy,
And, next his brother, holder up of Troy!'

93

This made him blush a little, out of shame,
To hear his praises sung with such a din,
And it was sport to notice, as he came,
How modestly he dropped his eyes and chin.
Criseyde could take his whole appearance in;
Down to her heart she let it softly sink,
Saying to herself 'O who has given me drink?'[7]

94

For her own thoughts she started to blush red,
As she remembered 'Heavens! This is he,
The man my uncle swears may soon be dead,
If he should get no mercy out of me.'
And in pure shame at such a notion, she
Pulled in her head and made the window fast,
While he and all the shouting crowd went past.

95

She began casting, rolling up and down
Within her thought, his excellence in war,
His royal state, his widely-spread renown,
His wit, his shape, his reputation for
Nobility; and yet what moved her more
Was that he pined for *her*, that such a youth
Should die for her – if he intended truth!

96

Now envious souls might quarrel with me thus:
'This was a sudden love! For how could she
So lightly give her love to Troilus,
And at first sight of him! Can such things be?'
Those who say that will get no good of me.
For everything must needs have a beginning
Ere all is done, and when it comes to winning

97

Her love, I do not say she suddenly
Gave it to him; but she began to incline
To like him first, and I have told you why.
His manhood and the thought that he would pine
On her account invited love to mine
Within her; but long service and devotion
Got him her love; it was no sudden motion.

98

And also blissful Venus, well arrayed,
Sat in her seventh house in heaven[8], and so
Was well disposed, with other stars in aid,
To cure the foolish Troilus of his woe;
And, to tell truth, she was not wholly foe
To Troilus in his nativity,
But somewhat favoured him, the luckier he.

99

And now no more of Troilus, let him go
Riding along, and let us turn as fast
Back to Criseyde, who sat with head hung low
All by herself, beginning to forecast
What course to set her mind upon at last,
If it should happen that her uncle's voice
Continued to press Troilus on her choice.

100

Lord! In her mind what arguments deployed
About this matter of which you have been told!
What it was best to do, and what avoid,
She turned them back and forth in fold on fold;
And now her heart was warm and now was cold,
And I shall write some part of this debate,
Which it has pleased my author to relate.

101

Prince Troilus in person well she knew
By sight, and also knew his gentle birth;
And so she thought 'Though it would never do
To grant him love, yet, seeing his great worth,
To be on terms of friendliness and mirth
With him would be an honour, and might be
Some ease to him and a support to me.

102

'I know, moreover, he is my King's son;
Since he now looks on me with such delight,
To flee him utterly would be to run
The risk, perhaps, of rousing him to spite,
And then I should be standing in worse plight;
Would it be wise for me, in such a case,
To purchase hate where I may stand in grace?

103

'Measure and temperance lie in all endeavour,
I know; if one prohibits drunkenness,
That does not mean that everyone for ever
Is doomed to drinklessness, or so I guess!
Knowing myself the cause of his distress,
Can I despise him? I don't think I should,
Since it seems certain that he means my good.

104

'And more than that, I've known for many a day
That he's no fool, his character is good;
Certainly, he's no boaster, so they say,
He's too intelligent, that's understood.
Nor will I cherish him, suppose I could,
Enough for him to boast, or have good cause
To boast; for I will sign to no such clause.

105

'Let us suppose the worst that could befall:
People might know he was in love with me.
Would that dishonour me? Why, not at all!
Can I prevent him? Not that I can see.
One hears about such cases constantly;
A man will love a woman without permission
From her; is she the worse for that condition?

106

'Think, too, that he is able to pick out –
Out of the whole of Troy – the loveliest
To be his love (her honour not in doubt);
For he is out and out the worthiest
Except for Hector, who is still the best;
And yet, to save his life now lies in me!
But such is love, and such my destiny.

107

'It is no wonder if he love me, though;
Heaven help me, well I know it – by the bye,
This is a thought I must let no one know –
I am among the loveliest, it's no lie,
For anyone, at least, that has an eye;
And so they say through all the town of Troy;
What wonder then if I should give him joy?

108

'I'm my own mistress, happily at ease,
Thank God for it, according to my state,
Young and untethered, where the pastures please,
I fear no jealousy, have no debate;
I have no husband now to say "Checkmate!"
Husbands are always full of jealousy,
Or masterful, or hunting novelty.

109

'What shall I do? What have I ever done?
Shall I not love – were I to think that best?
What! Heaven knows I could not be a nun.
And if I were to set my heart to rest
Upon this knight, who is the worthiest,
Keeping my honour safe and my good name,
By rights it should not do me any shame.'

110

But just as when the sun is shining bright
In March, a month which often changes face,
A gust of wind will set a cloud in flight
To overspread him in the blue of space,
A sudden, cloudy thought began to chase
Across her soul and overspread them all,
Those happy thoughts; fear almost made her fall.

111

The fear was this: 'Alas, since I am free,
Am I to love and put myself in danger?
Am I to lose my darling liberty?
Am I not mad to trust it to a stranger?
For look at others and their dog-in-manger
Loves, and their anxious joys, constraints and fears!
She who loves none has little cause for tears.

112

'For love is still the stormiest way of life,
In its own kind, that ever was begun;
There's always some mistrust, some silly strife
In love, some cloud that covers up the sun;
We wretched women! What is to be done
In all our grief? We sit and weep and think;
Our grief is this, that it's our grief we drink.

113

'And then there are these wicked tongues whose fashion
Is to speak harm; and men are so untrue;
Immediately they cease to feel their passion,
They cease to love; they're off to love anew;
But harm that's done is done, that's certain too:
Those are the very ones that passion rends;
But violent delights have violent ends.⁹

114

'How many are the times when we must own
That treachery to woman has been done!
Can any purpose in such love be shown?
And what becomes of it when it is gone?
No one can say, the answer is not known;
It has no substance, nothing solid in it;
Nothing to end with, nothing to begin it.

115

'How busy, if I love, I'll have to be,
Wooing the gossips! What a time I'll spend
Cajoling them, lest they speak harm of me!
For, without reason for it, they pretend
That it is very wrong to please one's friend.
But who can silence every wicked tongue,
Or stop the sound of bells while they are rung?'

116

But after that her thought began to clear;
She said 'Well, nothing venture, nothing win,
Like it or not!' Then a return to fear
Came with some other thought to hem her in;
Fear set her quaking, hope turned pale and thin,
Now hot, now cold; with these two to confuse her,
She rose and looked for something to amuse her.

117

And down the stairs immediately she went,
Into the garden with her nieces three,
And up and down they wandered in content,
Flexippe, Tarba and Antigone,[10]
In play together there, a joy to see,
And other of her women, a great rout
Followed her round the garden and about.

118

It was a wide, walled garden of pleached alleys,
And shadowy with blossom and with green,
All newly benched and sanded; little valleys
And little hills there were, and in between
They walked enlaced; Antigone, serene,
Antigone the Bright, began to sing
A Trojan song. It was a heavenly thing.

119

The Song of Antigone

O love, to whom I am, and ever shall
Be humble subject, and of purpose true,
To Thee, as best I may, I offer all
My heart's desire for ever, in revenue!
For never did thy heavenly grace endue
Any with blessedness so much as me;
I live secure in joy, from all fear free.

120

O blissful god, thou hast me sweetly fettered
In love; there surely is no creature living
Who could imagine how it might be bettered!
For, Lord, with neither quarrel nor misgiving,
The one I love is wholly bent on giving
Me tireless service true; a more unfeigned
There never was, nor less by evil stained.

121

He is the well of honour, and the ground
Of truth, the mirror of all goodliness,
Apollo-thoughted, Lord of new pleasures found,
Rock of my safety, very rootedness
Of virtue, and the slayer of distress;
And, sure, I love him best, as he loves me;
Good fortune follow him, where'er he be!

122

Whom should I thank but Thee, O god above,
For all this bliss in which I now begin
To bathe? Ah, Lord, I give Thee thanks for love!
This is the life, the right life, to be in,
To banish every form of vice and sin;
This turns me so to virtue, I intend
In heart and spirit daily to amend.

123

And whosoever says that love is vice,
Or servitude, through feeling its distress,
Is either envious or overnice,
Or is unable out of brutishness
To love at all; such are the folk, I guess,
Who defame love; nothing of him they know;
They talk, but never yet have bent his bow.

124

What, is the sun, which nature made so bright,
The worse because mere man has not the power
To look upon it with his feeble sight?
Is love the worse, because some wretch is sour?
No happiness that cannot face an hour
Of sorrow has any worth; let those whose bones
Are made of glass, beware of throwing stones!

125

But I, with all my heart and all my might,
As I have said, will love, unto my last,
My dearest heart, my own beloved knight,
In whom my soul has verily grown fast
As his in me, and shall till Time is past.
I feared love once, and dreaded to begin it;
Now I know well there is no peril in it.

126

The song was over and she ceased to sing;
After a moment, 'Niece,' inquired Criseyde,
'Who made that song? It is a charming thing,
And well-intentioned.' And her niece replied
'Madam, the loveliest girl, and best allied,
Of highest rank in all the town of Troy;
She leads her life in greatest honour and joy.'

127

'It certainly would seem so, by her song.'
Criseyde replied, and sighed in her delight.
'Lord! And can so much happiness belong
To lovers? Can they love as they can write?'
'Yes, truly,' said Antigone the White,
'And better; none that ever lived can tell
The bliss of loving, or describe it well.

128

'But never think that every wretch and sot
Knows the true bliss of love; it is not so.
They think it's love if one of them feels hot;
But not at all! It is their ignorance, though.
You have to ask the saints if you would know
If it is fair in Heaven; they can tell.
And ask a fiend if it is foul in Hell.'

129

Criseyde said nothing; then, from a world away,
She answered 'Yes . . . Evening has come at last.'
But every word that she had heard her say
She printed in her heart. The daylight passed.
Her fear of love lessened and faded fast;
Love sank into her heart and, terror fleeing,
Began on the conversion of her being.

130

The day's bright honour, and the eye of heaven,
Night's enemy – all this I call the sun –
Was westering swiftly as his car was driven
Downwards to earth; his daily course was run,
And all things white were growing dim and dun
For lack of light; the stars began to show;
She and her folk went in; and time to go.

131

And later when she wished to go to rest,
Being inclined to sleep, or so she said,
When gone were every visitor and guest,
Her womenfolk attended her to bed.
When all was hushed, she lay there still; her head
Was filled with everything she could recall
Of the day's doings; you have heard them all.

132

A nightingale upon a cedar green
Under the chamber window where she lay
Sang loudly out against the moony sheen,
And it may well have been, in its bird's way,
A lay of love; her heart grew light and gay.
And long she listened, but at last could keep
Awake no longer, and fell dead asleep.

133

Important (handwritten in left margin)

At once a dream descended on her rest;
There came an eagle, feathered white as bone,
Who set his curving talons to her breast
And tore her heart out, giving her his own
Into her body, left her there alone
– And yet she suffered neither fear nor smart –
And flew away, leaving her heart for heart.

134

So let her sleep, and let us turn once more
To Troilus riding back in bravery,
After the skirmish I described before;
There in his room he sits, while two or three
Messengers he had sent ran off to see
If Pandar could be found; and in the end
They came on him, and brought him to his friend.

135

This Pandarus came leaping in at once
And said 'Who's this that's taken such a beating
With swords and slings today? Is it that dunce
Young Troilus, who has a fever heating?'
And he began to joke, after this greeting,
'Lord how you sweat! Jump up, let's have a dish
Of dinner, and so to bed.' 'Well, as you wish.'

136

And off they went in haste, for they were bent
On supper and a quick return to bed;
Then their attendants closed the doors and went
Wherever private inclination led;
And Troilus, whose heart till then had bled
For woe, not knowing what news his friend would bring,
At last could say 'Well, do I weep or sing?'

137

Said Pandarus 'Lie still, and let me sleep;
It's all arranged; you can put on your hat;
And please yourself whether you sing or weep.
You'll have to trust me, but I tell you flat
She will do well by you, be sure of that,
And love you best, by God and on my oath,
Unless you fail in the pursuit, from sloth.

138

'I've got thus far in handling your affair –
From day to day, up to this happy morrow –
I've won her love – her friendship – for you; there!
For she has pledged herself; and you can borrow
On my security; I've lamed your sorrow,
I've cut its legs away.' As you have heard
It all, I needn't say another word.

139

And just as flowers in the chill of night,
Closed in themselves, will stoop upon their stalk,
Then hold their heads up to the morning's light
And spread their natural beauty where we walk,
So Troilus, on hearing Pandar talk,
Threw up his eyes, and cried with upturned face,
'O Venus, blessed be thy power and grace!'

140

To Pandar then he held up both his hands;
'Dear Lord, all that I have is yours!' said he,
'I'm free! You've burst my cruel iron bands;
A thousand Troys, though they were given me
One at a time, by God, could never be
So welcome or so gladdening to my heart;
It spreads for joy, O it will burst apart!

141

'Lord, what am I to do? How live? O when
Shall I next see her? Sweetest heart! My dear!
How drive away the long, long time till then?
How soon will you be going again to see her?
You will say "Wait, be patient, there's no fear",
But felons hanging, fighting for their breath,
Wait in the greatest agony for death.'

142

'Now, take it easy, for the love of Mars!
There is a time for everything, just wait
At least till night is over and the stars
Have disappeared, for it's as sure as Fate
I shall be there a little after eight;
Do as I tell you, then, as I implore you;
Or get some other man to do it for you.

143

'And God's my judge that always up till now
I've served you readily until tonight;
And this is no pretence, as you'll allow;
I've always done my best for your delight.
Do as I say, and you will be all right;
And if you won't, then seek your own relief,
And don't blame me if you should come to grief.

144

'I know you are a wiser man than I,
A thousand times; but still, if I were you
(God help me so!), the thing for you to try
Would be to write to her, this moment too,
In your own hand; a letter. That should do,
Begging her pity, saying you were ill;
Now don't give in to sloth, but show your will.

145

'I'll take it to her early in the day
And when you know that I am with her there,
Ride past upon a courser right away
In your best armour – but as if there were
Nothing particular happening. I'll take care
That she and I are in a window-seat;
We shall be looking down into the street.

146

'Salute us, if you like, but make it plain,
However, that your look is aimed at me;
And on your life be careful to refrain
From lingering there; God save us, that would be
Disaster! Just ride on with dignity;
We shall be talking of you, and I know
That when you have gone by, your ears will glow.

147

'As to your letter, you have sense enough
Not to be formal, or to show your wit
By being argumentative or tough;
Your handwriting should not be exquisite
Or clerkly; blot it with your tears a bit;
And if you hit on something good to soften
Her heart, avoid repeating it too often.

148

'For if the greatest harpist now alive,
Having the finest-toned, most glorious harp
That ever was, with all his fingers five,
And finger-nails that never were so sharp,
Kept warbling on one string, we all would carp
At his performance, for we should be bored
By those full strokes on that repeated chord.

149

'Don't jumble up discordant things together,
Medical terms, for instance, do not strike
The proper note in love; and take care whether
Your matter fits your form; they should be like;
For if a painter were to paint a pike
With donkey feet and headed like an ape,
It would not do; it would be just a jape.'

150

Now this advice appealed to Troilus
But still, he answered with a lover's sense
Of apprehension 'O, but Pandarus,
I'd be ashamed to write – it's no pretence –
For I might innocently give offence,
Or she refuse the letter, or resent it,
Then I should die and nothing could prevent it.'

151

Pandar replied 'You do as I suggest,
And let me take it to her, as I say;
For, by the Lord that made the east and west,
I hope to bring an answer right away,
Straight from her hand; and if you won't obey,
Well, let it go, and bitter be his pill
Who tries to give you help against your will.'

152

Said Troilus 'All right, then; I agree,
Since it's your wish; I will get up and write;
And I pray God in all sincerity
To speed the letter which I shall indite,
And your delivery of it. O White
Minerva, send me wit to write it well!'
And he sat down and wrote as I shall tell.

153

He called her his true lady, life and joy,
His sorrow's cure, his bliss, his heart's desire.
And all the other phrases they employ,
These lovers, as their cases may require;
Humbly at first he wrote, and, taking fire,
He tried to earn his way into her grace;
To tell it all would ask no little space.

154

And next he begged her with all lowliness,
Because he wrote in madness, not to chide
The audacity; he wrote under duress;
Love made him do it, or he would have died;
He begged her piteously to take his side,
And after that he said (and lied like thunder)
He was worth nothing, he was no great wonder,

155

And she must make allowance for his skill,
Which was but little; and he feared her so,
And argued his unworthiness until
He turned from that to dwell upon his woe,
But that was endless, it would never go;
His truth was sworn to her and he would hold it.
He read it over and began to fold it.

156

And as he did his tears fell salt and wet
Upon the ruby signet which he wore;
He set it neatly to the wax, and yet
He kissed the letter a thousand times before
He made an end, and, folding it once more,
Said 'Letter, what a blissful destiny
Awaits thee now, since she will look on thee!'

157

On the next day this Pandar took the letter
Off to his niece; he made an early start.
He swore it must be nine o'clock, or better,
And joked away and said 'Oh my poor heart!
How fresh it is! But how I feel it smart!
I never can sleep in May, I shan't tomorrow!
I have a jolly woe, a lusty sorrow!'

158

Now when she heard her uncle's voice, Criseyde,
With breathless heart, all eagerness to hear
The reason for his coming, thus replied
'Now tell me, on your honour, Uncle dear,
Whatever kind of wind has blown you here?
Tell us about your "lusty sorrow", do!
Where in love's dance can they have fitted you?'

159

'By God,' he said, 'I hop along behind!'
She laughed so much she thought her heart would burst.
'Mock on,' said Pandarus, 'that's right, be kind!
But I've some news for you, so listen first;
A stranger's come to town, and I conversed
With him, a Grecian spy, with something new
To say; I've come to pass it on to you.

160

'Let's go into the garden – lovely weather –
And be in private, it's a long affair.'
So off they sauntered, arm in arm together,
Down from her room and out into the air,
Far enough off for none to hear and stare;
And then he stopped, turned round and looked about,
And said to her, drawing the letter out,

161

'Look, he that is all yours, and at your free
Disposal, recommends himself to you,
Humbly, and sends this letter here by me;
When you have time, think it well over, do,
And try to find a kindly answer too,
For otherwise, God help me, to speak plain,
He cannot live much longer in such pain.'

162

She stood stock still at this, in sudden dread,
Not taking it; the meekness in her face
Began to change. 'Letters and notes!' she said
'Bring none of them to me, for heaven's grace;
And, dearest Uncle, in the present case,
I beg you put my interests before
His needs and pleasures. What can I say more?

163

'Consider now if it is reasonable –
And do not spare from favour or from sloth
To tell the truth – would it be suitable
To my condition – tell me on your oath –
To take it, or to pity him, or both,
Laying myself so open to attack,
Harming myself? For heaven's sake, take it back!'

164

On hearing this, Pandar began to stare
And answered 'Well! This is the greatest wonder
That ever I saw! Stop putting on this air
Of affectation; strike me dead with thunder
If I would stoop, to save the city yonder,
To bringing you a letter that could harm you,
Or one to him! What is there to alarm you?

165

'That's how you all behave, or almost all;
He who most longs to serve you, in your eyes,
Is least to be considered, let him fall!
It doesn't matter if he lives or dies.
By all I may deserve of you, be wise,
Take it, and don't refuse!' He caught her gown,
And in her bosom thrust the letter down.

166

'Throw it away, or tear it up, I say,
Let them all stare,' he said, 'we're in full view!'
'Well, I can wait till they have gone away.'
She answered, smiling, 'Uncle, I beg you, do
Take him whatever answer pleases you;
I will write nothing to him, let me state.'
'No? Well, I will,' he said, 'if you'll dictate.'

167

At that she laughed and said 'Let's go to dinner.'
He fell to jesting at himself, and passed
To other matters: 'Niece, I'm getting thinner;
It's love; and every other day I fast,
I suffer so!' All his best jokes at last
Came tumbling out, until his crazy chaffing
Made her afraid that she would die of laughing.

168

And when they had returned into the hall
She said 'Let us have dinner right away,
Uncle.' Her women answered to her call,
And to her room she went without delay;
But of her business there I have to say
That one thing which, for sure, she went to do
Was privately to read this letter through.

169

She conned it word by word, and line by line,
And found no lack of it; she thought it good,
Put it away and then went down to dine,
And came unseen on Pandarus, who stood
In a brown study, and caught him by the hood;
'Aha! You're caught!' she said, 'You didn't see!'
'Yes, I surrender! What's the penalty?'

170

They washed their hands and then sat down to eat,
And, about noontime, Pandar had the wit
To draw towards the window next the street,
And said 'Whose is that house just opposite?
The one out there, who decorated it?'
'Which house?' she said, and moved across to see,
And told him whose it happened then to be.

171

They fell in converse upon slender themes,
Both sitting by the window, in the splay,
Till Pandar saw the moment for his schemes
Had come, her servants having gone away.
'Now niece,' said he, 'Come out with it, I say!
That letter that you wot of, did he show
Up well in it? Of course, I wouldn't know.'

172

She didn't answer but began to hum,
But in the end she murmured 'So I think.'
'Well, for God's love, repay him for it, come!'
Her cheeks began to flame a rosy pink.
'I'll do the sealing, you shall do the ink!'
He knelt to her, 'A small reward, maybe,
But leave the sealing of it, do, to me!'

173

'Yes, I could write, of course,' she said, 'but then
The trouble is, I don't know what to say.'
'Now, niece,' said Pandar, 'don't say that again;
At least you're bound to thank him, anyway,
For his goodwill – unless you wish to slay!
And so, my little niece, for love of me,
On this occasion, don't refuse,' said he.

174

'Kind heaven, may all be well when all is done.'
She said, 'God help me, this is the first letter
That ever I wrote, or any part of one.'
And to her room she went alone, the better
To commune with herself and to unfetter
Her heart a little from its prison-plight
In her disdain, and set herself to write.

175

Of what she wrote him I shall only mention
The substance (if my grasp of it is sound);
She gave him thanks for every good intention
Towards her, but declined to give him ground
For greater hope; she never would be bound
In love, save as a sister; this, to please him,
She gladly would allow, if that could ease him.

176

She folded it, returned to where, alone,
Pandarus sat and stared into the street,
And on a golden cushion, on a stone
Of jasper, next to him she took her seat,
And said 'I never had a harder feat
As God's my witness, to accomplish. You
Have made me write it; you constrained me to.'

177

She gave it him; he thanked her and replied
'God knows that things unwillingly begun
Can often turn out well, dear niece Criseyde;
That you have been with difficulty won
Should gladden him, by God and yonder sun!
Because they say "Impressions lightly made
Are commonly among the first to fade."

178

'But you have played the tyrant far too long,
Your hard heart has resisted the engraver;
Now hesitate no longer, but be strong,
And though you still may wish to keep the flavour
Of cold formality, O give him savour
Of joy, and soon! Too studied a disdain
Can breed an answering scorn, to ease the pain.'

179

And just as they were arguing, just then,
Troilus turned the corner of the street
On horseback, with a company of ten,
Quietly riding like a little fleet,
Beneath his lady at her window-seat,
Towards the palace. Pandar, first aware,
Said 'Look at that! You see who's riding there?'

180

'Now don't run in, he's seen us, I suppose
And he may think you're trying to avoid him.'
'No, no,' she answered, turning red as rose;
And he saluted her (though fear destroyed him)
With humble looks; and yet it overjoyed him.
His colour came and went, and up he cast
A nod at Pandarus, and on he passed.

181

God knows whether he sat his horse aright,
Or looked his best on that eventful day!
God knows if he was like a manly knight!
Why should I drudge to tell you his array?
Criseyde, who saw it, I will briefly say,
Liked what she saw thus gathered in a glance,
His person, his array, his countenance,

182

His goodly manner and his gentle breed,
So much that never yet since she was born
Had she felt such compassion in his need
Of her, for all the hardness of her scorn.
I hope to God she now can feel the thorn;
She shall not pull it out this week, or next.
God send her more such thorns would be my text!

183

Now Pandar, standing close beside her there,
Sensing the iron hot, began to smite.
'Niece, let me ask you, if the question's fair,
Would you suppose a girl was doing right
If, for a lack of pity in her, in spite
Of innocence in him, she gave no heed
And brought his death upon him?' 'No, indeed!'

184

'God knows that's true, if ever truth there was!
You feel I am not lying, that is plain;
Look, there he goes a-riding!' 'So he does!'
'Well, as I've told you over and again,
Give up this foolishness of mad disdain
And speak to him – if but to ease his heart;
Don't let a scruple keep you so apart.'

185

He had to heave to make her grant the boon;
All things considered, it was not to be;
Why not? From shame. Besides it was too soon
To offer him so great a liberty.
It was her whole intention, argued she,
To love him unbeknown, if she so might,
And only gratify his sense of sight.

186

Pandar was thinking 'That will never do,
Not if I know it! Fantasies like these
Must not be entertained a year or two.'
Why make a sermon of his niceties?
He saw he must agree as one agrees
For the time being; and when evening fell
He rose and took his leave, and all was well.

187

He hurried homeward then, and as he sped
Upon his way, his heart was in a dance.
And Troilus he found alone in bed,
Like all these lovers, in a kind of trance;
Between dark desperation and the chance
Of hope he lay, and Pandar came in singing,
As if to say 'Just look at what I'm bringing!'

188

And said 'Who's taken to his bed so soon
And buried himself?' 'Friend, it is I,' said he.
'Why, if it isn't Troilus, by the moon!
You must get up at once; and you shall see
A charm that has been sent to you, through me,
To cure your ecstasy of sigh and sob,
If you've the strength to finish off the job.'

189

'Yes, with the help of God,' said Troilus,
And took the letter of Criseyde's inditing.
Said Pandar, laughing, 'God is good to us;
Here, take a light, and look at all this writing!'
Racing with joy, quaking with fear, a fighting
Rose in the heart of Troilus as he read,
And every word inspired hope or dread.

190

But in the end he took it for the best,
This letter of hers; for his attention lit
Upon a passage where his heart could rest;
Though she had veiled her meaning quite a bit,
He held to the more hopeful part of it;
So what with hope and Pandar's promised care,
He freed himself at least from sheer despair.

191

But, as we all can notice every day,
The more the wood and coal, the more the fire;
Increase of hope, be it for what it may,
Will very often bring increased desire,
Or, as an oak springs from a little spire,
So this same letter that she had returned him
Served to increase the passion that so burned him.

192

Therefore I have to say that day and night
This Troilus now hankered for her more
Than at the first, through hope; with all his might
He pressed ahead, and, helped by Pandar's lore,
He wrote to her of what he suffered for
Her sake, and, not to let the matter cool,
Sent word, by Pandar, daily as a rule.

193

All the observances that in these cases
A lover must perform, he also kept;
And, as the chance of fortune threw him aces
Or not, so he exulted or he wept;
Such throws as he received he must accept.
According to such answers as he had
His day was miserable, or was glad.

194

But it was always Pandarus to whom
He turned, in his complaining, for relief,
Begging advice and succour in his gloom,
And Pandarus, who saw his crazy grief,
Would nearly die of pity, and, in brief,
Busily searched his wits for what to do
To put an end to it, and quickly too,

195

And said 'Dear lord and brother, and dear friend,
God knows that when you suffer I feel woe,
If you could bring yourself to make an end
Of these sad faces! I can shape things, though,
With God's good help, within a day or so,
So as to bring you to a certain place
Where you can speak to her and beg for grace.

196

'And certainly – perhaps you mayn't have heard –
The experts in the arts of love do say
One of the things that makes a man preferred
Is if he finds the leisure time to pray
For grace, and some safe corner where he may.
Given a kindly heart, it must impress,
To see and hear the guiltless in distress.

197

'Perhaps you're thinking "Even were it so,
Supposing Nature move her to begin
To have some sort of pity on my woe,
Disdain would answer "You can never win
The spirit in her heart that rules within;
Though she may bend, she stands upon her stem."
Alas, my griefs! What help is that to them?

198

'But then remember that the sturdy oak,
When all the heavy hacking has been done,
Receives at last the happy felling-stroke;
There's a great rush and down it comes in one,
As do these rocks or mill-stones, at a run;
For heavy things will fall with greater force
And speed than will a lighter thing, of course.

199

'Now take a reed that bends to every blast
Quite easily; lull wind, and it will rise;
Not so an oak, which lies when it is cast
To ground; perhaps I need not moralize.
People are glad when a great enterprise
Is well achieved, stands firm, and none can doubt it;
And all the more if they took long about it.

200

'But, Troilus, putting these thoughts away,
I have a question for you, a request:
Which, of your many brothers, would you say
In your heart's privacy you loved the best?'
'Deiphebus, of course, above the rest.'
'Deiphebus? Well, in a day or so,
He'll ease your heart for you, and yet not know.

201

'Leave all to me; I'll work it if I can.
And off he went to see Deiphebus,
Whom he had always loved as Prince and man,
And was his best friend, next to Troilus.
And, to be brief, Pandar addressed him thus:
'Sir, let me beg of you to take my part
In a small matter which I have at heart.'

202

'Why, certainly! Whatever I can do,
God willing, shall be done without delay;
There's no one I would rather help than you,
Except my brother Troilus. In what way?
How can I help? You only have to say.
I don't remember ever taking part
Against a project that you had at heart.'

203

Pandarus thanked him, and in turn replied,
'Well, sir, there is a lady in this town
Who is my niece, and she is called Criseyde;
Now there are some who want to drag her down,
To steal her property and good renown,
And this is what has led me to beseech
Your help and friendship, Sir, without more speech.'

204

'O, is she not – this lady in distress,
Of whom you speak in such a distant way –
My friend Criseyde?' Pandarus answered: 'Yes.'
'Why, then, there's nothing more you need to say,'
Deiphebus said, 'believe it – and you may –
I'll be her champion too with spur and spear,
And if they hear of it, well let them hear.

205

'But, tell me, since you know what has occurred,
How should we act?' 'My Lord, if I may borrow
On your good nature, deign to send her word
To come and see you, say, some time tomorrow,
When she can privately unfold her sorrow.
Were she to bring her griefs to you, why then,
It would strike fear into these wicked men.

206

'And if I might make bolder still with you,
And burden you with something more than this,
Could you invite your brothers – one or two
To give her case a certain emphasis?
Then, I am sure, nothing could go amiss
In helping her, what with your interest
And that of other friends, as I suggest.'

207

Deiphebus, whose breed was of a kind
To do as honour and as bounty bade,
Replied 'It shall be done, and I can find
Still greater help; you need not be afraid.
Suppose for instance that I could persuade
Helen herself to minister to her needs?
Paris will follow too when Helen leads.

208

'For Hector, my Commander and my brother,
There is no need to beg for his support;
For I have heard him, one time and another,
Speak of Criseyde with praise of every sort
– He couldn't have spoken better; and, in short,
She has his good opinion. It's no task,
Getting his help; it's ours before we ask.

209

'And speak yourself, will you, to Troilus
On my behalf? Ask him to come and dine.'
'Sir, this shall all be done,' said Pandarus;
He took his leave, intent on the design,
And to his niece's house, in a straight line,
He went and found her rising from her table,
And down he sat himself, and spoke, when able:

210

'O blessed Lord, O God, how I have run!
Look, little niece! You see how I am sweating?
I doubt if you will thank me when I've done;
That wretched Poliphetes – you're forgetting?
Aren't you aware? – is at this moment setting
About new means to have you put on trial.'
'I? No!' she said, and paled in her denial.

211

'What is he after? Why does he so hound me?
It's very wrong. O what am I to do?
He's not alone in trying to confound me,
For there is Ántenor, Aeneas too,
Who are his friends in this – they make a crew.
But, for God's love, dear uncle, let it go;
If they take everything, well, be it so!

212

'Without all that, I have enough for us.'
'No!' answered Pandarus, 'it shall not be!
I've just been talking to Deiphebus,
Hector, and other lords, some two or three,
And made each one of them his enemy.
If I can help it he shall never win,
Whatever he does, whenever he may begin.'

213

And as they cast about for what was best
To do, Deiphebus in courtesy
Came personally to make it his request
To have the pleasure of her company
At dinner the next day, and willingly
She told him she was happy to obey;
He thanked her then, and went upon his way.

214

Then (to be brief) Pandar went off alone
To Troilus, to tell him what had passed,
And found him sitting, still as any stone.
He told him everything from first to last
And of the subtle dust that he had cast
In his brother's eyes; 'And now,' he said, 'it's done.
Behave yourself tomorrow and she's won!

215

'Speak, beg, implore her, piteously bewail,
Have no compunction, slackness, shame or fear,
Sooner or later one must tell the tale,
Believe it, and she'll lend a kindly ear;
You will in fact be saved by faith, my dear.
I know you feel afraid and in distress,
And what it is I bet you I can guess.

216

'You're thinking: "How am I to do all this?
From my sad face people are bound to see
I'm sick for love of her; they could not miss;
I'd rather die unknown in misery."
Don't think like that, it's imbecility.
I know you are afraid; if you look sick
We can make use of that; I have a trick.

217

'Go overnight, and sooner if you may,
Stay with your brother – as a relaxation,
As if to drive your malady away;
You do look ill, it's no exaggeration.
And then go off to bed in desperation
And say you can't endure a moment more;
Then lie right there and wait for what's in store.

218

'Say that your fevers usually take
A regular course and last until the morrow;
And let me see how nicely you can fake.
God knows that "sick is he that is in sorrow".
Now, off with you! Farewell! If I can borrow
The help of Venus, and you stay the pace,
She shall confirm you fully in her grace.'

219

'Alas,' said Troilus, 'there is no need
To counsel me to feign that I am sick,
For I am sick in earnest, sick indeed,
Sick unto death. I'm wounded to the quick.'
'All the less need,' said Pandar, 'for a trick;
The more you sweat, the less you're a deceiver;
People expect a man to sweat in fever.

220

'Keep close beside the trysting-place, and see
How well I drive the deer towards your bow.'
Then Pandarus departed equably,
And Troilus went homeward in a glow
Of joy, for never had he gloried so
In all his life; giving his whole assent
To Pandar, to his brother's house he went.

221

What need to tell you of the care and fuss
Of welcome that Deiphebus displayed,
Or of the fevered looks of Troilus,
Or of the pile of blankets that they laid
Upon him, or the entertainment made
To cheer him up? But it was all for naught;
He played his part as Pandarus had taught.

222

Before he slept (it cannot be denied)
Deiphebus had begged of him that night
To be a friend and helper to Criseyde.
God knows he granted this without a fight,
To be her friend entire, with all his might;
This was indeed no more to beg of him
Than if you were to ask a duck to swim.

223

The morning came, and time was drawing near
For dinner; fair Queen Helen took the street
Towards Deiphebus; her thoughts were clear;
This was a homely visit, just to meet
And gossip with her brother, and then eat
A quiet meal; and that was why she went;
God alone knew – and Pandar – what it meant.

224

Criseyde came too, as innocent as she.
Antigone and Tarba came as well.
But it is best to shun prolixity;
Let us speed on, for heaven's sake, to dwell
Upon the main effect; I have to tell
Why all these folk assembled for this meeting;
Let us pass over what they said in greeting.

225

Deiphebus did them honour, filled their glasses,
And fed them well with what could please; but still
He interjected plentiful 'alases',
Saying 'Dear brother Troilus is ill,
He's still in bed.' And, having sighed his fill,
He took great pains to gladden them again,
As best he could, happy to entertain.

226

Helen commiserated in his sickness
So faithfully, her pity seemed to flow,
And everyone with a surprising quickness
Became a doctor: 'This is how to go
About a cure . . .' 'There is a charm I know . . .'
But there sat one, silent among the rest,
And she was thinking 'I could cure him best.'

227

And after pitying, they began to praise him,
As folk still do; when someone has begun
To praise a man, others will quickly raise him
A thousand times yet higher than the sun:
'He is . . . he can . . . he'll do what few have done.'
Pandar gave ear to all their approbation
And did not fail to add his confirmation.

228

Criseyde heard every word of this and gave
It deep attention, not without delight;
Her heart was laughing, though her looks were grave,
For who would not feel glory if she might
Command the life or death of such a knight?
But I'll pass on without delaying you;
All that I tell has but one end in view.

229

The moment came to rise from where they sat
At dinner; so they did, and everyone
Talked for a little while of this and that
Till Pandar, breaking in upon their fun
Said to Deiphebus, 'May it be done
As I requested? Would you, if you please,
Say something of Criseyde's necessities?'

230

Helen, who held her hand, took up the phrase
And said 'We are all eager, if you would.'
Looked at Criseyde and, with a friendly gaze,
Added 'Jove never let him come to good
Who does you harm! We'll help you as we should;
Sorrow on us, and all true folk, I say,
If we don't make this fellow rue the day!'

231

'You know the story,' said Deiphebus
To Pandarus, 'you be the one to tell.'
'My lords and ladies, then, the case stands thus;
Why should I keep you waiting? Very well . . .'
He rang out the indictment like a bell,
And made this Poliphetes sound so grim
And heinous that they would have spat at him.

232

And each more violently than the other
On Poliphetes heaped his bitterest curse;
'He deserves hanging, though he were my brother,
And hanged he certainly shall be, or worse!'
Why drag the story out another verse?
Plainly at once all swore to be her friend
In all they could; on that she might depend.

233

Helen remarked to Pandar presently
'Touching this matter, does my brother know,
Hector, I mean? And Troilus, does he?
Yes; and now listen: shouldn't we make her go
– Since he is here – to Troilus, and show
Her troubles to him now? If you consent,
She could explain them all before she went.

234

'For he would have her grief the more at heart,
Because she is a lady in distress;
And, by your leave, I'll pop in for a start,
And tell you in a minute, even less,
If he's asleep; it might be a success.'
And in he leapt and whispered in his ear
'The Lord receive thy soul! I've brought the bier.'

235

This sally won a smile from Troilus,
And Pandar, with no more manoeuvring,
Went out to Helen and Deiphebus
And said 'So long as there's no lingering,
And not too many people, you may bring
Criseyde to see him, and he gives assurance
He'll hear her to the best of his endurance.

236

'But, as you know, the room is very small,
Even a few would make it rather warm;
I won't be answerable – listen, all! –
If you come thronging in you'll do him harm
And injure him; I'd rather lose my arm!
Whether it's better to postpone her visit
Let those decide who know; not easy, is it?

237

'I think it best, as far as I can tell,
For no one to go in but just you two,
Or me, perhaps; that would be just as well,
She doesn't know the details as I do;
I can present them quickly, she renew
Her plea for patronage, and slip away.
That cannot much disturb him, I dare say.

238

'And then, as she's a stranger, he'll forgo
His rest a little, as he never would
For you; another thing: I chance to know
He wants to tell you something for the good
Of Troy – a secret, so I understood.'
Neither of them suspecting his intent,
There was no further parley; in they went.

239

And Helen, in her soft and lovely way,
Saluted him, with all her womanly charm
Saying playfully 'You must get up, I say,
My handsome brother must not come to harm!'
And round his shoulders then she slipped an arm
And tried with all her wit to do him good,
Amuse and comfort him, as best she could.

240

And after that she said 'We beg of you,
I, and your brother, who is here with me,
Deiphebus – and Pandar begs you too –
Be friend and patron, give your sympathy
To poor Criseyde, for she is certainly
The victim of great wrongs, as Pandar knows;
He'll tell you how the case against her goes.'

241

This Pandarus began to file his tongue
To state her case; it slipped into the groove.
After a little, when his song was sung,
Troilus said 'As soon as I can move,
I gladly will be one of you, to prove
The justice of her cause with all my might.'
Queen Helen said 'And fortune speed the right!'

242

Pandarus asked him 'Would you mind if she
Took leave of you before she has to go?'
'Why, God forbid that she should not,' said he,
'If she will honour me by doing so.'
And after saying this, he added 'Oh
Deiphebus, and you, my sister dear,
I have to talk to you – I've something here,

243

'In which I certainly should be the better
For your advice,' and found beside his bed
(It happened so) a document or letter
Hector had sent him, asking advice, he said,
Whether some man deserved to lose his head,
I don't know who. And with the gravest air,
He begged of them to study it with care.

244

Deiphebus began unfolding it
In serious thought with Helena the Queen,
And out they roamed to read it, bit by bit,
Down the great stairway to an arbour green,
Studying it to see what they could glean;
And, roughly speaking, for about an hour
They read and pored upon it in their bower.

245

Now let them read; turn we to the event
And Pandar, prying like a man in haste,
To see if all was well; and out he went
Into the larger room, indeed, he raced;
'God bless this company!' he said, 'Make haste,
Dear niece, Queen Helen is awaiting you
Outside, my lady and their lordships too.

246

'Come, rise and bring your niece Antigone,
Or whom you will, no matter. I would say
The fewer of you the better; come with me
And see you thank them humbly for today,
All three of them, before you go away;
Seize the right moment for departure, lest
We stay too long and rob him of his rest.'

247

All innocent of Pandarus' intent,
Criseyde gave answer, in her ignorance,
'Let's go, dear Uncle.' Arm in arm they went,
And while she framed her words and countenance,
Pandarus, with a very earnest glance,
Said 'For God's love, you others, keep away,
Amuse yourselves; think of some game to play.

248

'Think where you are and who we have within
And in what state he is – God send a cure!'
Then, in an undertone, 'Come on, begin,
Go softly, little niece; and I adjure
You in the name of God to make all sure,
And by the Crown of Love to ease the pain
That you have caused; don't kill him with disdain.

249

'Shame on the devil! Think of who he is,
Think of him lying there in pain! have done!
Time lingered is Time lost, remember this;
You both will find that true, when two are one.
Secondly, all is safe; for there are none
Who yet have guessed; come off it, if you can,
While they are hoodwinked; on, and win your man!

250

'Titterings and pursuings and delays
Are feathers in the wind for folk to see;
Though you may later wish for happy days,
You will not dare, and why? For she and she
Exchanged a certain word, or he and he
A look. Lest *I* lose time, I dare not deal
With this at length; come, bring your man to heel!'

251

Now all you lovers that are listening here,
Think what a terrible predicament
For Troilus, who heard them drawing near!
He thought 'O Lord . . . O what has Fortune sent?
Am I to die, or shall I have content?'
He was to sue for love – his first assay!
Great God Almighty, what is he to say?

Book III

BOOK III

I

O blissful light, whose beams in clearness run
Over all Third Heaven[1], adorning it with splendour,
O daughter of Jove and darling of the Sun,
Pleasure of Love, O affable and tender,
The ready guest of noble hearts, defender
And cause of all well-being and delight,
Worshipped by thy benignity and might!

2

In heaven, in hell, in earth and the salt sea
Thy power is felt and is in evidence,
Since man, bird, beast, fish, herb and greening tree
Feel thee in season, eternal effluence!
God Himself loves, nor turns His countenance thence,
And there's no creature in this world alive
That without love has being or can thrive.

3

Thou first didst move Jove to those glad effects
Through which it comes that all things live and are,
Madest him amorous and, lo, he elects
His mortal loves; thou givest him, as far
As pleases thee, his pleasure, or dost bar,
Sending him in a thousand shapes to look
For love on earth; and whom thou wouldest, he took.

4

Yes, and fierce Mars for thee has slaked his ire;
Thou canst ennoble every heart and face
As it may please thee; those thou wilt set on fire
Learn to dread shame and shun whatever is base.
Courteous thou makest them, and fresh in grace,
And high or low, as his intent may be,
The joys a man may have are sent by thee.

5

Thou holdest realm and home in unity,
And art the steadfast cause of friendship too,
Thou knowest all that covered quality
Of things that makes us wonder what or who
It is that makes them tick[2]; where is the clue
Why she loves him, or he loves there or here,
And why this fish, not that, comes to the weir.

6

Thy law is set upon the universe;
And this I know, for lovers told it me,
That he who strives against thee fares the worse.
Now, lady bright, of thy benignity,
In reverence to those that worship thee,
Whose clerk I am, O teach me how to show
Some of the joy that, serving thee, they know.

7

Into my naked heart a sentience pour
With power, to show thy sweetness and delight!
Caliope, be present; I implore
Thy voice, for now is need! Thou seest my plight;
How shall I tell of Troilus' joy, or write
That all may honour Venus as they read it?
And to such joy, may God bring those who need it!

* * *

8

He lay there all this meanwhile, Troilus,
Learning the lesson suited to his case;
'By Jove,' he thought, 'I shall say thus and thus,
And thus entreat my darling for her grace;
That's a good phrase, and thus I'll set my face;
This I must not forget.' Unhappy man,
Pray God all goes according to his plan!

9

Lord, how his heart began to quake and thrum,
Hearing her step! His sighs came short and quick;
Pandar had led her in, and then had come
Closer, and twitched the curtain, by a trick
To peek inside, and said 'God help the sick!
Just look who's come to see you! There she stands,
The one who has your murder on her hands!'

10

He spoke as if he were about to weep.
'Ah! Ah!' cried Troilus, with a pitiful sigh,
'God knows if I am ill! I cannot sleep;
I cannot see – who is it standing by?'
'Sir,' said Criseyde, 'it's Pandarus and I.'
'You, sweetheart? O alas I cannot kneel
Or rise to show the reverence I feel.'

11

He raised himself a little, but she came
At once and softly laid her hands on his.
'You must not kneel to me; in heaven's name,
What do you mean?' she said; 'Two purposes
I have in coming, Sir; the first one is
To thank you; next to beg continuance
Of your protection, and your countenance.'

12

This Troilus, hearing his lady pray
For his support, lay neither quick nor dead:
Bashfulness left him not a word to say,
Not even if they'd come to take his head.
But, Lord, to see him suddenly turn red!
And, gentlemen, his lesson, learned so neatly,
To beg her favour, disappeared completely.

13

All this Criseyde had noticed well enough,
For she was wise, and loved him never the less,
Though he was not self-confident or tough,
Nor tried to fool her with some fine address;
But what he said, as soon as his distress
Began to lessen, if my rhyme will hold,
I'll tell you, as my ancient authors told.

14

With a changed voice, changed by his very dread,
Troilus answered. In a manner bare
Of all assurance, and now blushing red,
Now paling, to Criseyde, his lady fair,
With downcast, humble and surrendered air,
Twice he burst forth; one word was all his art,
And it was, 'Mercy, mercy, sweetest heart!'

15

Silent awhile, when he could speak again,
The next word was 'God knows that when I gave
Myself to you, as far as it has lain
In me to do so, and as God may save
My soul, I became yours, and to the grave,
Poor wretch, I shall be – not that I complain
Of suffering; none the less I suffer pain.

16

'This is as much, O sweet and womanly one,
As I may now bring forth; if it displease you,
I will revenge it on me and have done,
Soon, soon, and take my life, if that will ease you,
And death shall stay your anger and appease you;
Since you have heard me say somewhat, or try,
I do not care how soon I am to die.'

17

To see the manful sorrow that he felt
Might well have touched a heart of very stone,
Pandarus stood in tears, about to melt,
Nudging his niece anew at every moan;
'True are the hearts' he sobbed 'that weep alone!
O for the love of heaven, end our woe,
Or kill us both together, ere you go!'

18

'I? What?' she said, 'By heaven and in truth
I do not know what you would have me say.'
'Not know?' said he, 'Have pity on his youth!
For God's love, would you have him pass away?'
'Well then,' she said, 'I'll ask him, if I may,
What is the aim and end of his intent?
I never have truly gathered what he meant.'

19

'What I have meant? Ah, sweetest heart, my dear,'
Said Troilus, 'my lovely, fresh and free,
Let but the rivers of your eyes stream clear
In friendliness, once in a while, on me,
And give me your consent that I may be
He that, without a touch of vice, may ever
Offer his whole, true service and endeavour,

20

'As to his lady and his chief resource,
With all my heart and mind and diligence,
And to be comforted, or feel the force
Of your displeasure equal to my offence,
As death for any disobedience;
Deign me the honour, too, to use your power,
Commanding me in all, at any hour,

21

'And I to be your ever-humble, true,
Secret in service, patient in distress,
And in desire constant, fresh and new
Servant, to serve you in all eagerness,
In every inclination you express,
All it may cost accepting in good part,
See, that is what I mean, my sweetest heart.'

22

Said Pandarus 'Well! There's a hard request,
Reasonable for a lady to deny!
Now, by the Feast of Jupiter the Blest,
Were I a god, you should be marked to die,
You, that can hear this man lay all else by
To serve you until death, he is so fervent,
Yet you refuse to take him for your servant!'

23

Now fully at her ease, she turned her eyes
To look at him, serenely debonair,
And thought she need not hurry her replies;
But in the end she answered him with care,
And softly said 'My honour safe and fair,
And in such form as you have heard him proffer,
I will receive his service, at his offer,

24

'Beseeching him, for heaven's love, that he
Will, in all honour and without pretence,
As I mean well by him, mean well by me,
And guard my honour with all diligence.
If I can make him happy in this sense
Henceforward, then I will; this is no feigning;
And now be whole again, no more complaining.

25

'Nevertheless I warn you all the same,
Prince as you are, King's son and famous knight,
You shall have no more sovereignty or claim
On me in love than in such case is right;
And if you do amiss, I shall requite
It, though it anger you; but while you serve me,
Then I will cherish you as you deserve me.

26

'So in a word, dear heart, my chosen man,
Be happy; draw towards your strength again
And I will truly give you all I can
To pay you back in sweetness for your pain;
If I am she you need, you shall obtain
For every grief a recompense in bliss.'
And then she took him in her arms to kiss.

27

And down fell Pandarus upon his knees;
Casting his eyes and hands to heaven, he cried
'Immortal god, O deathless deity
– Cupid I mean – by this be glorified!
Venus, make melody! And, hark! outside
I seem to hear the bells of Troy a-ringing
For joy, without a hand to set them swinging!

28

'But ho! No more of this – and anyhow
They'll soon be coming back, when they have done
Reading that letter; there! I hear them now.
Criseyde, let me adjure you now, for one,
And you, for another, Troilus, my son;
Be ready at my house when I shall call –
You may be sure I shall arrange for all –

29

'To ease your hearts in practising your craft,
And let us see which of you wins the prize
For talking feelingly of love!' He laughed;
'You shall have leisure there to theorize.'
'How soon can this be done?' 'You must be wise,'
Said Pandarus, 'and wait till you are well;
It all will happen, just as you heard me tell.'

30

Deiphebus and Helen on their own
Started that moment to ascend the stair,
And, lord, how Troilus began to groan,
To blind his brother and his sister there.
Said Pandarus, 'It's time we went elsewhere;
Now, little niece, take leave of them, all three;
Leave them to talk, and come along with me.'

31

She took her leave of them most mannerly,
As well she could, and in return they bowed
And joined in doing her full courtesy;
When she had gone they sang her praises loud,
Spoke wonders of her excellence, and vowed
Her manners were enchanting, and her wit;
It was a joy to hear them praising it.

32

Now let her wend her way to her own place,
While we return to Troilus again;
He set at naught the letter and the case
Deiphebus had studied (but in vain).
From Helen and his brother, to be plain,
He longed to be delivered; it were best,
He said, to let him sleep; he needed rest.

33

So Helen kissed him and to where she dwelt
Set off, the others too; it all went right,
And Pandarus, as fast as he could pelt,
Came back to Troilus, in bee-line flight,
And on a pallet all that happy night
At blissful ease by Troilus he lay
Happy to talk until the break of day;

34

Yet, when they all had gone except these two,
And the great doors had shut away the town,
(To tell it shortly and without ado)
This Pandarus got up and sat him down
Freely on Troilus' bed, and with a frown,
Began to speak in a more serious way,
And I shall tell you what he tried to say.

35

'My dearest lord and brother, as God knows
– And so do you – it touched me to the quick
So long to see you languish in the woes
Of love, ever more desperately sick.
By every ingenuity and trick
Since then, I have been busy, ploy by ploy,
To bring you out of suffering into joy.

36

'And I've so managed matters, as you know,
That, thanks to me, you stand in a fair way
To prosper well. I say this not to crow;
Do you know why? I am ashamed to say;
To pleasure you I have begun to play
A game I'll never play for any other,
Not though he were a thousand times my brother.

37

'For you I have become since I began,
Half earnest, half in game, a *go-between*,
The kind that brings a woman to a man;
You know yourself what thing it is I mean.
For I have made my niece – and she is clean –
Place her whole trust on what is fine in you;
She will do all that you would have her do.

38

'God, who knows all, bear witness here for me!
There was no greed of gain in what I sought;
I only wished to abridge the misery
That was destroying you – or so I thought.
Good brother, now do everything you ought,
For God's dear love, to keep her out of blame;
As you are wise and good, protect her name.

39

'As well you know, people now think of her
As one enshrined and sainted, so to say.
The man is still unborn who could prefer
A charge that she had ever gone astray;
And woe is me that set her in the way
– My own dear niece – of what is yet to do!
I am her uncle and her traitor too.

40

'And were it known that I, by cunning measures,
Had put into her head the fantasy
Of being wholly yours to do your pleasures,
Why, all the world would cry out shame on me,
And say it was the foulest treachery
This deed of mine, that ever had been done.
She would be lost, and what would you have won?

41

'And so, before I take the step ahead,
Let me again beseech you, let me pray
For secrecy; we would be better dead
Than be betrayed in this, I mean to say;
Do not be angry with me for the way
I harp on secrecy; this high affair,
As you well know, demands as high a care.

42

'Think of the sorrows brought about ere this
By those who boast their conquests! One may read
Of many a sad mischance, of things amiss,
Day after day, just for this wicked deed;
And therefore ancient writers are agreed
And they have written, as we teach the young,
"The first of virtues is to hold your tongue."

43

'And were it now my purpose to engage
In a diffuse discussion, I could name
Almost a thousand from our heritage
Of ancient tales, of women brought to shame
By foolish boasters; you could do the same,
And proverbs too, against the vice of blabbing;
Even if it's the truth, it still is gabbing.

44

'O tongue, alas, that has so often torn,
And from so many a lady fair of face,
The cruel cry "Alas that I was born!"
And has kept fresh so many a girl's disgrace,
When what is boasted of in any case
Is oftenest a lie, when brought to test;
Braggarts are natural liars at the best.

45

'A braggart and a liar is all one;
As thus: suppose a woman granted me
Her love, and said that others there were none;
If I were sworn to this in secrecy,
And, after, went and blabbed to two or three,
I'd be a braggart, and, by the same token,
A liar too, because my word was broken.

46

'Look at such people! Are they not to blame?
What should I call them? What? What are they at,
These men that boast of women, and by name,
Who never promised either this or that,
And knew no more of them than my old hat?
God bless us all! It's little wonder then
Women are shy of dealing with us men.

47

'I do not say this as distrusting you,
Or any man of sense; but for the sot,
And for the mischief in the world now due
To folly as often as to wicked plot;
This blabbing vice – a woman fears it not
In men of sense, if she has been to school;
The man of sense takes warning from the fool.

48

'But to the point, my brother; to speak plain,
Keep everything that I have said in mind,
And keep it close! And now, cheer up again,
For when your moment comes, you then will **find**
Me true; I'll do your business in such kind
As will suffice you, if the Lord is good,
For all will happen as you wish it would.

49

'I know you mean her well, by Heaven I do!
And that is why I dared to undertake
Your business; what she now has granted you
You understand; the day is set to make
The contract. Well, I cannot keep awake,
Good night! Since you're in Heaven, say a prayer
To send me death, or let me join you there.'

50

Who could express the joy, the very bliss
That pierced the soul of Troilus when he felt
The effect of Pandar's promised help in this?
For all his former sorrows that had dealt
His heart so many a blow, began to melt
In joy; the luxury of sigh and tear
He felt no more, it seemed to disappear.

51

But just as all these woodlands and these hedges
That winter-long are dead and dry and grey,
Revest themselves in green and are May's pledges
To every lusty lad that likes to play,
So, to speak truth, and in the self-same way,
His heart grew suddenly so full of joy,
There never was a gladder man in Troy.

52

Turning to Pandar, upon whom he cast
An earnest look, a friendly one to see,
He said, 'Dear friend, it was in April last
As well you know (consult your memory)
You found me almost dead for misery
And worked on me, to bring me to confess
The secret cause of my unhappiness.

53

'You know how long it was that I forbore
To tell you, though I trust you best, and though
I knew there was no danger on that score.
Then tell me if you will, since this was so,
If I was loth that even you should know,
How would I dare tell others, in my fear
– I who am quaking now, lest someone hear?

54

'Nevertheless I swear, and by that Lord
Who as He pleases governs all whatever,
(And if I lie, Achilles with his sword
Cleave through my heart!) – swear, should I live for ever,
Who am but mortal man, that I could never
Dare – could, nor would – make boast to anyone
Of this, for all that's good beneath the sun.

55

'For I would rather die, and I determine
To do so, in the stocks, in prison, down
In foulest filth and wretchedness and vermin,
Captive of cruel King Agámenoun;
And this in all the temples in the town
Aye, and by all the gods too, I will swear
To you tomorrow morning, if you care.

56

'And as to all that you have done for me,
That is a thing I never can repay,
I know that well, not if I were to be
Killed for your sake a thousand times a day!
And there is nothing more that I can say
Except that from now on I'll be your slave
Wherever you go, and serve you to the grave.

57

'But here, with all my heart, I beg of you
Never to think I could be so insane
As to imagine – for you seemed to do –
That what you did in friendship for my pain
Was done in bawdry, like a pimp, for gain;
I'm not a madman, though I be a clod;
I know full well it wasn't that, by God!

58

'If there are men whose business in such dealings
Is done for money, call them what you must;
What you have done was done with noble feelings,
Done with compassion, fellowship and trust;
Distinguish love from what is done for lust.
There's a diversity to be discerned
Between things similar, so I have learned.

59

'And that you may be sure I could not blister
Your services by thinking them a jest,
Or shameful, there's Polyxena, my sister,
Or there's Cassandra, Helen and the rest,
Any of them, the fairest and the best
In the whole pack; just tell me which may be
The one you want, and leave the rest to me.

60

'And since this service has been done by you
To save my life, not for reward or fee,
I beg you, for God's love, to see me through
This great adventure; if it is to be
It needs you now; whatever you decree;
You make the rules, which, high and low I'll keep.
And now, good night, and let us go to sleep.'

61

Content in one another and at rest,
The world could hardly add a joy to theirs;
And in the morning they arose and dressed
And each went off upon his own affairs;
But Troilus who felt the burning airs
Of sharp desire and hope and promised pleasure
Did not forget wise Pandar's rule and measure,

62

And in a manlier way restrained his youth,
The reckless action, the unbridled glance,
And not a living soul, to tell the truth,
Could have imagined from his countenance,
Or what he said, a single circumstance;
Far as a cloud he seemed from everyone,
So well was his dissimulation done.

63

During the time of which I now am writing,
This was his life; with all his fullest might
By day he was in Mars' high service, fighting
The enemy in arms and as a knight;
And through the darkness to the early light,
He mostly lay, wondering how to serve
His lady better, and her thanks deserve,

64

And, soft as was his bed, I will not swear
There was no strain upon his mind; in fact
He turned and turned upon his pillows there,
Wishing himself possessed of what he lacked;
But in such cases, often men react
With as disturbed a pleasure as did he;
At least, this seems a possibility.

65

Certain it is, returning to my matter,
That all this meanwhile, so the story goes,
He saw her now and then, and, which was better,
She spoke to him, whenever she dared and chose,
And by agreeing then, beneath the rose,
(Ever the best way) settled, in their need,
How upon all occasions to proceed.

66

So hurried were their questions and replies
Anxiously spoken on the watch, (in fear
Lest anyone imagine or surmise
Something about it, reaching out an ear),
That there was nothing in the world so dear
To them as was their hope that love would send
A time to bring their speech to a right end.

67

But in the little that they did or said,
His prudent spirit took such careful heed
He knew by instinct what was in her head,
So that to her it seemed there was no need
To tell him what to do, still less, indeed,
What to avoid; love that had come so late
Had opened joy before her, like a gate.

68

And, to be brief (for I must mend my pace),
His actions and his words were so discreet,
He stood so highly in his lady's grace
That twenty thousand times she would repeat
Her thanks to God for having let them meet;
So schooled to do her service to the letter
He was, the world could not have shown a better.

69

She found him so dependable in all,
So secret, so obedient to her will,
That she could truly feel he was a wall
Of steel to her, a shield from every ill;
To trust in his good management and skill
She was no more afraid; he seemed inspired.
(No more afraid, I mean, than was required.)

70

And Pandarus was stoking up the fire,
Ready and punctual and diligent,
His only thought to speed his friend's desire;
So on he shoved, and back and forth he went
With letters from the city to the tent
Of Troilus; surely no one could attend
More carefully the wishes of a friend.

71

By some it is perhaps anticipated
That every word and message, look or smile
Of Troilus is now to be related
Just as they reached his lady all this while;
But it would make a long and tedious file
To read, of anyone in his position,
And have his words and looks on exhibition.

72

I have not heard of any writer who
Has tried it, nor, I think, has anyone;
I could not do it if I wanted to.
There was a deal of letter-writing done;
The matter, says my author, well might run
Another hundred verses; he ignored it.
How then should I be able to record it?

73

But to the great effect; I put it thus:
It was a concord quiet and complete
They now enjoyed (Criseyde and Troilus)
As I have said, and at this time was sweet;
Save only that they could not often meet
Or have the leisure to fulfil their speeches.
There came a time, which now my story reaches,

74

When Pandar, always doing what he might
To gain those ends of which you are aware,
(To bring together in his house, some night,
His lovely niece and Troilus, that there
They might talk over all this high affair
And bind it up to both their satisfaction)
Had, as he thought, discerned a time for action.

75

For he, acting with great deliberation,
Had forecast everything; his commonsense
Had given effect to this premeditation;
He had spared for neither trouble nor expense.
Come, if they liked, to have their conference,
Nothing should fail them; as for being caught
By spies, that was impossible, he thought.

76

No fear; he was down wind from every kind
Of chattering pie or spoilsport in the game;
So all was well, for the whole world was blind
To their affair, the wild bird and the tame;
The timber's there, all ready for the frame,
And we need nothing now but to be clear
As to the hour when she should appear.

77

And Troilus, to whom these careful schemes
Were fully known, waited as best he might;
He too had made arrangements, as it seems,
And found a pretext that would set things right
Should any note his absence, day or night,
While he was in the service of his love
– That he was sacrificing to the gods above,

78

Keeping a lonely vigil under vow
To hear Apollo's answer, and to see
The quivering of the holy laurel-bow
Before Apollo spoke out of the tree,
To tell him when the Greeks would turn and flee;
Let no one therefore – God forbid! – prevent him,
But pray Apollo's answer might be sent him.

79

Now there was little more to do, and soon
Pandar was up, for, briefly to explain,
Immediately upon the change of moon,
When earth, a night or two, was dark again,
And all the skies were gathering for rain,
Off in the morning to his niece he went,
And all of you have heard with what intent.

80

When he arrived, he started making fun
As usual, beginning with a jape
Against himself, and swore before he had done,
By this and that that she should not escape,
Or keep him running round her like an ape;
Certainly, by her leave, she was to come
That very night to sup with him at home.

81

She laughed at that and looked for an excuse,
And said 'It's raining, look! How can I go?'
'You must; don't stand there musing, it's no use;
And don't be late. It's got to be, you know.'
And they at last agreed it should be so,
'Or else – ' he swore it softly in her ear
'If you don't come to me, I shan't come here.'

82

And then she asked him, keeping her voice down,
Whether he knew if Troilus would be there.
He swore he wouldn't, he was out of town;
'But all the same,' he said, 'suppose he were,
Surely that need not weigh you down with care?
Rather than have him seen there, I would die
A thousand deaths; you need not fear a spy.'

83

My author has not cared to set it down
What she was thinking when he told her so,
(I mean that Troilus was out of town)
Or if she thought it was the truth or no;
At least she granted him that she would go
Without suspicion, being so besought,
And, as his niece, obeyed him as she ought.

84

Nevertheless she pressed her point on Pandar;
Although to dine with him would start no scare,
One must beware of many a goose and gander
Who love to dream up things that never were,
So let him choose his other guests with care;
'Uncle,' she urged him, 'since I trust you best,
Make sure that all is well; I'll do the rest.'

[131]

85

He swore to this by all the stocks and stones,
By all the gods that are in heaven as well,
On pain of being taken, skin and bones,
And cast as deep as Tantalus in Hell,
King Pluto's place. What more is there to tell?
When all was settled, Pandar took his leave;
She came to supper at the fall of eve,

86

Accompanied by certain of her men,
And by her lovely niece, Antigone,
And other of her women, nine or ten.
Who do you think was happy, answer me,
But Troilus? He stood where he could see
Out of a window in a closet-store,
Cooped there since midnight on the night before,

87

Unknown to anyone, save Pandarus,
Who, to resume, now met her in the hall
With every mark of joy and friendly fuss,
Embracing her, and then, as to a ball,
He led them in to supper, one and all,
When the time came and sat them softly down,
Needing, God knows, no dainties fetched from town!

88

And after supper they began to rise,
Eased and refreshed and happier by half;
Lucky the man best able to devise
Something to please her, or to make her laugh;
He sang; she played; he told a tale of chaff.
All things, however, have an end, and so
At last she took her leave, meaning to go.

89

O Fortune, O Executrix of Dooms,
O heavenly influences in the sky!
Truth is you are our herdsmen and our grooms,
And we your cattle, though we question why,
And think your reasoning has gone awry;
So with Criseyde, I mean: against her will,
The gods had their own purpose to fulfil.

90

Bent was the moon in Cancer, silver-pale,
And joined with Saturn and with Jupiter,
And such a rain from heaven, such a gale
Came smoking down that all the women there
Were terrified, quite overcome with fear;
Pandar made comment, laughing up his sleeve,
'Fine time, your ladyship, to take your leave!

91

'But, my dear niece, if ever in any way
I may have pleased you, let me beg of you
To do me a small favour; why not stay
And spend the night here? I implore you to.
It is as much your house as mine. Now, do!
It's not a joke, I really mean it so;
It would be a disgrace to let you go.'

92

She, knowing her advantage just as well
As half the world does, listened to his prayer;
The streets were flooding and the rain still fell.
It seemed as good a bargain to stay there
And grant the little favour with an air
And then be thanked, as grumble and then stay;
Going home now was not the better way.

93

'I will indeed,' she answered, 'Uncle dear,
If that is what you'd like, it shall be so;
I shall be very happy to stay here,
And I was joking when I said I'd go.'
'Thank you, dear niece,' he answered, 'joke or no,
To tell the truth you put me in a fright;
I am delighted you will stay the night.'

94

Thus all is well; and joy began to flower
All over again, the party warmed and spread;
But Pandar, if he'd had it in his power,
Would gladlier have hurried her to bed,
And so 'What a tremendous rain!' he said,
'Such weather is only fit for sleeping in,
That's my advice to you, so let's begin.

95

'Now, niece, you know where I am going to put you,
So that we shan't be lying far asunder,
And so you shall not hear (if that will suit you)
The noise of all this downpour and the thunder?
By God, right in my little closet yonder!
And I'll be in the outer room, alone,
And guard your women for you, on my own.

96

'Here in this central chamber, which you see,
Your women can sleep comfortably soft;
And right in there is where you are to be;
If you lie well tonight, "come once, come oft",
And never care what weather is aloft.
Some wine, now! Presently, when you think best,
It will be time for us to go and rest.'

97

And that was all; soon, if I may pursue,
Dessert was served, the traverse thereupon
Was drawn, and those with nothing more to do
About the room, departed and were gone,
And meanwhile it was raining, on and on
Amazingly; the wind blew loud and bleak;
People could hardly hear each other speak.

98

Then Pandarus, her uncle, as he should,
With certain of her women – three or four –
Escorted her to bed and, when he could,
He took his leave, and, bowing to the floor,
He said, 'Just here, outside this closet-door,
Across the way, your women will be near you;
You only have to call and they will hear you.'

99

Once she was in her closet and in bed,
With all her waiting-women ordered out
And sent to bed themselves, as I have said,
No one was left to skip or lounge about;
They had been scolded off, you needn't doubt,
(Such as were still astir) and told to keep
Their chambers and let other people sleep.

100

But Pandarus, who knew the ancient dance
At every step, and every point therein,
Saw all was well, with nothing left to chance,
And judged it was the moment to begin
His work, and from the door he took the pin;
Still as a stone, and with no more delay
He sat him down by Troilus right away.

101

To reach the point as quickly as I can,
He told him all the cunning artifice
Of the affair, and said 'Get ready, man,
You are about to enter Heaven's bliss.'
'O blessed Venus, send me grace for this!
I never had more need of it,' he cried,
'Nor ever have felt half so terrified.'

102

Said Pandarus 'Don't be at all afraid;
It will all happen just as you desire.
I promise you the gruel is well made,
If it is not I'll throw it in the fire.'
'Yet, blessed Venus,' Troilus prayed, 'inspire
My heart this night, as constantly as I
Serve, and shall serve thee better, till I die!

103

'And if it chanced the hour of my birth
Was governed by unfavourable stars,
If thou wert quenched, O Venus full of mirth,
By Saturn, or obstructed by fell Mars,
O pray thy Father to avert such jars
And give me joy, by him that in the grove,
Boar-slain Adonis, tasted of thy love.

104

'O Jove, by fair Europa's love and rape,
Whom, in a bull's form, thou didst bear away,
Help now! O Mars, thou with the bloody cape,
For Cypris' sake, hinder me not today!
O Phebus, think how Daphne in dismay
Clothed her in bark, and was a laurel tree;
Yet, for her love, send thou thy help to me!

105

'Mercury also, for the love of Hersé,
Cause of the rage of Pallas with Aglauros,[3]
Now help, and O Diana, in thy mercy,
Be not offended by the road before us!
And you, O Fatal Three, the sister-chorus,
That, ere my shirt was shaped for me, have spun
My destiny, O help this work begun!'

106

Said Pandarus 'You wretched mouse's heart,
Are you afraid that she is going to bite you?
Throw on this fur-lined mantle for a start
And follow me; allow me to invite you!
Wait, let me go in front of you, to light you.
And on the word, he lifted up the latch
And drew in Troilus after him, like a catch.

107

The stern wind snored so loudly round about
The house, no other noises could be heard;
Those that lay sleeping at the door without
Slept on securely there; they never stirred.
On sober tiptoe and without a word
Pandarus then, unhindered, crossed the floor
To where they lay, and softly closed the door.

108

As he came back towards her, quietly,
His niece awoke and called out 'Who is there?'
'My dearest niece,' he answered, 'only me;
Nothing to wonder at, you needn't fear.'
Then he came close and whispered in her ear
'For God's love, I beseech you, not a word!
Wake no one up; we might be overheard.'

109

'What? How did you come in? In heaven's name!
Didn't they hear you? But they must have done!'
'No, there's a little trap-door – that's how I came.'
Criseyde replied 'Then let me call someone.'
'What? God forbid! What foolish notions run
Into your little head! Speak softly, do,
Or else they'll think things they've no business to.

110

'A sleeping dog is better left alone;
No one will guess a thing, unless you make them;
Your women are asleep, as still as stone.
Why, you could blow the house up and not wake them!
They'll sleep till dawn and daylight overtake them.
And when I've finished what I've got to say,
As quietly as I came, I'll go away.

111

'Now, my dear niece, you surely understand,
For on this point you women think the same,
That when you've taken any man in hand
And called him "sweetheart" (it's a lover's name)
To play at blind-man's-buff with him – the game
Of having another lover all along –
Will do yourself a shame and him a wrong.

112

'Why do I say all this? You know quite well,
Better than any, that your love is plighted
To Troilus, who, as anyone can tell,
Is one of the finest fellows ever knighted;
You made him feel his feelings were requited
And that, except for fault in him, you never
Would play him false, though you should live for ever.

113

'Now this is how things stand; I have to say
That since I left, this Troilus, to be plain,
Has got into my room the secret way
– That's by the gutter – and in all this rain
– Unknown to anyone, I must explain –
Except to me, as I may hope for joy,
And by the faith I owe the King of Troy.

114

'He is in frantic pain, in such distress
That if he isn't fully mad by this,
He may run mad quite suddenly, unless
The Lord is good to him; the reason is
It has been told him by a friend of his
That you have promised love to one Horaste;[4]
For grief of which this night will be his last.'

115

Amazed to hear him saying this, Criseyde
Suddenly felt the heart in her turn cold,
And, with a sigh, impulsively replied
'Alas, I would have thought, whoever told
Such tales of me, my sweetheart would not hold
Me false so easily! Ah, wretched stuff
Of lying tales! I have lived long enough.

116

'Horaste, alas? I false to Troilus!
I've never even heard of him!' said she;
'What wicked spirit has maligned me thus?
Well, anyhow tomorrow he will see,
For I can clear myself as totally,
As ever woman did, if he will hear.'
And she began to sigh, and shed a tear.

117

'O God,' she said, 'that worldly happiness,
Called by the learned "false felicity",
Is intermingled with such bitterness;
A deep anxiety, God knows,' said she
'Gnaws at the root of vain prosperity!
For joys come rare and singly, perhaps never,
And no one has them always and for ever.

118

'O brittle happiness, unstable joy,
No matter whose you are, or how you spring,
Either one knows you for a transient toy
Or knows it not – one or the other thing;
How then can he who does not know it, sing
His joy in having joy? Does he not mark
His ignorance of the oncome of the dark?

119

'But if one knows that joy is transitory,
And every joy in worldly things must flee,
He that remembers this will lose the glory;
The very dread of losing it must be
Enough to ruin his felicity.
If then one sets no store on joy so brittle,
It follows surely that it's worth but little.

120

'And so I will conclude the matter thus,
That honestly, as far as I can tell,
There's no true happiness on earth for us;
But jealousy, thou Serpent out of Hell,
Thou envious madness, wicked infidel,
Why hast thou made my love mistrust me so,
Who never have offended, that I know?'

121

Said Pandar 'That's what's happened, anyhow.'
Said she 'But Uncle, who has told you this?
Why has my dear heart done this to me now?'
'You know, dear niece,' he answered, 'how it is;
I hope all will be well that is amiss,
For you can quench it; set his heart at rest,
And do so now, for that will be the best.'

122

'Why, then, tomorrow so I will,' said she,
'And then, God willing, he'll be satisfied.'
'Tomorrow? That would be a joke!' said he,
'No, that will never do, my dear Criseyde;
The learned say "It cannot be denied
That danger ever battens on delay."
Delays aren't worth a blackberry anyway.

123

'Niece, there's a time for everything, that's certain,
And, when the room's on fire, it's a flaw
To argue if the candle caught the curtain
Or how the devil they dropped it on the straw;
Far better put it out than hum and haw;
God bless us, while such talk is going on
The harm has happened and the bird is gone.

124

'And, little niece – now do not be offended –
If all night long you leave him in this woe,
God help me, I shall think your love pretended
And that you never cared. I dare say so
Since we're alone, we two; but I well know
You are too sensible for such a crime
As leaving him in danger all that time.

125

'*I never cared?* By God, I'd like to know
When you have cared for anyone,' said she,
'As I for him!' 'Indeed? Well, time will show;
But since for your example you take me,
Were I to leave him in this misery
For all the treasure in the town of Troy,
I pray God I may never come to joy.

126

'Now just reflect; if you, who are in love,
Can leave his life in dangerous distress,
And all for nothing, then by God above
It's worse than folly, it's sheer wickedness,
Straight malice, I should call it, nothing less.
What! Leave him in his present state of mind?
It's foolish, it's ungenerous, it's unkind.'

127

'Well,' said Criseyde, 'then will you do a thing
For me, and put an end to this upset?
Take this to him; it is my own blue ring;
There's nothing he would so much like to get,
Except myself. It is an amulet
To ease his heart; and tell him that his sorrow
Is groundless, as it shall appear tomorrow.'

128

'A ring? What next! Good gracious!' Pandar said,
'My dearest niece, that ring will need a stone
With power in it to awake the dead,
And such a ring I cannot think you own;
Where is your commonsense? It must have flown
Out of your head,' he said, 'to ruin you both;
O time, lost time! It is the curse of sloth.

129

'Do you not know a high and noble nature
Is neither moved to sorrow, nor consoled
By trifles? If a fool, or some low creature,
Fell in a jealous rage, I would not hold
His feelings worth a mite. He could be told
A few white lies some other day, you see;
But this is in a very different key.

130

'This is so noble and so tender a heart
He will choose death to give his griefs their due;
You may believe, however much they smart,
He will not speak his jealousies to you;
And therefore, lest his heart should break in two,
Speak to him now yourself of what's occurred,
For you can steer him with a single word.

131

'I've told you of the danger he is in;
His coming has been secret; none had sight
Of his arrival; where's the harm or sin
In seeing him? I shall be here all right;
But more than that, he is your chosen knight;
By rights you ought to trust him most of all,
And I am here to fetch him, at your call.'

132

So touching was this accident to hear,
So like a truth, moreover, on the face
Of it, and Troilus to her so dear,
His coming secret, and so safe the place,
Although she would be doing him a grace,
All things considered, as the matter pressed,
No wonder if she acted for the best,

133

And said 'As God may bring my soul to peace,
I feel for him, I grieve about his woe,
And I would do my best for his release
From pain, had I the grace; but even so
Whether you stay with me, or whether you go
To fetch him, till God clears my mind for me,
I'm in a dire dilemma, as you can see.'[5]

134

' "*Dilemma!*" Now, you listen to me in turn;
That means *The Donkeys' Bridge;*[6] it beats a fool,
For it seems hard to wretches who won't learn,
From sloth or wilful ignorance, at school
– Not worth a bean, such fellows, as a rule.
But you are wise, and what we have on hand
Is neither hard, nor easy to withstand.'

135

'Well,' she said, 'Uncle, do as you think just;
But I must first get up, you realize,
Before you bring him in; and since my trust
Is in you two, and you are both so wise,
Do everything discreetly and devise
A way to guard my honour and ease his soul;
For I am here as one in your control.'

136

Pandar replied 'That is well said, my dear,
A blessing on your wise and gentle heart!
But don't get up; you can receive him here,
There is no need to move, just play your part
And each will ease the other of all smart,
Please God! Venus, I worship thee! And very
Soon, as I dare to hope, we'll all be merry.'

137

Then Troilus went down upon his knees
At once, and reverently, beside her bed;
He greeted her with loving courtesies;
But, Lord! How suddenly she blushed deep red,
And not if they had come to take her head
Could she have said a word; she was struck dumb
Seeing him there, so suddenly had he come.

138

And Pandarus, who was so good at feeling
The mood of things, at once began to jest;
'Look, niece,' he said, 'see how this lord is kneeling!
Now there's a gentleman, by any test.'
He ran and fetched a cushion from the chest
'Now kneel away as long as you may please,
And may the Lord soon set your hearts at ease.'

139

I cannot say – she did not bid him rise –
If grief had put the matter from her mind,
Or if she simply took it in the guise
Of an observance, of a lover's kind;
And yet she did him favours, as I find;
She kissed him, sighing, and at last entreated
Him not to kneel, but rise up and be seated.

140

Said Pandarus 'Well, now you can begin;
Make him sit down, dear niece, a little higher
Beside you on the bed, up there within
The curtains, to hear better; I'll retire.'
And with that word he drew towards the fire
And took a light, and framed his countenance
As if to gaze upon an old romance.

141

She, being Troilus' lady as by right,
Stood on the clear ground of her faithfulness,
And though she thought her servant and her knight
Was one who never should so much as guess
At any untruth in her, yet his distress
Touched her – love-maddened, he had lost his head;
So, to rebuke his jealousy, she said:

142

'Look, dearest heart, because love's excellence,
Which no one may resist, would have it so;
Also because I know the innocence
Of your pure truth, and saw your service grow
From day to day, I came indeed to know
Your heart all mine; these things have driven me
To have compassion on your misery.

143

'And for your goodness, which to this very hour
I have found in you, dear heart and chosen knight,
I thank you to the best of my poor power,
Though that is less than you deserve of right,
And I, with all my heart and soul and might,
Swear that I am, and ever shall be, true
Whatever it may cost me, love, to you.

144

'This shall prove true, as you may well believe;
But, sweetest heart, what this is leading to
Has to be said, although you must not grieve
That I should say it and complain of you;
For finally the thing I hope to do
Is slay the heaviness and pain that fill
Our hearts, and bring redress to every ill.

145

'I cannot think, my darling, how or why
This jealousy, this wicked cockatrice,
Has crept into your heart so causelessly.
How gladly would I save you from that vice!
Alas that it – or even a small slice
Of it – should refuge in so fair a place!
May Jove uproot it, may it leave no trace!

146

'But O thou Jove, O Author of all Nature,
Is this an honour to thy deity
That there should fall on many a guiltless creature
Such injury, when guilty ones go free?
O were it lawful to complain to Thee,
For sanctioning unwarrantable pain
Through jealousy, how loud I would complain!

147

'A further grief is this, that people say
Nowadays "Jealousy is the soul of love."
A bushel of poison is excused today
By one small grain of fondness, which they shove
Into the mixture; God that sits above
Knows if it's more like love, or more like shame,
Or hatred; things should bear their proper name.

148

'Certain it is one kind of jealousy
Is more excusable than some I know,
As when there's cause; and some such fantasy,
So well repressed by pity, will not show;
It scarce does harm or speaks it – better so;
And bravely it drinks up its own distress
And I excuse it for its nobleness.

149

'Then there's a jealousy that comes from spite,
A furious, irrepressible intrusion;
But your dear heart is not in such a plight,
And I thank God for it; for your confusion,
So I would call it, is a mere illusion,
Of the abundance of your love for me,
Which makes your heart endure this misery.

150

'Sorry I am for it, but angry not;
Yet, for my duty and for your heart's rest,
Let me be judged on oath, or else by lot,
Or by ordeal; you shall choose the test,
And, for the love of God, may this prove best!
If I be guilty, take my life away;
What is there more that I can do or say?'

151

A few, bright, newly-gathered tear-drops fell
Then from her eyes, and suddenly she cried
'In thought or deed, O God, thou knowest well,
To Troilus was never yet Criseyde
Untrue!' And down she laid her head to hide
Under the sheet, at which she tugged and tore,
Then sighed and held her peace, said no word more.

152

And now God send me help to quench this sorrow!
– And so I hope He will, for He best may –
For I have often seen a misty morrow
That turned into a merry summer's day;
And after winter follows greening May;
We see it all the time, and read in stories
How bitter battles win to sudden glories.

153

This Troilus, on hearing what she urged,
You may imagine, had no thought of sleep;
It was not with a sense of being scourged
That he had heard and seen his lady weep,
But of the cramp of death; he felt it creep
About his heart at every tear she shed;
It wrung his soul in anguish by her bed.

154

Deep in his spirit, he began to curse
His coming there, to curse the very day
That he was born, for bad had turned to worse;
Lost was the service he had sought to pay
His lady; he too lost, a castaway;
'O Pandarus,' he thought 'your cunning wile
Is worthless to me . . . O, alas for guile!'

155

And loaded down with shame he hung his head,
Fell on his knees and sorrowfully sighed.
What could he say in answer, all but dead?
And she was angry that could best provide
The comfort he most needed. He replied
When he could speak, 'God knows that in this game,
When all is known, I shall not be to blame.'

156

And, as he spoke, his sorrow was compacted
And shut into his heart, without relief
Of tears; he felt his spirits so contracted,
Stunned, stupefied, by such excess of grief,
Oblivion came upon him like a thief,
His fears and feelings all fled out of town
And in a swoon he suddenly fell down.

157

This was no small calamity to see;
But all was hushed, and Pandarus moved fast;
'O niece, keep quiet, or we're lost!' said he,
'Don't be afraid.' But anyhow at last
In spite of all, he picked him up and cast
Him into bed, with 'Wretch! You can't be hurt?
Are you a man?' and stripped him to his shirt

158

And 'Niece,' he said, 'if you don't help us now
Your Troilus is lost, and all's forlorn!'
'I would indeed, if only I knew how,'
She said, 'And gladly; O that I was born!'
'Yes, niece, you should be pulling out the thorn
That's sticking in his heart,' said Pandarus,
'Say "All forgiven," dear, and stop this fuss.'

159

'That would be dearer to me, far more dear,'
She said 'than all the good under the sun!'
And then she stooped and whispered in his ear
'I am not angry with you, love; have done!
I swear it, not with you or anyone,
O speak to me, for it is I, Criseyde!'
In vain; he neither wakened nor replied.

160

They felt his pulse and she began to soften
His hands and temples with her tender touch,
Sought to deliver him and kissed him often
To loose his bonds, recall him from the clutch
Of bitter swooning; and they did so much
That, at long last, he started to draw breath,
Seeming to dawn out of the dark of death.

161

Reason took back her power on his mind,
Deeply abashed and humbled by her kiss,
And, with a sigh, as he began to find
Himself awake, he said 'O what's amiss?
Merciful God! You wrong yourself in this!'
And she gave answer, calling him by name,
'Are you a man? O Troilus, for shame!'

162

And then she laid her arm across his breast
Forgave him all, and kissed him where he lay
Many a time; he thanked her with the best
Of all that welled into his heart to say,
And she gave answer in as kind a way
As came to her, to cheer him and delight,
And do away the sorrows of the night.

163

Said Pandarus 'For aught I can surmise,
I and this candle serve no purpose here;
When folk are sick a light may hurt their eyes;
So, for the love of God, since you appear
To be in happy plight, let no more fear
Hang in your hearts, and may all discord cease.'
He bore the candle to the mantelpiece.

164

Soon after that, though there was little need,
She took his oath and forced him to unsay
His jealousy; and after that, indeed,
She saw no cause for sending him away;
For trifles lighter than an oath will sway
On many occasions; as I dare to guess,
He that loves well means no ungentleness.

165

But still she taxed him with the charge of treason,
Questioning him of whom, and where, and why
He had been jealous, since there was no reason,
And what the sign he had been prompted by.
She pressed him busily for a reply,
Or else (she let him think) she had no doubt
It was a plot designed to find her out.

166

And, briefly, that the matter might be mended,
He felt obliged to answer when she ceased;
And, to avoid more trouble, he pretended
She had not smiled at such and such a feast;
Surely she might have looked at him, at least!
And so on. Almost everyone produces
Rubbish like that when fishing for excuses.

167

Criseyde replied 'But, sweet, if it were so,
What harm was there in that? I did not mean
You any harm. By heaven, you should know
My very thoughts are yours, and clear and clean!
None of your arguments are worth a bean!
Are these your childish jealousies? I thank you!
You're like a little boy; I ought to spank you!'

168

Troilus sorrowfully began to sigh,
The fear that she was angry grew so strong;
He seemed to feel the heart within him die;
'Alas,' he said, 'I have been ill so long,
Have mercy on me if I did you wrong!
I promise never to offend you more;
I am in your hands, with much to answer for.'

169

'For guilt, a mercy flows to take your part;'
She answered, 'and I have forgiven you;
Yet keep this night recorded in your heart,
Lest you should fall again, if tempted to;
Promise me this' 'My dearest heart, I do.'
'And now that I have punished you for this,
Forgive it me, my darling, with a kiss.'

170

This Troilus, by sudden bliss surprised,
Put all into God's hand, as one who meant
Nothing but well, and, suddenly advised
By impulse, took her in his arms and bent
Her to him; Pandarus with kind intent
Went off to bed, saying 'If you are wise,
No fainting now, lest other people rise.'

171

What is there for the hapless lark to do
When taken in the sparrowhawk's fierce foot?
I can say nothing more; but, of these two,
For those to whom my story may be soot
Or sugar – I follow what my author put,
And must, though I delayed a year, express
Their joy, as I have told their heaviness.

172

Criseyde, on feeling herself taken thus,
As says my author in his ancient book,
In the enfolding arms of Troilus
Lay trembling, like an aspen leaf she shook.
And Troilus with glory in his look
Gave thanks to the bright gods and all their train.
So we may come to Paradise through pain.

173

And then this Troilus began to strain
Her in his arms and whispered, 'Sweetest, say,
Are you not caught? We are alone, we twain,
Now yield yourself, there is no other way.'
And soon she answered him, as there she lay,
'Had I not yielded long ago, my dear,
My sweetest heart, I should not now be here.'

174

O true it is that he who seeks a cure,
As of a fever or a long disease,
Must, as we see all day, perforce endure
To drink the bitterest medicines to the lees;
And so we drink down pain to bring us ease,
As did these lovers in their fresh adventure;
They found their cure through pain, and long indenture.

175

And now the sweetness seemed to be more sweet
Because they had endured the bitter thorn;
For out of woe and into bliss they fleet,
Such as they had not known since they were born.
And better so than both to be forlorn!
For love of God, let women all take heed
And do as did Criseyde, if there be need.

176

Criseyde unloosed from care or thought of flight,
Having so great a cause to trust in him,
Made much of him with welcoming delight,
And, as the honeysuckle twists her slim
And scented tendrils over bole and limb
Of a tall tree, so, free of all alarms,
They wound and bound each other in their arms.

177

And as a nightingale that is abashed
And holds her peace, having begun to sing,
Because she may have heard the hedges crashed
By cattle, or the shout of shepherding,
Then, reassured, will let her music ring,
Just so Criseyde, now that her fears were still,
Opened her heart to him and showed her will.

178

Like one who sees his death is taking shape,
And die he must for all that he can see,
Whom suddenly a rescue and escape
Bring back from death to new security,
For all the world, to such new ecstasy
With his sweet lady won, came Troilus;
God grant no worse a fortune fall to us!

179

Her delicate arms, her back so straight and soft,
Her slender flanks, flesh-soft and smooth and white
He then began to stroke, and blessed as oft
Her snowy throat, her breasts so round and slight,
And in this heaven taking his delight,
A thousand, thousand times he kissed her too,
For rapture scarcely knowing what to do.

180

And then he said 'O Love, O Charity,
Who, with thy mother, Cytherea the sweet,
After thyself is to be worshipped, she,
Venus, the planet of all kindly heat,
And next to you, Hymen I also greet,
For never to the gods was man beholden
As I, from cold care brought, to grace so golden!

181

'Benignest Love, thou holy bond of things,
Who seeks thy grace but renders thee no praise,
Lo! His desire would fly, but has no wings;
And were it not thy bounty deigns to raise
Those that best serve thee, labouring many days,
All would be lost, for what could they inherit
Unless thy grace were greater than their merit?

182

'Since thou hast helped me that could least deserve thee
Among the many numbered in thy grace,
And, when I was near death, hast let me serve thee
And hast bestowed me in so high a place
There is no bliss beyond it in all space,
What can I say but "Praise and reverence
Be to thy bounty and thy excellence!"'

183

And having spoken thus, he kissed Criseyde,
At which she felt, be certain, no displeasure;
'Ah, would to God that I but knew,' he cried
'How I might please you best, my heart, my treasure!
For was there ever man had such a measure
Of joy as I, on whom the loveliest
I ever saw has deigned her heart to rest?

184

'Here mercy is proved greater than deserving,
And every feeling proves it so in me,
For I, bright lady, whom I live in serving,
Cannot deserve your generosity;
Yet think, although I serve unworthily,
Needs must I shall learn better to deserve you
In virtue of the honour it is to serve you.

185

'And, for the love of God, my lady dear,
Since He created me to serve your will
– I mean, it is His will that you should steer
My course of life, to save me or to kill –
Teach me to earn your thanks and to fulfil
Your wishes, so that I may never chance
On your displeasure, through my ignorance.

186

'O fresh and womanly love, I dare to give
This certain promise: truth and diligence,
These you will find in me, and while I live
I will be perfect in obedience;
And should I fail you, in presence or absence,
Let me be killed for it, if it seems good
To you, my darling, in your womanhood.'

187

'Indeed,' said she, 'dear heart of my desire,
Ground of my joy, my garner and my store,
I thank you for it with a trust entire
As it is thankful; let us say no more,
It is enough; for all was said before.
And, in a word that asks for no release,
Welcome, my lover, my sufficing peace.'

188

Of all their ecstasies and joys, the least
Was more than I have power to convey;
But you, if you have tasted, judge the feast
Of their delight, the sweetness of their play;
I can say little, but at least I say
In safety, yet in dread, with night above,
They learnt the honour and excellence of love.

189

O blissful night, that they so long had sought,
How wert thou kindly to them both, how fair!
Would that my soul could such a night have bought,
Yes, or the least among the joys were there!
Away with coldness and away with care
And in this bliss of heaven let them dwell,
Surpassing all that tongue of man can tell.

190 (192)⁷

These very two, in their embraces left,
So loath a moment to be disentwined,
Lest in their parting they should be bereft
Each of the other, or awake to find
It was a dream, a fancy of the mind,
Each to the other whispered in their kiss
'Can this be true? Or am I dreaming this?'

191 (193)

Lord, how he gazed at her, how blissfully!
His hungry eyes now never left her face,
And still he said 'Dear heart, O can it be
That you are truly in this very place?'
'Yes, yes, indeed I am, by heaven's grace.'
Criseyde gave answer with so soft a kiss
His spirit knew not where it was, for bliss.

192 (194)

With many kisses Troilus again
Touching her fluttered eyelids made reply
'Clear eyes, you were the cause of all my pain,
The humble nets my lady caught me by!
Though mercy may be written in her eye,
God knows the text was difficult to find;
How was I bound without a thong to bind?'

BOOK III

193 (195)

Then in his arms he took and held her close,
And sighs welled up in him and took their flight
A hundred times, nor were they such as those
Men sigh in grief or sickness, but the right
And easy sighs of passion and delight,
Sighs on the quickening pulse of love within,
That none will wish away when they begin.

194 (196)

Soon after this they spoke of many things
Seeking their great adventure to unfold,
And made a playful interchange of rings,
Though what the posy was we are not told;
Yet well I know there was a brooch of gold
And blue, set with a ruby heart, she took
And pinned upon his shirt, so says the book.

195 (197)

Lord! Do you think some avaricious ape
Who girds at love and scorns it as a toy,
Out of the pence that he can hoard and scrape,
Had ever such a moment of pure joy
As love can give, pursuing his foul ploy?
Never believe it! For, by God above,
No miser ever knew the joy of love.

196 (198)

Misers would answer 'Yes'; but, Lord, they're liars!
Busy and apprehensive, old and cold
And sad, who think of love as crazed desires;
But it shall happen to them as I told;
They shall forgo their silver and their gold
And live in grief; God grant they don't recover,
And God advance the truth of every lover!

197 (199)

I wish to God those wretches that dismiss
Love and its service sprouted ears as long
As Midas [8] did, that man of avarice;
Would they were given drink as hot and strong
As Crassus [9] swallowed, being in the wrong,
To teach such folk that avarice is vicious
And love is virtue, which they think pernicious.

198 (200)

These very two whose tale I have to tell,
Deep in the new assurance that was theirs,
Played in their talk and found it joy to dwell
On every detail, all the whens and wheres
And hows of their first meetings, and the cares
That now were passed, their heavy hearts, their sadness,
Which, I thank God, had all been turned to gladness.

199 (201)

And ever more in speaking of some pain
Or woe remembered, but now past and done,
They broke into their tale to kiss again,
And so another rapture was begun;
They yielded all their strength, since they were one,
Recapturing their bliss to feel at ease,
And weigh their joys with former miseries.

200 (202)

I will not speak of sleep, for reason swears
That sleep is nothing to my purpose here;
And heaven knows it was not much to theirs.
But lest this night that they had bought so dear
Escape them vainly – which was not to fear –
They packed its moments up with all the treasure
Of tenderness and gentle-natured pleasure.

201

However, though I cannot tell it all
As excellently as my author can,
Yet I have given – and, with God's help, shall –
The gist and substance of that learned man;
And if, in reverence of love, my plan
Has added more, it was my simple wit
Intending well; do what you like with it.

202

For these my words, here and in every part
Of this, are spoken under the correction
Of you that have a feeling for love's art,
And I submit them all to your reflection;
Add or diminish, make your own selection
Of my poor language; let it be your care,
I beg you! To return to where we were,

203

When the first cock, common astrologer,
Began to beat his breast and then to crow,
And Lucifer, the morning's messenger
And star of day, began to rise and show,
And eastwards there appeared (for those who know)
Fortuna Major,[9] she, with stricken heart
Spoke thus to Troilus, that they should part:

204

'Life of my heart, my trust, and my delight,
Alas that I was born, alas, I say,
That day should part the lovers of the night!
But it is time to go; you must away,
Else I am lost for ever and a day;
Couldst thou not, night, have hovered on us, and kept
All dark, as when with Jove Alcmena slept?

205

'O dark of night, since books and learned folk
Affirm that God created thee to hide
This world, at certain times, in thy black cloak,
That rest to men should never be denied,
The beasts should bellow at thee, and men chide,
Since, broken with labour all the heavy day,
They get no rest from thee, that fleest away.

206

'Alas, too briefly is thy business done,
Swift night! May God, the Lord of Nature, hear,
And, for the malice of thy downward run,
Curse thee, and bind thee to our hemisphere,
Never beneath the earth to reappear!
For through thy reckless hurrying out of Troy
I have as hastily forgone my joy.'

207

This Troilus, who at these sayings felt
(As then it seemed to him in his distress)
His heart in tears of blood begin to melt,
Like one that never yet such bitterness
Had tasted out of joy so measureless,
Enfolding his dear lady, his Criseyde,
In straining arms, lamentingly replied;

208

'O cruel day, denouncer of the joy
That love and night have stolen and made their prize,
Accursèd by thy coming into Troy,
For every chink has one of thy bright eyes!
Envious day! Wherefore so many spies?
What hast thou lost? What dost thou seek of us?
God quench the light in thee for doing thus!

209

'How has love injured thee, or been at fault,
Pitiless Day? Thine be the pains of Hell!
Many a love lies slain by thy assault,
For where thou pourest in they cannot dwell.
Is this the place to proffer light? Go sell
Thy merchandise to such as carve or paint;
We do not need thee, source of our complaint!'

210

And he began to chide the titan sun:
'Fool that thou art! No wonder men deride thee
To lie all night with Dawn, as thou hast done,
And yet to let her slip from close beside thee
To trouble other lovers; off! and hide thee
In bed again, thou and thy precious Morrow!
A curse upon you both, God give you sorrow!'

211

He sighed profoundly, turning to continue
To her, and said 'Lady of weal and woe,
Lovely Criseyde, their very root and sinew,
Shall I arise, alas, and let you go?
I feel my heart will break and overflow;
How shall I live a moment if I do,
Since all the life I have is lived in you?

212

'What shall I do? Indeed I know not how,
Or when, alas, if ever, we shall see
A time to be again as we are now;
And, for my life, God knows what that can be
Since even now desire is biting me
And I shall die unless I may return!
How can I keep away from you and burn?

213

'Nevertheless my own, my lady bright,
If I could but be certain it was true
That I, your humblest servant and your knight,
Was set as firmly in your heart, as you
Are set in mine – if this I only knew,
It would mean more to me than Troy and Greece
Together, and I could endure in peace.'

214

To which Criseyde made answer straight away
Sighing profoundly; this was her reply:
'The game has gone so far since yesterday,
That Phoebus first shall tumble from on high,
And doves be one with eagles in the sky,
And every rock in earth shall break apart,
Ere Troilus be sundered from my heart.

215

'For in my heart you are so deeply graven
That though it were my wish to turn you out,
As sure as God may bring my soul to haven,
Were I to die in torture, have no doubt,
I could not do it; therefore be without
These creeping fancies of the brain, I say,
For God's dear love, or I shall pine away.

216

'That you should hold me ever fast in mind,
As I hold you, is all that I beseech;
And if I knew that I was sure to find
It so, it were as far as joy could reach;
But dearest heart, with no more waste of speech,
Be true to me, or pity on us both,
For I am yours, by God and this true oath.

217

'And so feel sure of me, and no more sadness!
This is a thing I never said before
Nor shall to any; should it give you gladness
To come again and visit me once more,
I long for it as much as you, be sure,
As God may comfort me; I give you this.'
She took him in her arms with many a kiss.

218

Against his will (but still it had to be)
This Troilus rose up and left their bed,
Put on his clothes and kissed her tenderly
A hundred times; and on his way he sped,
And with the voice of one whose spirit bled
He said 'Farewell my dearest heart, my sweet,
And may God grant us safe and soon to meet.'

219

Her grief had left her not a word to say,
So bitter did their parting seem, so dire;
And to his palace Troilus made way
As woebegone as she, yet still on fire
(To tell the truth), still wrung by the desire
To be again where he had been in bliss;
Nothing effaced the memory of this.

220

Back at his royal palace, quickly too,
He softly stole to bed, hoping to slink
Into long sleep, as he was wont to do;
But all for nought, he couldn't sleep a wink;
Into his fevered heart no sleep would sink.
He burned with passion for her now, who seemed
Worth more, a thousand fold, than he had dreamed.

221

Within him up and down began to wind
Her every word and gesture, stored with treasure,
Firmly impressed for ever on his mind,
To the least point of the remembered pleasure;
And at the memory, in no small measure,
Desire would blaze again, and longing grew
More than before, yet nothing could he do.

222

Criseyde herself, in the same manner, nursed
Within her heart the thought of his affection,
His sovereign worth, how she had met him first,
His gentle breeding and his circumspection,
And gave her thanks to love for this protection,
Longing to have him with her as before
And entertain her dearest heart once more.

223

Now Pandarus, when day had come again,
Went in to see his niece, and up he stepped
And said 'I am afraid this dreadful rain
Left you but little leisure . . . Have you slept?
Did you have happy dreams? Now *I* was kept
Awake all night, yes, many were kept waking,
And some of us there are whose heads are aching.'

224

He came in close and said 'Well, how do you do
This merry morning? How are you feeling, niece?'
'Never the better', she replied 'for you,
Fox that you are! May all your cares increase!
God knows you are the author of this piece.
For all your outward shows and words so white,
Little they know, who know you but by sight.'

225

And, saying this, she made a move to hide
Under the sheet, for she was blushing red;
But Pandar, lifting up a corner, pried
Within, remarking 'Well now, strike me dead!
Where is that sword of mine? Chop off my head!'
And, with a sudden thrust, his hand slipped past
Under her neck; he kissed her then at last.

226

I will pass over all that needs no saying;
God let him off his death, and so did she;[11]
There they were, laughing happily and playing,
There was no reason why they should not be.
But to my purpose in this history;
When the time came, home to her house she went;
Pandarus had accomplished his intent.

227

Now let us turn again to Troilus;
In bed he lay, long, in a restless mood.
He had sent secretly for Pandarus
To come to him as quickly as he could;
He came at once, as may be understood;
Not once did he say 'no'; gravely instead
He greeted him and sat beside his bed.

228

This Troilus, with all the force of feeling
That ever in the heart of friendship dwelt,
Threw himself down in front of Pandar, kneeling,
And would not rise again from where he knelt
Till he had poured the gratitude he felt
Forth in a thousand thanks, and blessed the morrow
Pandar was born to bring him out of sorrow.

229

'O friend of friends,' he said, 'the very best
That ever was or will be, truth to tell,
Who brought my soul to Heaven and to rest
From Phlegethon, the fiery flood of Hell,
Though I should serve you, though I were to sell
My life for you a thousand times a day,
That were a mote of what I ought to pay.

230

'The sun above, with all the world to see,
Has never yet, my life on it, set eye
On one so inly good and fair as she,
Whose I now am, and shall be till I die;
That I am hers I thank and glorify
Love that appointed me to this high end;
And I thank you for your kind office, friend.

231

'It was no little thing for you to give;
Yours is a debt I never can repay;
I owe my life to you – and why? I *live*,
Dead but for you and buried, many a day!'
And having spoken, back in bed he lay.
And Pandar listened with a sober eye
Till he had done, and then he made reply:

232

'Dear friend, if I've done anything for you,
It was a pleasure to me; in God's name
Believe it, I was very glad to do
Whatever I could for you – but all the same,
(Don't be offended!) I should be to blame
Unless I warned you; you are now in joy;
Beware, for it is easy to destroy.

233

'Think that of Fortune's sharp adversities
The most unfortunate of all, at last,
Is to have known a life of joy and ease,
And to remember it when it is past.
Therefore be careful; do not go too fast;
Never be rash, though you are sitting warm,
For if you are you'll surely come to harm.

234

'You are at ease; that is a good beginning;
But it's a certainty, as sure as fire
Is red, that keeping is as hard as winning
And needs as great a skill; bridle desire,
For worldly joy hangs only by a wire
As one can see; day after day it snaps;
And so go softly, there is need perhaps.'

235

'I hope, God helping me in my design,'
Said Troilus, 'I shall bear myself in such
A way as not to risk, through fault of mine,
The loss of anything, by too rash a touch;
Nor do you need to speak of this so much;
If you but knew my heart and its intention,
You would not think this matter worth a mention.'

236

He told him of the gladness of the night,
Why he had dreaded it at first, and how,
And said 'O friend, as true as I'm a knight,
And by the faith I owe the gods, I vow
I never had it half as hot as now;
But this I know, the more desire bites me
To love her best, the better it delights me.

237

'And I can hardly tell you how it is,
But now I feel full of fresh quality,
Quite unlike anything I felt ere this.'
Pandar replied to this judiciously:
'One who has known what heaven's bliss can be
Will feel quite differently, I do not doubt it,
From what he did when first he heard about it.'

238

To sum things in a word, this Troilus
Could never tire of speaking in her praise,
And would asseverate to Pandarus
The bounty of his lady and her ways,
And thank and welcome him with cheerful phrase;
The tale was ever freshly spun with wonder,
Till night came down and put the friends asunder.

239

Soon after this – for Fortune still was steady –
There came the blessed moment of sweet news
When Troilus had warning to be ready
To meet Criseyde again; they were to use
The self-same means; he felt his heart suffuse
Itself in joy of sweet anticipation
And gave the gods all thanks and adoration.

240

The form and manner of the thing was treated
Just as before; she came, with him ahead;
Therefore I think it need not be repeated,
And, to go plainly to the point instead,
In joy and safety they were put to bed
By Pandar, when the moment suited best;
And thus they were in quiet and at rest.

241

You needn't ask of me, since they are met,
Whether they were as happy as before;
Blissful as was their first encounter, yet
Their second was a thousandfold the more;
Gone were the sorrows and the fears of yore,
And both of them, indeed, if truth be told,
Knew as much joy as human heart can hold.

242

This is no little thing for me to say;
It stuns imagination to express.
For each began to honour and obey
The other's pleasure; happiness, I guess,
So praised by learned men, is something less.
This joy may not be written down in ink,
For it surpasses all that heart can think.

243

But cruel day would make them catch their breath
At its approach; it signed to them again,
And what they felt was like the stroke of death;
The colour in their faces showed the strain,
And they began once more in their disdain
To call day traitor, envious and worse,
Laying the daylight under bitter curse.

244

'Alas!' said Troilus, 'now I, for one,
Can see how Pyrois,[12] and those other three
Swift steeds, that draw the chariot of the sun
Have used some by-path, out of spite to me,
And day has come so soon and suddenly;
The sun has hastened; he shall pay the price;
I never more will do him sacrifice.'

245

Soon, of necessity, the daylight bid
Them part; and then, all speech and greeting done,
They separated as before they did
And set a time to meet and be at one.
Many a night renewed their love begun,
And Fortune led them for a time in joy,
Criseyde and this King's son, this Prince of Troy.

246

Deeply fulfilled, in happiness and song,
Troilus led his life from day to day;
He jousted, spent and feasted with the throng,
Gave presents, decked himself in fine array,
And was surrounded by a world as gay
And fresh in heart as any he could find,
Fitting the natural temper of his mind.

247

His fame rose up, and with a voice so great
Throughout the world, for generosity
And honour that it rang at heaven's gate;
Being in love for him was ecstasy,
And in his inmost heart, it seems to me,
He thought there was no lover upon earth
So happy as he; love had declared its worth.

248

No loveliness that nature might allot
To any other lady that he met
Was able to undo one little knot
About his heart in her enchanted net,
He was so close-enmeshed, was so beset
By it, to loosen him or set him free
Was quite impossible, or seemed to be.

249

And often taking Pandar by the arm
Into the garden, in a joyous mood,
He fashioned feasts of language on her charm,
Praising Criseyde, praising her womanhood,
Praising her beauty; it was more than good,
It was a heaven, to hear his praises ring,
And in this manner then he used to sing:

250

'Love that is ruler over earth and sea,[13]
Love whose commandment governs heaven on high,
Love that has made a wholesome amity
In neighbour states to join and guide them by,
That couples lovers in a holy tie,
And gives the law of love to friends as well,
Bind thou this harmony of which I tell!

251

'How that the universe, of faith so stable,
Varies its seasons with harmonious sway,
So that the elements, for all their babel,
Hold a perpetual bond that lasts for aye,
So Phoebus can bring forth his rosy day,
And so the moon has lordship over night;
This is love's doing; worshipped be his might!

252

'So that the sea, so greedy in its flowing,
Constrains his floods within a certain bound,
To hold them well in check at their fierce growing,
Lest earth and all for ever should be drowned: —
Were love to drop the bridle, then the ground
Of all that lives in love would burst apart,
And lost were all that Love now holds in heart.

253

'For so God willed, the Author of all Nature,
To circle every heart in His great bond
Of love, whose power not a single creature
Should know how to escape or go beyond,
And which can twist cold hearts to make them fond,
Able to love, and to feel pity too
For the unhappy heart, and help the true.'

254

In all the dangers of the town's defence
He was the first to arm him as a knight,
And certainly, to trust the evidence,
Was the most dreaded soldier in a fight,
Except for Hector; hardiness and might
Came to him out of love – the wish to win
His lady's thanks had changed him so within.

255

In time of truce, out hawking he would ride,
Or else out hunting – lion, boar, or bear –
(For lesser beasts than these he left aside);
And riding back would often be aware
That she was standing at her window there,
Fresh as a falcon coming from her pen,
And she was ready with a greeting then.

256

Of love and virtue chiefly was his speech
And he despised all baseness; you may guess
There never was occasion to beseech
Him to do honour to true worthiness,
Or bring relief to any in distress.
And glad he was if any man fared well
Who was a lover too, when he heard tell.

257

He thought a man was lost, to tell the truth,
Unless on love's high service he was bent
– I mean such folk as had the right of youth;
And he had language for the sentiment
Of love, and was so strangely eloquent
About love's ordinances, lovers thought
He always spoke and acted as he ought.

258

And though of royal blood, he showed no pride
And harassed no one set in lower place;
To each and all benign, on every side
He earned the thanks of every smiling face;
This was love's will, all honour to love's grace!
Pride, avarice, envy, anger, in a trice
Were rooted out, and every other vice.

259

O my bright lady, thou, Dioné's daughter,[14]
And thou, Sir Cupid, blind and wing'd, her son,
And O ye Nine,[15] by Helicon's[16] fair water,
That on Parnassus hill[17] have loved to run,
You that have guided all that I have done,
Since it's your will to leave me, and we sever,
What can I do but honour you for ever?

260

Through you I have accomplished in my song
The full effects of love in Troilus,
His joys and griefs – for certain griefs belong
Among them, as the story comes to us.
My third book therefore is concluded thus,
With Troilus in happiness, at rest
In love, with his Criseyde, his own and best.

Book IV

BOOK IV

1

How short a time, lament it as we may,
Such joy continues under Fortune's rule,
She that seems truest when about to slay,
And tunes her song, beguiling to a fool,
To bind and blind and make of him her tool,
The common traitress! From her wheel she throws
Him down, and laughs at him with mops and mows.

2

For she began to turn her shining face
Away from Troilus, took of him no heed,
And cast him clean out of his lady's grace,
And on her wheel she set up Diomede,
A thought for which my heart begins to bleed;
The very pen with which I now am writing
Trembles at what I soon must be enditing.

3

For how she left him, how Criseyde forsook
Her Troilus, or was at least unkind,
Must henceforth be the matter of my book,
For so they write who keep the tale in mind.
Alas, alas, that ever they should find
Cause to speak harm of her! And if they lie,
On them should fall the infamy, say I.

4

O Daughters of Old Night, you Furies Three,
In endless lamentation, endless pain,
Megaera, Alecto and Tisiphone,
And Roman Mars, the slayer of the slain,
Help me to write the Books that still remain
Of Troilus and Criseyde, and of the strife
In which he lost his love, and lost his life.

* * *

5

There, in a mighty host, as I have said,
The Greeks were ranged, encamped about Troy town;
It happened that when Phoebus' golden head
Laid on the Lion's breast, was shining down,
Hector and many a noble of renown
Fixed on a day to sally forth and fight
And do the Greeks what injury they might.

6

I do not know how long it was between
This, their decision, and the day they chose,
But came the day when, armoured bright and clean,
Hector and many a gallant man arose,
With spear in hand, or carrying great bows;
And out they went to battle and appeared
Before their foes, and met them beard to beard.

7

All the long day, with weapons sharply ground,
Arrows and darts and swords and dreadful maces,
They battled; many a horse and man were downed,
Their axes hacked away at brains and faces;
But in their last encounter (so the case is)
The night came down, the Trojans were misled,
And, having had the worst of it, they fled.

8

And on that day the Greeks took Ántenor,
Despite Polydamas or Monesteo,
Xantippus, Sarpedon, Polynestor,
Polites, and the Trojan lord, Ripheo.
And other lesser folk, like Phebuseo[1];
The day's disaster, for the folk of Troy,
Bred fear in them, a heavy loss in joy.

9

Nevertheless a truce was then arranged
(The Greeks requested it) and they began
To treat of prisoners to be exchanged
And paid great sums in ransom, man for man;
And soon through every street the rumour ran
In town and out; it came to every ear,
And Calkas was among the first to hear.

10

When Calkas knew for certain these awards
Would hold, he joined the Greeks at interview,
Thrusting himself among the older lords,
And took his seat as he was wont to do;
Then, changing countenance, he begged them to
Be silent for the love of God, and pay
Respect to him and what he had to say.

11

And thus he said: 'My lords and masters all,
I was a Trojan, everybody knows;
And Calkas is my name, if you recall.
Twas I who first brought comfort to your woes,
Foretelling your success against your foes.
Your work will soon and certainly be crowned;
Troy will be burnt and beaten to the ground.

12

'And in what form and manner, in what way,
To blot this city out and gain your ends,
Often enough you all have heard me say,
As each, I think, among you apprehends.
I held the Greeks my very special friends
And so I came to you in person here,
And what was best to do I then made clear,

13

'Without considering my loss in treasure,
Weighed with your comfort – loss of income too –
Thinking, my lords, in this to give you pleasure,
I left my goods behind and came to you.
The loss was nothing, though, with that in view;
For I surrender, as I hope for joy,
On your behalf, all that I have in Troy,

14

'Save for my daughter, whom I left, alas,
Sleeping at home when out of Troy I crept;
O stern, O cruel father that I was!
Hard-hearted resolution to have kept!
Would I had brought her naked as she slept!
For grief of which I may not reach tomorrow,
Unless you lords take pity on my sorrow.

15

'Because I saw no moment until now
For her deliverance, I held my peace;
But now or never; if you will allow,
I very soon may joy in her release.
O help, be gracious to me, Lords of Greece!
Pity a poor old wretch, and take his part!
It was to comfort you he broke his heart.

16

'You now have captured, chained, and may condemn
Plenty of Trojans; if you willed it, she
My child, could be exchanged for one of them;
Now, in the name of generosity,
Out of so many, give up one to me!
And why refuse this prayer? Troy will fall
And you will conquer people, town and all.

17

'Upon my life it's true, believe you me;
Apollo told me faithfully about it,
And I have checked it by astronomy,
By lot and augury, you needn't doubt it;
The time is near when you, who stand without it,
Shall witness flame and fire as they flash
Above the town, and Troy shall turn to ash.

18

'For Phoebus certainly and Neptune,[2] too,
Who made the walls of this accursed town,
Are in high wrath against it and will do
Vengeance on all its folk, and bring it down,
And on Laomedon who wore the crown
In times gone by, but would not pay their hire;
And so these gods will set the town on fire.'

19

Telling his story on, this old, grey man,
Humble in speech and in his look as meek,
(While the salt tears from either eyelid ran
And left their stain upon his grizzled cheek,)
Went on imploring succour from the Greek
So long that they, to cure him of these sore
Lamentings, handed over Ántenor

20

To Calkas; who so glad of it as he?
Pressing his needs upon them then, he plied
All those appointed for the embassy,
Begging that Ántenor should now provide
The offset for King Thoas and Criseyde.
And when King Priam's safeguard had been sent,
At once to Troy the emissaries went.

21

Told of the reasons for this embassy,
King Priam, issuing a general writ,
Assembled Parliament immediately,
With the result – I give the gist of it –
The embassy were told they would permit
The exchange of prisoners, and what else was needed;
They were well pleased; and so the plan proceeded.

22

This Troilus was present in his place
When Ántenor was asked against Criseyde;
It brought a sudden change into his face,
To hear those words was almost to have died.
But he said nothing, for his tongue was tied;
Were he to speak, they might spy out his passion;
So he endured his grief in manly fashion.

23

And full of anguish and of grisly dread,
He waited for what other lords might tend
To say of it; two thoughts were in his head:
First, if they granted it, which heaven forfend,
Was how to save her honour? and how contend
Against the exchange? What could he do or say?
He wildly cast about to find a way.

24

Love drove him fiercely to oppose her going,
Rather to die, indeed, than let her go;
But reason said 'What? Speak without her knowing?
You cannot think of it, as well you know;
Gain her consent, or she will be your foe,
And say it was your meddling had revealed,
Your love, so long and carefully concealed.'

25

So he began to think it might be best,
If parliament decided she be sent,
To acquiesce in what they might suggest
And be the first to tell her their intent,
And leave her then to tell him what she meant
To do, which he would make his whole ambition,
Though all the world should be in opposition.

26

Hector, on hearing how the Greeks suggested
Taking Criseyde instead of Ántenor,
Gave them a sober answer; he protested:
'Sirs, she is not a prisoner of war,
Who ordered this? What do they take us for?
For my part, I would wish it were made clear
It's not our practice to sell women here.'

27

A noise of people started up at once,
As violent as the blaze of straw on fire
(Though, as misfortune willed it, for the nonce
Their own destruction lay in their desire)
'Hector!' they cried, 'What evil spirits inspire
You thus to shield this woman, and to lose
Prince Ántenor? That is no way to choose!

28

'He is a wise commander and a bold,
And we have need of men, as one can see.
One of the greatest, worth his weight in gold;
Hector have done with all this fantasy!
Hear us,' they said, 'King Priam! We agree.
We give our voices to forgo Criseyde;
Let them deliver Ántenor!' they cried.

29

O Juvenal,[3] how true your saying, master,
That men so little know what they should yearn
To have, that their desire is their disaster;
A cloud of error lets them not discern
What the best is, as from this case we learn:
These people were now clamouring to recall
Prince Ántenor, who brought about their fall.

30

It was his treason gave the Greeks possession
Of Troy; alas, too soon they set him free!
O foolish world, look, there is your discretion!
Criseyde, who never did them injury,
Shall now no longer bathe in ecstasy,
But Ántenor – 'he shall come home to town,
And she shall go' they shouted up and down.

31

And so, deliberately, Parliament
Took Ántenor and yielded up Criseyde
By the pronouncement of the President,
With many a 'No!' from Hector, who still tried
To save her; he and others were denied,
They spoke in vain; she was obliged to go,
For the majority would have it so.

32

Then all departed out of Parliament;
And Troilus – there is no more to say –
Went swiftly to his room; alone he went
Save for a man or two of his, but they
Were quickly told to take themselves away,
Because he wished to sleep, or so he said,
And down he flung himself upon his bed.

33

And as the leaves are torn by winter's theft
Each after other till the tree is bare,
And nothing but the bark and branch are left,
So Troilus lay bereft of comfort there,
Fast bound within the blackened bark of care,
And on the brink of madness, being tried
So sorely by the exchanging of Criseyde.

34

First he rose up and every door he shut
And window too; and then this sorrowful man
Sat himself down upon his bedside, but
More like a lifeless image, pale and wan,
And from his breast the heaped-up woe began
To burst in fury forth, under the spell
Of madness, and he did as I shall tell.

35

As a wild bull that lunges round and reels
Hither and thither, wounded to the heart,
And roars remonstrance at the death he feels,
So Troilus with violent fit and start
Lunged round his room, fists battering his heart,
Head beating wall and body flung to ground,
In utter self-confusion round and round.

36

His eyes in pity lent his heart relief,
Swift as twin wells, in tears they streamed away,
The high, convulsive sobs of bitter grief
Reft him of speech, and he could barely say
'O death! Alas, dost thou not hear me pray?
Wilt thou not let me die? Accursed be
The day when Nature formed and fashioned me!'

37

But after, when the fury and the rage
By which his heart was twisted and oppressed,
In time began a little to assuage
Themselves, he lay upon his bed to rest,
The tears gushed forth again and shook his breast;
The wonder is a body can sustain
The pain I speak of, aye, or half the pain.

38

And then he said 'Fortune, alas for woe!
What have I done? In what have I offended?
Have you no pity, to deceive me so?
Is there no grace to save me? Is all ended?
Must Criseyde go because you so intended?
How can you find it in your heart to be
So cruel, Fortune, so unkind to me?

39

'Have I not, Fortune, ever held you high
Above all other gods? You know it well.
Will you deprive me thus of joy? Ah, why?
O Troilus, of thee what will they tell
Save that, a wretch of wretches, down he fell
From honour into misery; thence to wail
Criseyde, alas, until his breath should fail?

40

'Alas, O Fortune, if my life in joy
Roused your foul envy and displeasure, then
Why did you not take Priam, King of Troy,
My father, or let die my brethren?
Or have me killed, the wretchedest of men,
Cumbering earth, useless to all, and lying
Like one not fully dead, yet ever dying?

41

'Though all were taken, if Criseyde were left me,
I should not care whither you chose to steer;
But it is she of whom you have bereft me;
Aye, that has been your style for many a year,
To rob a man of what he holds most dear,
To prove thereby your fickle violence;
So I am lost and there is no defence.

42

'O very Lord of Love! Alas, O Lord,
Who best do know my heart, my every thought,
What sorrowful future can my life afford
If I forgo what was so dearly bought?
And since Criseyde and I by you were brought
Into your grace, and there our hearts were sealed,
How can you suffer this to be repealed?

43

'What shall I do? As long as I am master
Of my poor life of care and cruel pain,
I will cry out against this great disaster;
Alone as I was born, I will complain.
I'll never see the sunshine or the rain;
Like Oedipus, in darkness I shall end
My sorrowful life and die without a friend.

44

'O weary spirit ranging to and fro
Why fleest thou not out of the woefullest
Of bodies that were ever friend to woe?
O soul, lurking within me, leave thy nest,
Take wing out of my heart, and break! my breast;
Follow Criseyde, follow thy lady dear,
Thy rightful place is now no longer here!

45

'Sorrowful eyes that found their happiness
In gazing into hers that were so bright,
What are you good for now in my distress?
For nothing but to weep away your sight,
Since she is quenched that was your only light!
In vain it is I have you, eyes of mine,
Since she is gone that gave you power to shine.

46

'O my Criseyde, O sovereign excellence,
Who shall give comfort to the sorrowful soul
That cries his pain with such a vehemence?
Alas, there's no one; death will take his toll,
And my sad ghost, enamoured of its goal,
Will seek thee out to serve thee; O receive it!
What does the body matter, since I leave it?

47

'And O you lovers high upon the wheel
Of happy Fortune in your great endeavour,
God send you find a love as true as steel
And may your life in joy continue ever!
And when you pass my sepulchre, ah never
Forget your fellow who is resting there;
He also loved, unworthy though he were.

48

'O old, unwholesome, evil-living man,
Calkas I mean, alas, what ailed you, Sir,
To turn into a Greek, since you began
A Trojan? You will be my murderer;
Cursed was your birth for me! May Jupiter
Grant this to me, out of his blissful joy,
To have you where I want you, back in Troy!'

49

A thousand sighs that burnt like a live coal
One, then another, issued from his breast,
And mingled with the sorrows of his soul
Feeding his grief, giving his tears no rest;
He was so lacerated, so oppressed,
So utterly checkmated by this chance,
He felt no joy or grief, but lay in trance.

50

Pandarus, who had heard in Parliament
What every lord and burgess had replied,
And how they all had given their consent
To have back Ántenor and yield Criseyde,
Went nearly mad, he was so mortified;
Not knowing, in his misery, for the nonce,
What he was doing, he rushed away at once

51

To Troilus; the Squire at his door
On duty opened it anon for him,
And Pandarus, though weeping more and more,
Into the chamber, that was dark and dim,
Pressed onward silently; he seemed to swim
In his confusion, knew not what to say;
For very woe his wits were half astray.

52

All lacerated both in looks and mood,
In grief, with folded arms, a little space
Before this woeful Troilus he stood,
And gazed upon his pitiable face.
His heart turned chill to see his sorry case,
It slew his heart to see his friend in woe
And misery, or he imagined so.

53

And the unhappy Troilus who felt
The presence of his friend instinctively,
Like snow on sunny days began to melt,
While sorrowing Pandarus, in sympathy,
Was weeping too as tenderly as he.
So speechlessly they gazed, without relief;
Neither of them could speak a word, for grief.

54

But in the end the woeful Troilus
Near dead with suffering, burst into a roar,
A sorrowful noise indeed, and spoke him thus,
Through sighs and sobs that shook him to the core,
'O Pandar, I am dead; there's nothing more.
Did you not hear in Parliament' he cried
'They've taken Ántenor for my Criseyde!'

55

And Pandarus, dead-pale, could only nod
And answer, very miserably, 'Yes;
I've heard – I know about it all. O God,
Who ever would have thought it? Who could guess?
If only it were false! It is a mess
Which, in a moment – how was one to know? –
Fortune has planned, to be our overthrow.

56

'In all the world no creature, I suppose,
Ever saw ruin stranger than have we,
Whether by chance or accident who knows?
Who can avoid all evils, who foresee?
Such is this world; in my philosophy
No one should think that Fortune is at call
For him alone; for she is common to all.

57

'But tell me, Troilus, why are you so mad,
Taking it all to heart, the way you do?
What you desired you at least have had;
By rights that ought to be enough for you.
What about *me*? I've never had my due
For my love-service, never a friendly eye
Or glance! It is for me to wail and die.

58

'Besides all this – and you must know as much
As I do here – the town and roundabout
Is full of ladies, fairer than twelve such
In my opinion; I will search them out
And find you one or two, you needn't doubt;
Be happy then, again, my own, dear brother;
If she is lost, we can procure another.

59

'What! God forbid our pleasures all should spring
From one sole source, or only in one way;
If one can dance, another girl can sing,
One is demure, another light and gay,
One knows her way about and one can play;
Each is admired for her special grace;
Both heron-hawk and falcon have their place.

60

'As Zeuxis[4] wrote (so wise and full of phrases)
"New love will often chase away the old."
Remember, circumstances alter cases.
Self-preservation, we are always told,
Comes first; the fires of passion will turn cold
By course of nature; since it was casual pleasure,
You can forget about it at your leisure.

61

'For just as sure as day will follow night,
New love, or work, or other predilection,
Or the mere fact of seldom having sight
Of someone, can obliterate affection.
One of these ways, to sever the connexion,
And shorten what you suffer, shall be sought;
Absence will surely drive her from your thought.'

62

He spoke whatever came into his head
To help his friend, and, following his brief,
He did not care what foolishness he said,
So long as it might bring him some relief.
But Troilus, so nearly dead for grief,
Paid little heed, whatever it was he meant;
In at one ear and out the other it went.

63

At last he stirred and answered as he leaned
Upon his elbow, 'Friend, your remedy
Would suit me well enough, were I a fiend.
What! to betray one that is true to me?
Shame on the thought of all such villainy!
Better to have me killed before your eyes
At once, than have me do as you advise.

64

'She that I love, whatever you reply,
To whom my heart is given as to none,
Shall have me wholly hers until I die;
I have sworn truth to her and that is done.
I will not be untrue for anyone;
I live and die her man, I will not swerve;
No other living creature will I serve.

65

'And where you tell me you can find a creature
As fair as she, have done with it! Take care,
For there's no other being in all nature
To equal her, and so make no compare,
For your opinion I will never share
Touching all this, and you can spare your breath;
To listen to you is a kind of death.

66

'You tell me solemnly to love some other,
To start afresh and let my lady go;
It isn't in my power, my dear brother,
And if it were I would not have it so.
Can you play racquets with it, to and fro,
Nettle in, dock out, and shift from here to there?
Bad luck to her that takes you in her care!

67

'The way you are behaving, Pandarus,
Is like when someone sees a man in woe
And saunters up to him, and argues thus:
"Don't think about it and the pain will go."
You'll have to turn me into granite though,
Strip me and rifle me of every passion,
Before you cure me in that easy fashion.

68

'Death well may drive the life out of my breast,
Which a long grief will surely undermine,
But never shall my soul be dispossessed
Of her love's dart, but down to Proserpine,
When I am dead, I'll go, and there resign
Myself to live in pain, and broken-hearted,
Eternal grief, that she and I are parted.

69

'You made an argument along the line
That it should prove a lesser misery
To lose Criseyde, because she once was mine,
And I had had a full felicity.
Why gab like that? Haven't you said to me
Often enough that it was worse to fall
From joy, than not to have known joy at all?

70

'But tell me, since you think it is so easy
To change in love, and wander to and fro,
How comes it that your feelings are too queasy
To change the one that causes you such woe?
Empty your heart of her and let her go,
Exchange her for some other, sweeter diet,
Some lady that will cause you no disquiet.

71

'If you, whose love is dogged by unsuccess,
Still cannot drive that love out of your mind,
I that have lived in joy and happiness
With her, as much as any man could find,
Could I so soon forget her? Are you blind?
Where have you been mewed up so long, how spent
Your time, who are so good at argument?

72

'No, no. God knows that everything you've said
Is worthless; for, befall what may befall,
I mean to die; would I indeed were dead
And no more words; come, Death, the end of all
Our sorrows, come, O hear me when I call!
Happy the death that's called for not in vain,
And, often called, will come to end all pain.

73

'I know that when I lived my life in quiet
To keep thee off I would have paid thee hire;
Thy coming now would be my sweetest diet;
There's nothing in the world I more desire,
O Death! My griefs have set my heart on fire,
Drown me in tears at once, or take thy dart
And with thy cold stroke quench both heat and heart.

74

'And since thou slayest so many of the best
Against their will, unasked for, day and night,
Do me this service now at my request,
Deliver the world of me and do me right,
The wretchedest of men that Fortune's spite
Ever struck down; it's time for me to die,
Since in this world I serve no purpose, I.'

75

The tears welled up into his eyes, distilling
Like drops from an alembic, and as fast;
And Pandar held his tongue and stood unwilling
To venture further, with his eyes downcast.
The thought however came to him at last
'By heaven, rather than my friend should die,
I'll say a little more to him, or try.'

76

'Dear friend,' he said, 'you are in great distress,
And since you think my arguments at fault,
Why don't you help yourself and take redress,
Using your manhood now to call a halt
To all these tears? Carry her by assault!
These niceties are nothing but self-pity;
Get up and take Criseyde and leave the city!

77

'Are you a Trojan? Where's your resolution?
Not take a woman who's in love with you
And who would say it was the best solution?
What foolish scruples are you listening to?
Get up at once, and stop this weeping, do,
Show us your manhood and within the hour
I'll die for it, or have her in our power.'

78

And Troilus, whose voice began to soften,
Replied 'You may be certain, brother dear,
That I have thought of this, and very often,
And more than what you have suggested here;
But why I haven't done it will appear
When you have heard what I have got to say;
Then, if you wish to lecture me, you may.

79

'First, as you know, this city is at war
Just for a woman carried off by force;
I'm one there could be no allowance for,
As things stand now, in such a wicked course;
I should be blamed by all and be a source
Of trouble to the town, if I withstood
My father's word; she leaves for the town's good.

80

'And I have also thought – should she consent –
To beg her of my father, as a grace;
That would accuse her, to her detriment.
Nor can I offer purchase in this case,
For since my father, in so high a place
As Parliament, has given it his seal,
He could not now consider my appeal

81

'Yet most I dread her heart might be perturbed
By violence, were I to play that game,
For if the town were openly disturbed
It must result in slander on her name,
Which I would rather die for, than defame;
And God forbid that ever I prefer
Saving my wretched life to saving her.

82

'So I am lost, for all that I can see,
For it is certain, since I am her knight,
Her honour is a dearer thing to me
Than I myself, it must be, as of right.
Desire and reason tear me in their fight;
Desire counsels "ravish her!", but reason,
So fears my heart, forbids me such a treason.'

83

And still he wept away with tears unceasing
And said 'Alas, what will become of us?
I feel my love increasing and increasing
And hope diminishing, my Pandarus,
For reasons ever more calamitous!
Alas, alas, why will my heart not burst?
There's little rest in love, from last to first.'

84

'As for myself,' said Pandarus 'you're free,
Do as you like; but if I had it hot
And were a Prince, I'd take her off with me,
Though all the city shouted I should not;
I wouldn't give a penny for the lot.
When all the shouting's over and the thunder,
It ends in whispers and a nine-days'-wonder.

85

'You're so considerate, you go so deep;
Think of yourself! The time is past and done
For weeping now; better if others weep!
Especially since you and she are one.
Get up and help yourself, for, by the sun,
It's better to be blamed and pointed at
Than to lie here and perish like a gnat.

86

'It's not a vice in you, there is no shame
In holding back the woman you love most;
Maybe she'll think it's foolish of you, tame,
To let her go and join the Grecian host;
Fortune favours the brave! It is her boast
To help the hardy in a thing like this,
And thwart all wretches for their cowardice.

87

'And if Criseyde turns peevish, should she grieve
A little, you may make your peace at will
Hereafter; as for me, I can't believe
That even now she'd take it very ill;
Fear nothing! Let your quaking heart be still;
Remember Paris; Paris is your brother;
He has a love, and why not you another?

88

'And, Troilus, there's one thing I can swear;
If she – Criseyde – your darling and your bliss –
Loves you as truly now as you love her,
God knows that she will never take amiss
What you may do to remedy all this;
And if she leaves you, if she thinks it fit,
Then she is false; love her the less for it.

89

'And so take heart! Remember, you're a knight;
For love the laws are broken every day;
So show your courage, show your strength and right,
Have pity on yourself and throw away
This awe you feel; don't let this wretched day
Gnaw out your heart; set all at six and seven,
And if you die a martyr, go to heaven.

90

'And I will stand beside you. No retreat!
Even if I, and all my kith and kin,
Lie dead as dogs for it upon the street
Thrust through with bloody wounds. So count us in!
You'll find me friend, whether you lose or win.
But if you'd rather die in bed upstairs,
Good-bye! To Hell with anyone who cares!'

91

These words brought Troilus to life again
And he replied 'Well, thanks for that, dear friend;
You needn't goad me so; I suffer pain
Greater than you can give. Now, hear the end:
Whatever happens I do not intend
To carry her off, except by her consent,
Not if it kills me. That was what I meant.'

92

'Why, so did I! And I've been saying so
All day,' said Pandar, 'have you asked her yet?
Is that why you are sad?' He answered 'No.'
'Then what dismays you, if you haven't met?
How can you know that she would be upset
If you should carry her off? Why should you fear?
Has Jove come down and whispered in your ear?

93

'Get up and wash your face; and see it's clean.
Pretend that nothing's happened; see the King,
Or he may wonder where you can have been;
Throw dust into his eyes – yes, that's the thing,
For even now he may be ordering
Someone to fetch you, ere you are aware;
Cheer up, and let me deal with this affair.

94

'For I am certain that I can contrive it
Somehow, somewhere, some time tonight, for you
To see your lady where you can be private;
Then by her words, and her appearance too,
You'll soon perceive what she would have you do,
And all her mind; talk over what is best;
Farewell for now, for on this point I rest.'

95

Impartial rumour that is wont to bring
A false report as swiftly as a true,
Had darted through all Troy on eager wing
From man to man, telling the tale anew,
How Calkas' daughter, she, the bright of hue,
In Parliament, not even argued for,
Had been delivered up for Ántenor.

96

And very soon the rumour reached Criseyde;
She, for her part, had never given thought
To Calkas, cared not if he lived or died;
She called down curses on the man who brought
The treaty of exchange, but never sought
To question it, for fear it might be true;
She dared not ask of anyone she knew.

97

As one who long had set her heart and mind
On Troilus, and who had there made fast,
So that the world itself could not unbind
Such ties of love, or Troilus be cast
Out of her heart as long as life should last,
She burned with love and terror, to and fro;
What would be best to do she did not know.

98

But, as one sees in town and roundabout,
Women like visiting their friends to chatter;
Criseyde was soon the centre of a rout
Supposing her delighted at the matter;
So gossip and congratulating patter,
Dear at a penny, full of bright regret,
Poured from these city ladies when they met.

99

Said one 'I am as happy as could be
On your account; you'll see your father, dear!'
Another said 'Indeed? I can't agree!
We have seen all too little of her here.'
Then said a third 'Let's hope that she will clear
The air and bring us peace on either side,
And may the Lord Almighty be her Guide!'

100

These femininities and gossipings
She heard as one whose thoughts are far away;
God knows her heart was set on other things;
Her body sat and heard them say their say,
But the attention of her spirit lay
On Troilus; she sought him with the whole
Speechless desire and passion of her soul.

101

These women, fancying that they could please her
Expended all their tales on her for naught,
For no such vanities had power to ease her,
Since all the while she listened she was caught
In flames of other passions than they thought;
She felt her heart would die of misery
And weariness in such a company.

102

She was no longer able to restrain
The tears within her, they began to well
And give their signal of the bitter pain
In which her spirit dwelt and had to dwell,
Remembering from what Heaven to what Hell
She now had fallen, since she must forgo
The sight of Troilus; she sighed for woe.

103

And every fool of those who sat about her
Supposed that she was weeping for the pain
Of having to depart and do without her
And never be amused by her again;
Her older friends were ready to explain,
Seeing her weep, that it was human nature,
And they wept too for the unhappy creature.

104

And so these women busily consoled her
For things of which she had not even thought,
Believing she was cheered by what they told her;
'She ought to be more cheerful, yes she ought,'
They urged her; and the comfort that they brought
Was such as, with a headache, one might feel,
If someone came and clawed one by the heel.

105

But after all this foolish vanity
They took their leave, and home they hurried all.
Criseyde, invaded by her misery,
Went up into her chamber from the hall,
Fell on her bed for dead, and to the wall
She turned, intending never thence to rise,
As I shall tell you, and, with countless cries,

106

Her rippled hair, the colour of the sun,
She tore, and wrung her fingers long and slender,
Calling on God for pity upon one
Who only wished for death to save and end her;
Her cheeks that once were bright, now pale and tender
With tears, bore witness to her sad constraint,
And sobbing thus, she spoke in long complaint:

107

'Alas!' she said, 'That I must leave this nation,
Wretched, unfortunate and full of woe,
Born under an accursèd constellation,
And, parted from my knight, compelled to go!
Sorrow upon the daylight, in the glow
Of which these eyes first saw him riding there,
Causing me, and I him, so much despair!'

108

And upon that there started from her eyes
Tears like an April shower, and as fast,
She beat her white breast, and a thousand cries
She gave for death to come to her at last,
Since he that eased her sorrow in the past
Must be forgone; and in this grief and need
She felt herself a creature lost indeed.

109

'What shall I do?' she said, 'And what will he?
How shall I live if we are thus divided?
And O dear heart I love so faithfully,
Who will console your misery as I did?
Calkas, on your head be the sin, misguided
Father! O Argyve, his wife,
Sorrow upon the day you gave me life!

110

'To what end should I live and sorrow thus?
Can a fish live out of its element?
What is Criseyde without her Troilus?
How should a plant or creature find content
Or live, without its natural nourishment?
There is a proverb, I have heard it said,
"The green that has least root is soonest dead."

111

'Thus I resolve to do: since sword and dart
I dare not handle, for their cruel pain,
From the dread day on which I must depart,
Unless I die of grieving, sorrow-slain,
I never shall touch meat or drink again
Till I unsheathe my soul and end my breath,
And in this way I'll do myself to death.

112

'My dresses, Troilus, shall be unpearled,
They shall be black, my dearest heart and best,
In token, love, I have forgone the world,
Who once was wont to set your heart at rest;
And in my Order, till by death possessed,
I shall observe, you being absent thence,
The rule of grief, complaint and abstinence.

113

'The sorrowing soul that harbours in my heart
I leave to you – with yours it shall complain
Eternally, for they shall never part.
For though on earth we parted, once again
In the far field of pity, out of pain,
Known as Elysium, we shall meet above,
Like Orpheus and Eurydice, his love.

114

'Thus, dearest heart, for Ántenor, alas,
I soon shall be exchanged, is that not sure?
What will you do? Can such a sorrow pass?
How shall your tenderness of heart endure?
Forget your grief, my love! Be that your cure,
Forget me also, for I tell you true
I'll gladly die if all be well with you.'

115

Could they be ever written, said, or sung,
Her words of lamentation and distress?
I do not know; but if my simple tongue
Should venture to describe her heaviness,
I should but make her sorrow seem far less
Than what it was, and childishly deface
Her high complaint; here it shall have no place.

116

Pandar, who had been sent by Troilus
To see Criseyde, when, as you heard me say,
It was agreed it would be better thus
(And he was glad to serve in such a way)
Came to Criseyde in secret, where she lay
Upon her bed, in torment and in rage,
As he came in upon his embassage.

117

And this was how he found her when they met;
Her tears fell salt upon her bed of care,
And bathed her breast and countenance with wet;
The mighty tresses of her sunnish hair,
Hanging about her ears unbraided there,
Were a wild symbol of her martyrdom
And death; her spirit longed for it to come.

118

And, seeing him, she started thereupon
To hide her teary face and turn away,
And this made Pandar feel so woebegone,
That he could hardly bring himself to stay,
It was too much for him. And I must say
That if Criseyde had made lament before,
She did so now a thousand times the more.

119

In bitterest complaining, thus she cried:
'O Pandarus, first cause, as well I know,
Of many a cause of joy to me, Criseyde,
That is transmuted now to cruel woe,
Tell me, am I to welcome you, or no?
You were the first to bring me to the bliss
Of serving love; and must it end like this?

120

'Ends love in sorrow? Yes, or people lie;
Aye, and all worldly bliss, it seems to me.
Bliss has a goal that sorrows occupy,
And whosoever thinks this cannot be,
Wretch that I am, let him but look at me
That hate myself, and ever more shall curse
My birth, and feel I move from bad to worse.

121

'Whoever sees me, sees all grief in one,
Pain, torment, lamentation, bitterness,
None but inhabits my sad body, none!
Anguish and languishment and woe, distress,
Vexation, smart, fear, fury, giddiness . . .
Indeed I think the very heavens rain
Down tears in pity of my cruel pain.'

122

'Ah my dear niece, my sister in dejection,'
Said Pandarus, 'what do you mean to do?
Have some regard, some thought for your protection;
Will you let sorrow make an end of you?
Stop it! Here's something you must listen to:
I have a word for you, so pay attention,
Sent you by me from Troilus, I may mention.'

123

Criseyde then turned towards him in a grief
So great, it was a very death to see.
'Alas,' she said, 'what word can bring relief?
What has my dearest heart to say to me
Whom I may never see again? Does he
Lack tears upon my going? Should he care
To send for them, I have enough to spare.'

124

The visage that she showed had paid the price;
She looked like one that they had come to bind
Upon her bier; her face, once Paradise,
Had changed and seemed as of another kind;
The fun and laughter one was wont to find
In her, and all her joyfulness, had flown
From poor Criseyde, and there she lay alone.

125

About her eyes there was a purple ring
That circled them in token of her pain
And to behold her was a deadly thing,
And Pandar was unable to restrain
Tears that came gushing from his eyes like rain.
Nevertheless, as best he could, he tried
To give these words from Troilus to Criseyde:

126

'Niece, I suppose you've heard of the to-do;
The King, and others, acting for the best,
Have made exchange of Ántenor and you,
The cause of all this trouble and unrest.
But how these fatal doings have oppressed
Your Troilus no earthly tongue can say;
For very grief his wits have gone astray.

127

'Ah, we have been so wretched, he and I,
It nearly killed us both; but thanks to keeping
To my advice, he has made shift to dry
His eyes and somewhat to withdraw from weeping;
And I am sure that he would fain be sleeping
By you tonight. Together you may find
Some remedy, of one or other kind.

128

'This, short and plain, is all I have to say
– As far as I can gather, anyhow;
And you, in all this tempest of dismay,
Cannot attend to lengthy prologues now;
Send him an answer, if your tears allow,
And, for the love of God, I beg you, dear,
Stop weeping before Troilus comes here.'

129

'Great is my grief,' she answered, as before,
Sighing like one in deadly, sharp distress,
'But yet to me his sufferings weigh still more;
I love him better than myself, I guess.
Is it for me, alas, this heaviness
Of heart, of which he piteously complains?
Indeed this sorrow doubles my own pains.

130

'Grievous to me, God knows, it is to part,'
She said, 'yet it is harder still for me
To look into the sorrow of his heart,
For that will be my death, as I foresee.
Yes, I shall surely die. And yet,' said she
'Bid him to come, ere threatening death may sack
The city of my soul in its attack.'

131

Having said this, she buried her face flat
Upon her forearms, shedding many a tear.
Pandarus said, 'Alas! Ah, why do that?
You must get up, you know the time is near;
Rise up and quickly, he will soon be here!
You must not let him find you blubbered red,
Unless you wish to send him off his head.

132

'If he could see you making this to-do,
He'd kill himself; and if I had expected
This fuss, I'd not have let him visit you
For all the wealth King Priam has collected;
Since to what end his course would be directed
I know too well; and therefore you must try
To stop this woe, or, flatly, he will die.

133

'Prepare yourself, dear niece, to render aid,
To mitigate his sorrows, not to heat;
And touch him with the flat and not the blade;
Use all your wisdom, set him on his feet.
How would it help, were you to fill a street
With tears, though both of you should drown in them?
No time for tears; but time for stratagem.

134

'Here's what I mean: I'll bring him here, and, knowing
You'll be at one in what you fix upon,
I trust you'll find a way to stop your going,
Or to return soon after you have gone.
Women are quick to see a long way on;
Let's see if you can make your wit prevail,
And if you want my help it shall not fail.'

135

'Go,' said Criseyde, 'and, Uncle, honestly,
With all the power I have I will refrain
From weeping in his sight; and eagerly
I'll work to make him happy once again;
I will explore my heart in every vein,
For there shall lack no salve to heal his sore
In anything that I'm to answer for.'

136

So off went Pandar seeking Troilus.
He found him in a temple all alone,
Like one whose life had lost its impetus
And who cared nothing for it; at the throne
Of every pitying god he made his moan
Imploring to be taken from earth's face,
Sure as he was to find no better grace.

137

And, to speak briefly, it would be no lie
To say he was so overcome by care
As utterly to have resolved to die
That day; all argument had led him there,
Telling him he was lost, and to despair;
'Since all that comes, comes by necessity,
Thus to be lost is but my destiny.

138 5

'And certainly, I know it well,' he cried,
'That, in His foresight, Providence Divine
Forever has seen me losing my Criseyde,
(Since God sees everything) and things combine
As He disposes them in His design
According to their merits, and their station
Is as it shall be, by predestination.

139

'But all the same, whom am I to believe?
Though there are many great and learned men,
And many are the arguments they weave,
To prove predestination; yet again
Others affirm we have free choice; but then
Those ancient men of learning are so sly:
On whose opinion am I to rely?

140

'Some say "If God sees everything before
It happens – and deceived He cannot be –
Then everything must happen, though you swore
The contrary, for He has seen it, He."
And so I say, if from eternity
God has foreknowledge of our thought and deed,
We've no free choice, whatever books we read.

141

'No other thought, no other action either,
Could ever be but such as Providence
(Which cannot be deceived about it neither)
Has long foreseen, without impediments.
If there could be a variation thence,
A wriggling out of God's foreseeing eye,
Then there would be no Providence on high.

142

'God then would have no more than an opinion,
With nothing steadfastly foreseen or sure;
It were absurd to say of His dominion
That it would lack a knowledge clear and pure,
Or had the doubtful knowing men endure;
To guess such errors into Deity
Were false and foul, a wicked blasphemy.

143

'Yet there's another view maintained by some
Who wear their tonsures very smooth and dry;
And they would say "A thing is not to come
Because divine foreknowledge from on high
Foresaw it; rather, that the reason why
It was foreseen was that it had to be,
Which Providence foresaw, presumably."

144

'So, in this manner, this Necessity
Just crosses back onto the other side
Of the debate; things do not have to be
Because foreseen, that has to be denied.
But if they are to be they cannot hide
From Providence; things certain to befall
Must be foreseen for certain, one and all.

145

'I mean – and I am labouring in this –
To question which is cause of which, and see
Whether the fact of God's foreknowledge is
The certain cause of the necessity
By which things come about eventually,
Or if the fact that they must come about
Is what makes God foresee them; there's the doubt.

146

'Yet I won't strive to show, nor have I shown,
How causes stand in order, but infer
That, of necessity, a thing foreknown
For certain, will most certainly occur,
Whether or not we seem to register
That God's foreknowledge made it come to pass;
Yet it will come, for good or ill, alas!

147

'If there's a man there, sitting on the seat,
Then, of necessity, it follows fair
Enough that your opinion is no cheat
When you conjecture he is sitting there;
And yet again, as I am well aware,
The contrary opinion stays as strong,
As thus – now listen, for I won't take long –

148

'I say, if the opinion you declare
Is true (that he is sitting there), I say
That of necessity he's truly there;
And so necessity goes either way:
Necessity that he be on display
Necessity in you to see him so,
And that's necessity in both, you know.

149

'But you may say "He is not sitting there
Because the fact you think he is is true,
But rather, he was sitting on that chair
From long before, and so was seen by you."
And I say, though indeed it may be due
To his being there, yet the necessity
Is common to you, interchangeably.

150

'In just this way (it makes undoubted sense)
I can construct – or so it seems to me –
My argument about God's providence
And about all the things that come to be;
And by this reasoning we all can see
That whatsoever things on earth befall
Come of necessity, predestined all.

151

'Although whatever comes about, I mean,
Must therefore be foreknown – as who can doubt? –
And though it does not come because foreseen,
Yet it still follows, and one can't get out
Of this, that things which are to come about
Must be foreseen; or, if foreseen, take shape
Inevitably; there is no escape.

152

'And this is quite sufficient anyway
To prove free choice in us a mere pretence;
What an absurdity it is to say
That temporal happenings – the things of sense –
Are causes of eternal prescience!
Now truly, it's as false as it is odd
To say things cause the Providence of God!

153

'What might I think, had I such thought in store,
Except that God foresees what is to come
Because it is to come, and nothing more?
So might I think that all things, part and sum,
That once had being, but are dead and dumb,
Caused providence, ere they were in the making,
To know them, and to know without mistaking.

154

'Above all this, I have yet more to show,
That just as, when I know a thing to be,
That thing must of necessity be so,
So, when a thing that I can know and see
Is coming, come it will; necessity
Of things to come, foreknown before their day,
Can never be evaded any way.'

155

Then said he thus: 'Almighty Jove on high,
That knowest our sad case infallibly,
Have pity on my sorrow, let me die,
Or from our trouble bring Criseyde and me.'
And as he knelt there in his misery,
With all these thoughts debating in his head,
Pandar came in, and (you shall hear it) said:

156

'Almighty God enthroned in heaven above!
Whoever saw a man behaving so?
Why, Troilus, what are you thinking of?
Always your own worst enemy, as though
Criseyde had gone already! Don't you know
We have her still? Why kill yourself with dread?
The very eyeballs in your skull look dead.

157

'Haven't you lived for many years, dear brother,
Without her, happily and well at ease?
And were you born for her and for no other?
Did nature only fashion you to please
Criseyde? You should be thinking thoughts like these;
Just as with dice chance governs every throw,
So too with love; its pleasures come and go.

158

'Yet of all wonders this I find most strange,
Why you should weep so, when, as you'll admit,
You have no notion what they will arrange,
Or whether she has ways of stopping it.
You haven't yet made trial of her wit;
It's time enough to stick your neck out when
Your head's to be cut off; start weeping then!

159

'You pay attention, then, to what I say;
I've spent some time with her; she spoke to me
(As was agreed between us, by the way),
And all the time I kept on thinking, she
Had something locked in her heart's privacy
By which she hopes – if I have any ear –
To find a means to hinder what you fear.

160

'So I'd advise you, at the fall of night,
To go and see her and to make an end
Of this; and Juno in her splendid might
Will, as I hope, send grace and be our friend.
My heart is saying "They shall never send
Criseyde away!" So set your heart at rest;
Hold to your purpose, for it is the best.'

161

'You have said well, that's just what I will do,'
Said Troilus, and yet he sighed for woe,
Then stammered out another word or two,
And when he saw that it was time to go
He went alone, and secretly, as though
All was as usual, and took his way
To where she was, and did as I shall say.

162

The truth is this, that when at first they met
Pain in their hearts gave them so sharp a twist
Neither could say a word in greeting, yet
They fell into each other's arms and kissed.
Which was the sorrier at such a tryst
Neither could say; grief has a way of robbing
The soul of words; they could not speak for sobbing.

163

The tears that in their sorrow they let fall
Bitter beyond all tears of nature's kind,
Smarted as wood of aloes does, or gall;
Tears bitterer than these I do not find
The woeful Myrrha[6] wept through bark and rind;
In all the world there's none so hard of heart
But would have felt compassion for their smart.

164

But when the weary spirits of these twain
Returned to them, to where they ought to dwell,
And felt a little lessening of pain
By long lament and ebbing of the well
Of tears, their hearts beginning to unswell,
At last, and with a broken voice, Criseyde,
Hoarse from her sobbing, looked at him and cried:

165

'O Jove, have mercy on me, I am dying!
Help, Troilus!' And then she laid her face
Upon his breast, and speechless from her crying,
She felt her soul was gliding into space
Leaving for ever its appointed place;
She lay, a greenish pallor in her features,
That once had been the loveliest of creatures.

166

And he began with passion to behold her
Calling her name; but there she lay for dead,
Speechless and cold, her head upon his shoulder,
Her eyes thrown back and upward in her head.
He, at a loss what should be done or said,
Kissing her cold mouth over and again,
Suffered, God alone knew – and he – what pain!

167

He roused himself, and laid her on the bed;
No sign of life she gave that he could see,
Stretched out in length she lay there, seeming dead,
'Alas!' his heart was sighing, 'woe is me!'
And when he saw her lying speechlessly,
He said, all bare of bliss, and heavy-hearted,
That she was gone, her spirit had departed.

168

When he had long lamented and complained,
Had wrung his hands and said what was to say,
And his salt tears upon her breast had rained,
He brought himself to wipe those tears away
And pitifully he began to pray,
Saying 'O Lord, that sittest on Thy throne,
Pity me too, that follow her alone!'

169

Lifeless she lay, cold and insentient,
There was no breath in her, for all he knew;
This was for him a pregnant argument
That she had left the world, and left him too;
And when he saw there was no more to do,
He dressed her limbs and body in the way
They use for those that wait their burial day.

170

And after this, sternly and cruelly,
Out of its sheath he drew his naked sword
To kill himself, sharp though the pain might be,
That soul might follow soul in one accord
Whithersoever Minos[7] gave the word,
Since, by the will of Fortune and of Love,
He must no longer live on earth above.

171

And then he said, filled with a high disdain,
'O cruel Jove, O Fortune so adverse,
This is the sum of all, since you have slain
Criseyde, by treachery, and can do no worse
To me; fie on your double dealings, curse
Your cowardly power that cannot break my vow!
No death can part me from my lady now.

172

'I'll leave this world, since you have slain her thus,
And follow her below, or else above;
Never shall lover say that Troilus
Dared not, for fear, to die beside his love;
I'll join her, that I can be certain of.
Since you forbid our love for one another
Here, yet allow our souls to find each other.

173

'And O thou city that I leave in woe,
And Priam, thou, and all my brethren here,
Farewell! Farewell my mother, for I go;
And, Atropos,[8] make ready thou my bier.
And thou, Criseyde, ah, sweetheart, ah, my dear,
Receive my spirit!' So he thought to cry
With sword at heart, in readiness to die.

174

But, as God willed, her spirit was restored;
She broke from swoon, and 'Troilus!' she cried,
And he gave answer, letting fall his sword,
'Are you alive, O lady mine, Criseyde?'
'Yes, sweetest heart,' she sighingly replied,
'Thanks be to Cypris'; he in new delight
Began to comfort her as best he might.

175

He took her in his arms with kisses soft,
And strove to comfort her by every art,
So that her spirit, flickering aloft,
Came back again into her woeful heart,
When, glancing somewhat downward and apart,
She saw the naked sword where it was lying;
Fear came upon her and she started crying,

176

And asked what made him draw it; he replied
By telling her the cause that now had passed,
And how he would have stabbed himself and died;
She gazed at him again, and then she cast
Her arms about his body, firm and fast;
'O what a deed!' she said beneath her breath,
'Merciful God, how near we were to death!

177

'And if I hadn't spoken, by God's grace,
You would have killed yourself?' 'Yes, certainly.'
'Alas, alas,' she said 'O heavy case!
For by the Lord above that fashioned me,
I wouldn't live a moment more,' said she
After your death – not to be crowned the Queen
Of all the countries that the sun has seen!

178

'But with that very weapon – there it is –
I also would have killed myself,' she said,
'But O, no more! We've had enough of this;
Let us rise up at once and go to bed
And talk about the woes that lie ahead;
For, by that night-light which I see there burning,
I know that daylight will be soon returning.'

179

They lay in bed, but, though their arms were lacing,
It was not thus that they had lain before;
Now they looked misery in their embracing,
Lost was the bliss that they had known of yore;
Why were they born? Ah, would they were no more!
So they bewailed, until a thought awoke
Within her, and to Troilus she spoke:

180

'Listen, my sweetheart, well you know' said she
'That if a man does nothing but complain
About his griefs, and seeks no remedy,
It is mere folly and increase of pain;
And since we came together here again
To find some remedy out, or make a plan
To cure our woes, it's time that we began.

181

'I am a woman, as you know full well,
And sudden intuitions come to me
Which, while they still are hot, I have to tell.
Neither of us, as far as I can see,
Ought to give way to half this misery;
Surely we have the cunning to redress
What is amiss, and end this heaviness.

182

'The truth is that our misery of heart
(For all I know) comes from no more than this:
Only that you and I are forced to part;
Considered well, there is no more amiss.
If that be all, it's not a precipice!
For though we part, there may be ways to meet,
And that is all there is to it, my sweet.

183

'I'm positive of bringing things about
So that, once gone, I can return to you;
Of that I have no shadow of a doubt,
And certainly, within a week or two,
I shall be here again; that this is true
I can convince you in a word or so,
For there are heaps of ways, as I can show.

184

'I won't take long – no sermon, no confusion,
For time once lost one never can recall;
I promise to go straight to my conclusion,
Which is, it seems to me, the best of all;
And yet forgive me if my choice should fall
Upon a scheme that causes you unrest,
For, honestly, I'm speaking for the best.

185

'However, let me make the protestation
That, in the words that I am going to say,
I'm only showing my imagination
Of means to help ourselves the easiest way;
And do not take it otherwise, I pray,
For in effect I'll do as you decide;
That's no demand, and shall not be denied.

186

'Now listen: as you well have understood,
My going is agreed by Parliament
So firmly, to withstand it is no good,
As far as I can judge; that's evident.
Since no consideration can prevent
The course of things, banish it from your mind,
And see what other measures we can find.

187

'I know the separation of us two
Will cruelly distress us, and annoy:
Those who serve love have painful things to do
From time to time, if they would have the joy.
That I shall be no further out of Troy
Than half a morning's ride is a relief,
And ought to lessen the effect of grief.

188

'If they don't mew me up but leave me loose,
My own and best, then day by day, my dear,
Since, as you know, it is a time of truce,
You shall have news of me, you need not fear,
And long before it's over I'll be here;
You'll then have Ántenor, your chosen man,
And me as well; be happy if you can!

189

'Think of it this way: "My Criseyde has gone;
But what of that? She'll come back right away."
"And when, alas?" "A little later on,
Ten days at most, that I can safely say."
How happy shall we be that golden day,
To live together, evermore, in Troy!
Why, the whole world could never tell our joy!

190

'And, as things are, I often notice, too,
To keep our secret, (which we have to hide),
You do not speak to me, nor I to you,
For a whole fortnight; you go out to ride
But I don't see you; can you not abide
Ten days to save my honour, and make all sure
In our adventure; is that much to endure?

191

'Then, as you know, my family is here,
That is, except my father; only he
Has gone; and all the things I hold most dear
Are here together, you especially,
Whom, above all, I would not cease to see
For all the world – wide as it is to rove;
Else let me never see the face of Jove.

192

'Why do you think my father should so prize me,
Or long for me, unless he fears the spite
Of people in this town who may despise me
Because of him and his unhappy flight?
What does he know about my present plight?
If he but knew how happy I am here,
My going would be nothing we need fear.

193

'You see how every day, and more and more,
They treat of peace; there is some indication
That we are almost ready to restore
Queen Helen, if the Greeks make reparation;
And, if there were no other consolation,
The fact they purpose peace on either part
Is one that should a little ease your heart.

194

'If it be peace, my dearest, then the tidings
Will, of their nature, force us to contrive
Intercommunication; there'll be ridings
Thither and back, the place will be alive
All day, as thick as bees about a hive,
And everyone will be in a position
To come and go, and will not need permission.

195

'And if no peace should follow, even so,
If never such a peace or treaty were,
I *must* come back; for where am I to go?
And how in heaven should I stay out there
Among those men-at-arms, in constant fear?
And so, as God may guide the soul He made,
I see no cause for you to be afraid.

196

'And here's another way that may unfold,
If you're not satisfied to leave things thus;
My father, as you know, is getting old;
Old men are usually covetous,
And I've just thought of a fine trick for us
To catch him by – and all without a net! –
If you agree; so listen to me yet.

197

'It often has been said that, in the end,
To keep the wolf at bay you kill a sheep;
That is to say, you often have to spend
A part of what you have, if you would keep
The rest of it; now gold is graven deep
Upon the heart of every covetous man;
So let me tell you how I mean to plan.

198

'The valuables here in town with me
I'll take to give my father, and will say
They're sent in trust and for security
By certain of his former friends, and they
Desire him fervently without delay
To send for more, and send most speedily
While the town still remains in jeopardy.

199

'It shall be an enormous quantity
(So I shall say) but, lest the news get out,
It can be sent by no one but by me.
I'll show him, too, if peace should come about,
That I have friends at Court, and they, no doubt,
Will soften Priam's rage and plead his case,
So that he soon will be restored to grace.

200

'So, what with one thing and another, sweet,
I shall enchant him with my words, and cause
Him to suppose all heaven is at his feet:
As for Apollo's servants and their saws,
Their calculations are not worth three straws;
Gold and his lusts shall blind him, and with these
I'll shape him to whatever ends I please.

201

'And if by auguries, as I believe
He will, he tries to show that I am lying,
I will find means to pluck him by the sleeve
And so disturb him in the act of trying
His sortilege, or say he's falsifying;
(Gods are ambiguous in their replies,
And for one truth they'll tell you twenty lies.)

202

And "Fear first made the gods, so I suppose"
I'll say to him; it was his coward heart
That made him misinterpret, when he chose
To run away from Delphi,⁹ for a start,
So I shall say to him; and if my art
Doesn't convert him in a day or two,
Then you may kill me: I will force you to.'

203

And truly it is written, as I find,
That all she said was said with good intent,
And that her heart was true as it was kind
Towards him, and she spoke just what she meant
And almost died of sorrow when she went;
She purposed to be true, as she professed,
Or so they write who knew her conduct best.

204

But he, all ears and heart to what she said,
And hearing her devisings to and fro,
Truly believed the notions in his head
Were much like hers; but yet . . . to let her go!
The heart within misgave him and said *no*;
Yet in the end he saw he had to force
Himself to trust her, as the surest course.

205

And so the anguish of his circumstance
Was quenched in hope, and so, at last, the night
Was softened in the joy of amorous dance;
And as the birds, whenever sun is bright,
Sing high in the green leaves and take delight,
So these two took their joy, and made communion
Of loving speech, and cleared their hearts in union.

206

Nevertheless Criseyde was going to leave him:
The dreadful thought was ever in his mind,
And, fearful that her promises deceived him,
He begged her piteously 'Be true and kind!
Keep to your day and do not lag behind
Among the Greeks! Come quickly back to Troy,
Or I shall lose all honour, health and joy.

207

'As sure as that the sun will rise tomorrow,
(And O God, guide Thou me upon my way,
Wretch as I am, out of this cruel sorrow),
I mean to kill myself if you delay.
But though my death means little, still I say
Before you cause me so much misery,
My own dear heart, stay here in Troy with me.

208

'For truly lady, truly my Criseyde,
Whatever cunning shifts you may prepare
Likely enough will fail when they are tried;
There is a saying "He who leads the bear
Has many a thought which Bruin doesn't share."
The wisdom of your father is admitted;
The wise may be outrun, but not outwitted.

209

'It's difficult to limp and not be spied
By cripples, for it is a trick they know;
Your father's subtleties are Argus-eyed,[10]
And though his goods were taken long ago
His subtleties are with him still, I know.
You won't deceive him with your woman's wile,
And that is all my fear; you lack the guile.

210

'I do not know if peace will ever be;
But, peace or no, in earnest or in game,
Calkas went over to the enemy,
He joined the Greeks, and foully lost his name;
He never would return to us, for shame.
And so that way, as far as I can see,
Cannot be trusted; it's a fantasy.

211

'Then you will find your father will cajole
You into marriage; he knows how to preach.
He will commend some Greek, and charm your soul
With praises of him, ravish you with speech,
Or force you into it; it's in his reach.
And Troilus, whom you will never pity,
Firm in his truth, will perish in this city.

212

'Over all this, your father will dispraise
Us all, and say we cannot save the town;
He'll tell you that the Greeks will never raise
The siege; that they have sworn, for their renown,
To slay us all; our walls shall be torn down.
Thus he will say: I dread that he may scare
You with his reasons into staying there.

213

'And you will see so many a lusty knight
Among the Greeks, distinguished, sure to please,
Each with intelligence and heart and might
To do his best to put you at your ease,
And you will tire of the rusticities
Of us fool-Trojans (though remorse may hurt you)
Unless true constancy should prove your virtue.

214

'And this is so unbearable to think
It rends the soul out of my breast; for O,
There could no good opinion of it sink
Into my heart, should you decide to go.
Your father's cunning will destroy us, though,
And if you leave me, as I said before,
Then think of me as dead and nothing more.

215

'So, with a humble, true and piteous heart,
I beg you to be merciful, and pray
A thousand prayers out of my bitter smart
And misery to do as I shall say:
Let us steal off together right away!
For think what folly it is, when we can choose,
To grasp a shadow, and a substance lose!

216

'I mean there is a chance for us, ere dawn,
To steal away, and be together so;
What sense is there in seeing it withdrawn
So as to join your father? Risk to go,
Uncertain if you can return or no?
It would be madness, as it seems to me
To court such danger, when you could be free.

217

'And to speak vulgarly, we both have treasure
That we can take with us, and it will spread
To let us live in honour, and in pleasure,
Until the time will come when we are dead.
By this we can avoid our present dread;
To every other way you can invent,
My heart, most certainly, will not consent.

218

'And you need have no fear of taking hurt
Through poverty, for I have friends elsewhere,
And kindred; though you came in your bare shirt,
You would not lack for gold and things to wear;
We would be honoured if we settled there.
Let us go now, for it is plain to me
This is the best, if you will but agree.'

219

Criseyde gave answer, sighing, 'As you say,
All this, my true love, we could surely do;
As you imagine, we could steal away,
Or have a dozen other means in view
That later we'd regret, and sorely too.
As God may help me in my greatest need,
Your fears are groundless, yes, they are indeed.

220

'For when my father's cherishing of me,
Or when my fear of him, or other fear,
Pleasure, estate, marriage, or anything
Makes me untrue to you, my dearest dear,
May Saturn's daughter, Juno the Severe,
Drive me as mad as Athamas,[11] to dwell
Eternally in Styx, the pit of Hell!

[233]

221

'And this I swear by every god supernal,
And every goddess too and patroness,
Terrestrial nymph and deity infernal,
Satyr and faun, the greater and the less,
Rough demi-gods that haunt the wilderness;
Cut, Atropos, my thread of life and kill
If I be false! Now trust me if you will.

222

'O Simois, like an arrow running clear
Through Troy and ever downward to the sea,
Bear witness to the words I utter here,
And on the day when I shall prove to be
Untrue to Troilus, O turn and flee
Back on thy course, flow upward to thy well,
And let me sink, body and soul, to Hell!

223

'As for the thing you spoke of – thus to go,
Abandon all your friends and steal away,
May God forbid you ever should do so
For any woman! Troy has need today
Of all her men; and there is this to say:
If this were known, my life and your good name
Would lie in balance. Save us, Lord, from shame!

224

'And if so be that peace should come again
– One sees it daily, anger giving place
To amity – how could you bear the pain,
Not daring to return and show your face?
Do not expose yourself to such disgrace;
Do not be hasty in this hot affair,
For hasty men are men who suffer care.

225

'What do you think the people round about
Would make of it? That's very easily said;
They'd think, and they would swear to it no doubt,
It was not love that drove you, but you fled
Out of voluptuous lust and coward dread.
Then all your honour would be lost, my dear,
That honour which has ever shone so clear.

226

'And think a little of my own good name,
Still in its flower; how I should offend,
What filth it would be spotted with, what shame,
Were we to run away, as you intend!
For though I were to live to the world's end
What justice could I ever hope to win?
I should be lost; that would be grief and sin.

227

'And therefore let your reason cool your dish;
It's said they win who suffer patiently.
To have a wish one must give up a wish,
And make a virtue of necessity
By exercising patience; think that he
That would be lord of Fortune must ignore her;
Only a wretch will fear and fall before her.

228

'And believe this, my sweetheart; sure I am
That ere the moon, Lucina the Serene,
Has entered Leo, passing from the Ram,[12]
I will return; and what I say I mean,
As ever help me Juno, Heaven's Queen!
On the tenth day; if death should not prevail
Against me, I'll be with you, without fail.'

229

'Provided this is true,' said Troilus,
'Well, I'll endure it, up to the tenth day,
Since I can see that things must needs be thus;
But for the love of heaven, still I say
Let us at once steal secretly away,
Ever together, as now, and be at rest;
My heart keeps saying that will be the best.'

230

'Merciful God! What life is this?' said she,
'Ah! Do you wish to kill me in my woe?
I see it now; you have no trust in me,
Your words show well enough that this is so.
Now for the love of Cynthia white as snow,
Mistrust me not without a cause, unheard,
Untried, for pity's sake! You have my word.

231

'Think, it is sometimes wiser to forget
Time present for a better time in view;
Heavens above, you haven't lost me yet!
What's to be parted for a day or two?
Drive out the fantasies that lurk in you,
Have trust in me and lay aside your sorrow,
Or else I will not live until tomorrow.

232

'For if you knew how bitterly it smarts,
You would abandon this. Dear God! You know
How the pure spirit in my heart of hearts
Weeps when I see you weep, I love you so!
Also because I shall be forced to go
Among the Greeks; and if I knew not how
To come back here again, I should die now.

233

'Am I so foolish that I never could
Imagine anything, or find a way
Of coming back the day I said I would?
Who can hold back a thing that will not stay?
My father? No! for all his subtle play.
And if I should succeed, my leaving Troy
Will turn some other day to greater joy.

234

'So I beseech you from my very heart,
If there is anything that at my prayer
You would consent to do before we part,
And for the love I love you with, my dear,
O let me see you cheerful, free of care,
A happy face – for that will ease the aching
About my heart, which is at point of breaking.

235

'And there is one thing more,' she said 'my own,
I beg of you, my heart's sufficiency,
Since I am wholly yours and yours alone,
While I am absent, let no gallantry
With other ladies take your thoughts from me!
I never cease to fear it; it is said
Love is a thing of jealousy and dread.

236

'There lives no lady underneath the sun,
If you – which God forbid – should prove untrue,
That would be so betrayed, or so undone
As I, who think of truth as lodged in you;
Were I to find it other than I do,
It would be death; therefore, unless you see
Good reason, do not be unkind to me.'

237

'As God, from whom no secret can be hidden,
May give me joy, since first you caught my eye
No taint of falsehood, bidden or unbidden,
Has ever crossed my heart,' he made reply,
'And never shall until I come to die.
And well you may believe that this is so,
Though more I cannot say; but time will show.'

238

'Most loving thanks, my dearest,' answered she,
'May blissful Lady Venus, whom I serve,
Keep me from death until, in some degree,
I can requite you well, who well deserve;
And while I have my wits, which God preserve,
I shall do so, for I have found you true,
And honour will rebound to me from you.

239

'It was no royal state, or high descent,
No vain delight, nor any worthiness
In war or military tournament,
Pomp, riches, or magnificence of dress
That led me on to pity your distress,
But moral virtue, grounded in truth of heart,
That moved me to compassion from the start.

240

'Your noble heart, the manhood that you had,
And the contempt for all that was not right,
(It seemed to me) – all that was base and bad,
Like rudeness, or a vulgar appetite –
And that your reason bridled your delight;
These things, so far above what others give,
Have made me yours, and shall do, while I live.

[238]

241

'For this the length of years shall not undo,
Nor Fortune the Inconstant shall deface;
And Jupiter, whose power can renew
The sorrowful in gladness, send us grace
That we may meet together in this place
Within ten nights, and ease our hearts of woe;
And now farewell, for it is time to go.'

242

At last their long lamenting reached its close
With many kisses as they lay embraced,
The dawn came on, and Troilus arose
And, looking at her, felt the bitter taste
Of death's cold cares; and then, in troubled haste,
He took his leave of her and went away;
Whether he was sad, I need not say;

243

For the imagination hardly can
Grasp, or perception feel, or poet tell
The cruel pains of this unhappy man,
For they were greater than the pains of Hell.
He saw that she must leave the citadel;
His heart was of its very soul bereft;
Without a word, he turned away and left.

Book V

BOOK V

1

And there approached that fatal destiny
Which lies in the disposal of Jove's frown
And to you angry Furies, sisters three,
Is, for its execution, handed down;
Because of which Criseyde must leave the town
And Troilus live on in pain and dread
Till Lachesis no longer spin his thread.

2

Now golden-headed Phoebus, high aloft,
Had three times melted in his sunny sheen
The winter snows, and Zephyrus as oft
Had brought the leaves again in tender green
Since Troilus, son of Hecuba the Queen,
First fell in love with her, for whom his sorrow
Was all for this: she was to leave that morrow.

* * *

3

At prime of day the sturdy Diomede
Stood ready at the gates; he was to lead
Criseyde to join the Greeks, but she indeed
Was at a loss, she felt her spirit bleed.
And, truly, not in all the books we read
Can there be found a woman so cast down
Nor ever one so loth to leave a town.

4

And Troilus with neither plan of war,
Nor counsel, lost to joy for ever more,
Now waited desolate at his lady's door,
She that had been the root and flower before
Of all his happiness and joys of yore.
Now, Troilus, farewell to all your joy,
For you will never see her back in Troy!

[243]

5

It's true that while he waited in this trance
He laboured, in a manly way, to hide
His grief; it barely changed his countenance;
But at the gate whence she was due to ride
With certain folk, he hovered on the side;
He was so woebegone, (although of course
He did not speak), he scarce could sit his horse.

6

He shook with rage, his heart began to gnaw
Within, when Diomede prepared to mount;
He muttered to himself at what he saw
'O baseness, shame, to suffer this affront!
Why not redress or bring it to account?
Were it not better die in the endeavour
Than to endure this misery for ever?

7

'Why don't I fall on them, give rich and poor
Something to do before I let her go?
Why don't I bring all Troy into a roar?
Why don't I kill this Diomede, and show
Some courage? Why not, with a man or so,
Steal her away? What more must I endure?
Why don't I help myself to my own cure?'

8

But why he would not do so fell a deed
I have to tell you, why he chose and willed
It not to be; he feared that it would breed
A battle, and Criseyde might well be killed;
And that is why his wish was unfulfilled,
Otherwise certainly, as you have heard,
It had been done without another word.

9

At last Criseyde was ready for the ride
Sighing 'Alas!' with sorrow in her face;
But go she must, whatever might betide;
There is no remedy in such a case.
She rode out at a melancholy pace;
What wonder if she felt a bitter smart
Forgoing Troilus, her own dear heart!

10

And he, by way of showing courtesy,
With hawk on hand, and with a splendid rout
Of knights, rode forth and kept her company.
They passed the distant valley far without
And would have ridden further yet, no doubt,
Most gladly; it was grief to turn so soon,
But turn he had to, that unhappy noon.

11

Just at that moment Ántenor appeared
Out of the Grecian host, and every knight
Was glad and gave him welcome as he neared;
And Troilus, though very far from light
Of heart, obliged himself, as best he might,
At least to hold his tears; his eyes were dim
As he kissed Ántenor and welcomed him.

12

And here at last he had to take his leave;
He cast his eyes upon her piteously
And, riding closer, took her by the sleeve
To plead his cause, and touched her soberly;
Ah, Lord! She started weeping tenderly.
Softly and slyly he contrived to say
'Now do not kill me, darling, keep your day.'

13

With that he turned his courser round about;
His face was very pale. To Diomede
He spoke not, nor to any of his rout;
This Greek, the son of Tideus, took good heed;
 Here was a craft in which he knew his Creed,
And more than that; he took her leading-rein,
And Troilus to Troy rode home again.

14

This Diomede who led her by the bridle,
Now that the Trojans could no longer stay,
Thought 'Well, this is no moment to be idle;
I have the work, so I should get the pay;
I'll talk to her; it will beguile the way.
As I was taught a dozen times at school
"He who forgets to help himself's a fool."'

15

Nevertheless he understood enough
To think 'It will for certain come to naught
If I should speak of love, or make it tough,
For doubtless, if she treasures in her thought
Him I suspect, she cannot well be brought
To let him go so soon; I'll try to find
A means, and yet not let her know my mind.'

16

This Diomede, who knew his way about,
Chose the right moment when to fall in speech
With her of this and that, and ask right out
Why she was in distress, and to beseech
Her to command him – were it in his reach
To put her at her ease; if she but knew it,
She only had to ask and he would do it.

17

For truly, and he swore it as a knight,
There was not anything to give her pleasure
He would not do with all his heart and might,
If it could ease her heart in any measure;
He begged her to allay and not to treasure
Her grief, and said 'We Grecians will take joy
In honouring you, as much as folk in Troy.'

18

He also said 'I know you find it strange
– No wonder either, it is new to you –
To drop these Trojan friendships in exchange
For ours of Greece, people you never knew.
But God forbid there should not be a few
Among the Grecian hosts that you will find
As true as any Trojan, and as kind.

19

'And as, a moment since, I made a vow
To be your friend, helpfully if I might,
Since I have more acquaintance with you now
Than other strangers, I will claim a right;
From this time on, command me, day or night;
And though it should be painful, I will do
Whatever may delight your heart and you.

20

'And I would have you treat me as your brother
And do not hold my friendship in disdain;
And though you grieve for some great thing or other
– I know not what – I know my heart would fain
Relieve you, had we leisure, of your pain;
If it be more than I can well redress,
I am right sorry for your heaviness.

21

'You Trojans and we Greeks have long been loth
To love each other, and many a day will be;
Yet there's one god of love we worship both;
So, for the love of God, my lady free,
Hate whom you will, but have no hate for me;
No one could serve you, trust me this is true,
That would be half so loth to anger you.

22

'And were it not that we are near the tent
Of Calkas (who can see us, by the way)
I would go on to tell you all I meant;
This must be sealed up for another day.
Give me your hand; I am and shall be aye,
God helping me, while life shall last, alone
Above all other men, your very own.

23

'And that's a thing I never said before
To any woman born; and I can vow
I never yet have had a paramour
And never loved a woman, up till now;
So do not be my enemy! Allow
For lack of eloquence in me, and spurn
Me not for it, for I have much to learn.

24

'Though it may seem a wonder, lady bright,
To hear me speak of love so quickly, yet
I have heard tell that many at first sight
Have loved, who up till then had never met;
Nor do I have in me the power to set
Myself against the god, whom I obey,
And ever will; have mercy, then, I say.

25

'Such admirable knights are in this place
And you so beautiful – that one and all
Will strain in rivalry to stand in grace
With you; but should such happiness befall
Me as to be the one that you will call
Your servant, there's not one of them so true
As I shall be, till death, in serving you.'

26

Criseyde made slight rejoinder, though she heard,
Oppressed with grief and wondering what to do,
But in effect she hardly caught a word,
A sentence here and there, a phrase or two.
She thought her sorrowing heart would burst right through
Her breast; and when she saw her father there
She sank upon her saddle in despair.

27

Nevertheless, to Diomede she proffered
Her thanks for all his pains, and his display
Of welcome, and the friendship he had offered,
Which she accepted in a civil way;
She would be glad to do what he would say
And she would trust him, as indeed she might,
Or so she said, beginning to alight.

28

Her father took her in his arms and cried,
As twenty times he kissed her on the cheek,
'Welcome, my own dear daughter!' She replied
That she was glad to see him, ceased to speak
And stood before him, mute and mild and meek.
And here I leave her with her father thus,
And I turn back to tell of Troilus.

29

To Troy this woeful Troilus returned
In sorrow, above all other sorrows' force,
With felon look, a face where fury burned.
Abruptly he dismounted from his horse
And through his palace took his angry course,
Heedless of everything, to seek his room,
And no one dared break in upon his gloom.

30

There to the griefs till then within him pent
He gave large issue; 'Death!' he cried at first,
Then, in the frantic throes he underwent,
Cursed Jove, Apollo, Cupid, said his worst
Of Ceres, Bacchus, Cypris, and he cursed
His birth, himself, his fortune and his nature
And, save his lady, every earthly creature.

31

To bed he went and wallowed, turned and lay
In fury, as Ixion does in Hell,
And so continued until nearly day;
His heart began a little to unswell
Relieved by tears that issued from their well;
And piteously he called upon Criseyde,
Crying aloud, and this is what he cried:

32

'Where is my own, my lady loved and dear?
And where is her white breast? Where is it? Where?
Where are her arms? And where her eyes so clear,
That this time yesternight were with me here?
Now I may weep alone, full many a tear!
And wildly grasp about, but in her place
I only find a pillow to embrace.

33

'How shall I do? When will she come again?
Alas, I know not! Why did I let her go?
Ah! would to God that I had then been slain!
My sweetest heart, Criseyde, my darling foe,
My lady, only love and only woe,
To whom I give my heart for ever! See,
See, I am dying, will you not rescue me?

34

'Who gazes on you now, my guiding star?
Who in your presence sits? Or who stands near?
Who now can comfort you in your heart's war?
Since I am gone, to whom do you give ear?
Who speaks for me, for me in absence here?
No one, alas! I grieve and that is why;
I know you fare as evilly as I.

35

'How am I to endure for ten whole days,
When, the first night, I suffer so much pain?
How will she do, sad creature? In what ways,
Seeing her tenderness, will she sustain
Her grief for me? O. ere you come again,
Piteous and pale and green your face will be
With longing hither to return, to me.'

36

And when he fell in fitful slumberings,
After a little he began to groan,
For dreams would visit him of dreadful things
That well might be: dreaming he was alone
In some appalling place and making moan,
Or dreaming he was prisoner to bands
Of enemies; his life was in their hands.

37

His body thereupon would give a start
And with that start he found himself awake
With such a tremor felt about his heart
The terror of it made his body quake;
And there were sudden noises he would make
And he imagined he had fallen deep
From a great height; and then he had to weep,

38

And spend such pity on his misery;
Wonder it was to hear his fantasies;
Then, in a moment, he would mightily
Console himself – a madness, a disease,
He said it was, to have such fears as these;
Again his bitter sorrows overbore him,
And any man would have felt sorry for him.

39

Who could have told, or fully have unfurled
His torment, his lament, his flow of brine?
No one alive or dead in all the world!
I leave you, gentle reader, to divine
That grief like his, for such a wit as mine,
Is far too great, and I should work in vain;
To think about it cuts me to the brain.

40

In heaven still the stars were to be seen,
Although the moon was paling, quickly too,
As the horizon whitened with a sheen
Far to the east, as it is wont to do
When Phoebus with his rosy car is due;
He was preparing for his journey thus
When Troilus sent word for Pandarus.

41

This Pandarus, who all the previous day
Had been unable, even for an hour,
To see him, though he'd sworn to get away
– For he was with King Priam in the Tower,
And so it simply wasn't in his power
To make a move – now, with the morning, went
To Troilus, who, as I say, had sent.

42

He found it easy in his heart to guess
That Troilus had lain awake in woe
And needed now to talk of his distress;
He did not need a book to tell him so.
And to his chamber he made haste to go
The shortest way, greeted and gravely eyed him,
And then sat down upon the bed beside him.

43

'My Pandarus,' said Troilus, 'the sorrow
I undergo I cannot long endure.
I feel I shall not live until tomorrow,
So I would lay my plans, to make all sure,
And fix my funeral and sepulchre.
As for my property and all the rest,
Dispose of it for me as you think best.

44

'But for the fire and for the burial flames
In which my body shall be burned and freed,
And for the feasting and the funeral games
To grace my wake, I beg of you, take heed;
See that all's well; and offer Mars my steed,
My sword and helmet; also, brother dear,
My shield to Pallas, she that shines so clear.

45

'The powdery ash to which my heart will burn
I beg of you to gather and preserve
In such a vessel as they call an urn,
A golden one; give it to her I serve,
For love of whom I die; I did not swerve.
So give it her; do me this courtesy
And beg her keep it in my memory.

46

'I know it from my malady, and by
My present dreams and some from long ago,
That I am certainly about to die.
Besides, the owl they call Escaphilo[1]
These two nights past has shrieked for me, and so
I pray for Mercury, if he please, to fetch
This soul of mine and guide a sorrowful wretch!'

47

Pandarus answered 'Listen, Troilus;
Dear friend, as I have often said before,
It is mere madness in you, sorrowing thus
Without a reason; I can say no more.
He that to all advice will close the door
Is one for whom I know no remedy;
Leave him to stew in his own fantasy.

48

'But, Troilus, I beg you; tell me, do,
Whether you think that ever anyone
Loved with so passionate a love as you?
God knows they have, and many so have done;
Many have had to let a fortnight run
Without their ladies, and have made no fuss;
What need is there? It's quite ridiculous.

49

'For, day by day, as you yourself can see,
A man may part from lover or from wife,
When they are sundered by necessity,
Aye, though he loves her better than his life;
But all the same he will not be at strife
Within himself; for, as you know, dear brother,
Friends cannot always be with one another.

50

'What do they do who see their lovers wedded
Because of powerful friends, as happens oft,
And in their spouses' bed behold them bedded?
God knows they take it wisely – fair and soft,
Because good hope will keep their hearts aloft;
And if they can endure a time of grief,
As time has hurt them, time will bring relief.

51

'That is the way to take it; let it slide!
Try to enjoy yourself, have no concern;
Ten days are not so long for you to bide;
For since she gave her promise to return,
No one will make her break it; she will learn
Some way of coming back, so fear no ill;
I'll lay my life upon it that she will.

52

'As for those dreams of yours and all such folly,
To Hell with them! Imagination teems
With stuff like that; it's from your melancholy
That troubles you in sleep, or so it seems.
A straw for the significance of dreams!
I wouldn't give a bean for them, not I!
No one can tell you what they signify.

53

'The temple priests incline to tell you this,
That dreams are sent as Heaven's revelations;
They also tell you, and with emphasis,
They're diabolical hallucinations;
The doctors say that glandular liquations
Engender them, by fast – or gluttony;
How can the truth be contradictory?

54

'Others will say they come from an obsession;
Some fixed idea a fellow has, a theme;
And this will cause a vision-like impression.
Others report from books that it would seem
A thing quite natural for men to dream
At certain times of year, according to
The moon; believe no dream. It will not do.

55

'All very well, these dreams, for poor old wives,
Who trust in birds and auguries and howls
That send them all in terror of their lives!
– Ravens foreboding death and screeching owls –
Belief in them is false and it befouls;
O that a creature with a noble mind
Like man, should trust in garbage of the kind!

56

'Let me beseech you, then, with all my heart,
Forgive yourself for all that's gone astray.
Let's talk no more; get up and make a start.
Let's think how we may drive the time away
And how our lives will freshen on the day
When she comes back – and soon it will be too! –
For that's the best, God help us, we can do.

57

'Rise up, recall the lusty life in Troy
That we have led! And so we shall contrive
To fleet the time until our time for joy
Shall bring us back again our bliss alive;
The languors of a day or two – twice five –
We shall forget about, or somehow stifle,
So that the whole affair shall seem a trifle.

58

'I've seen a lot of gentlefolk about,
And we are meanwhile in a state of truce.
Let's have some fun and join the lusty rout
At Sárpedoun's, a mile away; get loose,
And cheat the time by putting it to use!
Drive it along to meet that blissful morrow
When you will see her, cause of all your sorrow!

59

'Rise up, I say, dear brother Troilus;
It does no honour to you, don't you see,
To weep and linger in your bedroom thus.
One thing is absolutely sure, trust me,
If you lie here a day or two, or three,
People will say it is a coward's trick,
You daren't rise up and fight, you're feigning sick.'

60

And Troilus replied 'O brother dear,
As anyone that ever suffered pain
Will know, it is no wonder to appear
In sorrow, or to weep, or to complain,
For one who feels the smart in every vein;
Though I complain and weep, I have the right,
Since I have lost my cause of all delight.

61

'Forced by necessity to make a start,
I will get up, as soon as ever I may,
And God, to whom I sacrifice my heart,
Send us in haste the tenth, the happy day!
There never was a bird so glad of May
As I shall be when she returns to Troy,
The cause of all my torment, and my joy.

62

'But what do you advise,' said Troilus,
'Where we can best amuse ourselves in town?'
'Well, my advice, by God,' said Pandarus,
'Is to ride out and see King Sárpedoun.'
This for a while they argued up and down,
Till, in the end, Troilus gave consent
And rose; and off to Sárpedoun they went.

63

He was a man whose life had been a fable
Of honour, liberality and worth;
And all that could be offered on a table
And that was dainty, though it cost the earth,
He gave them day by day; there was no dearth,
So people said, the greatest and the least;
The like was never seen at any feast.

64

Nor could you hope to find an instrument
Delicious by the use of wind or string
In all the world, however far you went,
That tongue can tell of or that heart can bring
To mind, but blended at their banqueting;
And never was a company so fair
To look on as the ladies dancing there.

65

Of what avail was this to Troilus
In his despondency? It went for nought.
For all the while his heart, so dolorous,
Sought for Criseyde; insistently it sought.
Ever and only she was all his thought,
Now this, now that, in his imagination;
What banqueting could bring him consolation?

66

Since, of these ladies at the feast, the gem
Was lacking for him, with Criseyde away,
It was a grief for him to look at them,
Or listen to the instruments in play;
She being absent in whose hand there lay
The key of his heart, it was his fantasy
That no one had a right to melody.

67

There was no hour of the day or night,
When there was nobody to overhear,
But that he said 'My darling, my delight,
How has it been with you since you were here?
How I would welcome you again, my dear!'
Fortune had caught him in her maze, alas!
And fitted him a helmet made of glass.[2]

68

The letters she had written him moreover,
In former days, that now were gone for good,
A hundred times a day he read them over,
Refiguring her lovely womanhood
Within his heart, and every word and mood
Out of the past, and thus he battled on
Till the fourth day; then said he must be gone.

69

'Is it a firm intention, this of yours,
Pandar, for us to linger, you and I,
Till Sárpedoun has turned us out of doors?
Were it not better now to say good-bye?
For heaven's sake this evening let us try
To take our leave of him and disappear
For home, for honestly I won't stay here.'

70

Said Pandarus: 'What did we come here for?
To borrow a light and then run home again?
I don't know where we could have found a more
Delightful host, gladder to entertain
Than Sárpedoun; and isn't it quite plain
He likes us? Don't you see that if we fled
So suddenly, it would be most ill-bred?

71

'We told him we were paying him a visit
For a whole week; so suddenly to change
And take our leave is hardly proper, is it?
After four days! He'd think it very strange.
Let's stick by what we've chosen to arrange.
And since you've promised him that you would stay,
Stand by your word; we then can ride away.'

72

Thus Pandar, with much trouble and persuasion,
Forced him to stay awhile and show his face;
But when the week-end came, they took occasion
To bid the King farewell and leave the place;
Said Troilus: 'Now Heaven send me grace
That I may find, upon my homecoming,
Criseyde returned!' And he began to sing.

73

'Nuts!' muttered Pandar softly to himself,
Who, in his heart of hearts, was thinking thus:
'All this hot stuff will cool upon a shelf
Ere Calkas sends Criseyde to Troilus!'
But still he swore 'She will come back to us,
What your heart says is right,' he japed away,
'She will come back as soon as ever she may!'

74

When they had reached the palace of his friend
There they dismounted in the evening light
And to his chamber took their way, to spend
The time in talking on into the night;
And all their talk was of Criseyde the Bright.
And, later, when it pleased them, having fed,
They rose from supper and they went to bed.

75

When morning came and day began to clear,
This Troilus stirred and awoke, and cried
To Pandarus 'Dear brother, do you hear?
For heaven's sake let us get up and ride;
Let us go see the palace of Criseyde;
For since we are not yet to have the feast,
There is the palace to be seen at least.'

76

To lull suspicions in his followers,
He made pretence that he had work to do
In town, and to the house that still was hers
They started off – how sad he alone knew;
It seemed to him his heart would break in two;
And when he found the doors were sparred across
He almost fell to earth, so great the loss.

77

And taking in all that his eyes now told
– For barred was every window in the place –
He felt as if a frost had fallen cold
Upon his heart; the colour of his face
Changed to a deadly pallor; quickening pace,
Without a word, he rode ahead so fast
That no one saw his countenance as he passed.

78

Then said he thus: 'O palace desolate,
O house of houses that was once so bright,
O palace, empty and disconsolate,
O lantern quenched, from which they stole the light,
Palace that once was day and now is night,
Ought not you to fall, and I to die,
Since she is gone that we were guided by?

79

'O palace, crown of houses, now forsaken,
But once illumined by the sun of bliss,
O ring from which the ruby has been taken,
Cause of a joy that now has come to this,
Since I may do no better, I would kiss
Your cold, cold doorway, but for all this rout
Of people; farewell shrine, whose saint is out!'

80

He turned and cast his eyes on Pandar then;
His face was changed and pitiful to see;
As he rode on with him he spoke again,
As far as he had opportunity
Of his old joys and his new misery,
So sadly, with a face so dead and grim
That anybody would have pitied him.

81

So he went onward, riding up and down,
And memories poured in at every glance,
Passing the very places in the town
That once had had such power to entrance:
'Look, it was there I saw my lady dance!
And in that temple with her shining eyes
She took me first, my darling, by surprise.

82

'And yonder, once, I heard her lovely laughter,
I heard her laughter and I saw her play,
And it was blissful; then, a little after,
Just there, she once came up to me to say
"O love me, sweetheart, love me well today."
And it was there she gazed at me so sweetly
That until death my heart was hers completely.

83

'And at that corner, in the house you see,
I heard my loveliest of ladies sing,
So womanly, and how melodiously!
How well, how clear, with what a pleasing ring!
Still in my soul I hear it echoing,
That blissful sound; and there's the very place
In which she first received me into grace!'

84

And then he thought: 'Ah, Cupid, blessed Lord,
When I recall the past, the purgatory
I have endured, how fiercely thou hast warred
Against me, it would make a book, a story.
What need was there to add unto thy glory
By this poor victory on me and mine,
What joy in slaying what is wholly thine?

85

'Well hast thou wreaked upon me, Lord, thine ire,
Thou mighty god, so fearful to annoy!
Have mercy, Lord, thou knowest I desire
Thy favour more than any other joy,
And will profess Thy faith, in whose employ
I mean to livè and die, and ask no boon
Save that Thou send me back Criseyde, and soon!

86

'Constrain her heart with longing to return,
As, to behold her, thou constrainest me!
Then it will surely be her whole concern,
And she'll not tarry! Ah, Cupid, do not be
As cruel to our blood and monarchy
As Juno to the blood of Thebes, for whom,
And for her rage, the Thebans met their doom!'

87

And after this he visited the gate
Through which, at such a lively pace, Criseyde
Had ridden out, and he began to wait
In restless hope; and up and down he plied
His horse, and said 'Alas, I saw her ride
Away from here; O God, in Heaven's joy,
Let me but see her riding into Troy!

88

'To think I guided her to yonder hill,
Alas! And it was there I took my leave.
I saw her ride away, I see her still;
The sorrow of it is enough to cleave
My heart! And hither I came home at eve,
And here must linger on, cast out from joy,
And shall, until I see her back in Troy.'

89

Often enough he thought himself undone,
Defeated, pale, shrunken to something less
Than what he was, imagined everyone
Was saying 'What has happened? Who can guess
Why Troilus is in such deep distress?'
All this was nothing but his melancholy;
A fantasy about himself, a folly.

90

Another time he would imagine – weighing
What people whispered as they cast an eye
Upon him – they were pitying him, saying
'I am right sorry Troilus will die.'
And in these thoughts a day or two went by
As you have heard; such was the life he led,
Like one who halted between hope and dread.

91

It gave him pleasure in his songs to show
The reason of his grief, as best he might;
He made a song of just a word or so,
To ease his heart and make his sorrow light,
And when he was alone and out of sight
He softly sang about his lady dear
In absence, and he sang as you shall hear:

92

'O star of love, since I have lost thy light,
Shall not my heart lament thee and bewail
In darkening torment, moving night by night
Towards my death; the wind is in my sail.
If the tenth night should come, and if it fail,
Thy guiding beam, if only for an hour,
My ship and me Charybdis³ will devour.'

[265]

93

But after singing it, he very soon
Fell once again to sighing, as of old,
And every night rose up to see the moon
As was his habit, and to her he told
His sorrows all, and yet he would make bold
To say 'Yet moon, the night your horns renew
I shall be happy – if all the world is true!'

94

'Old were the horns I saw you wear that morning
When my dear lady rode away from here
Who is my cause of torment and of mourning
And therefore, O Lucina, bright and clear,
For love of God, run swiftly round thy sphere;
For when thy horns begin again to spring
Then she will come who has my bliss to bring.'

95

Longer the day and longer still the night
Than they were wont to be, or so he thought;
The course the sun was taking was not right,
It made a longer journey than it ought;
'Phaeton⁴ is not dead, as I was taught,'
Said Troilus, 'I fear he is alive
And has his father's cart, but cannot drive.'

96

Fast up and down the walls he used to walk
Gazing towards the Grecian armaments,
And thus would commune with himself and talk
'Yonder my lady lies, at all events,
Or, maybe, yonder, where I see those tents!
And thence must come this air so sweet and soft,
Touching my soul and raising it aloft!

97

'Surely this breath of wind, that more and more,
Moment by moment, comes to fan my face,
Is of her sighing, for her heart is sore;
I prove it thus, that in no other place
In the whole city but this little space
Feel I a wind whose sound is like a pain,
And says "Alas! When shall we meet again?"'

98

Through this long time of waiting drove he thus,
Till the ninth day and night had fully passed;
And always at his side was Pandarus,
Busily finding comfort to the last;
He did his best to lend a lighter cast
To all his thoughts, gave hope that on the morrow
She would return to him and end his sorrow.

99

Upon the other hand there was Criseyde
With her few women in the Grecian throng,
And many times a day 'Alas!' she cried,
'That ever I was born! Well may I long
For death! Alas that I have lived too long!
What can I do that things may turn to good?
All is far worse than I had understood.

100

'Nothing will bring my father to relent
Or let me go; I cannot find a way
To wheedle him; when the ten days are spent,
Deep in his heart my Troilus will say
That I am false to him – and well he may.
No one will thank me for it, either side;
Alas that I was born! Would I had died!

101

'And if I were to put myself in danger,
Stealing away by night, might I not fall
Into some sentry's hand, and, as a stranger,
Be taken for a spy? But, worst of all,
Some ruffian Greek, fresh from a drunken brawl
Might come on me and, true as is my heart,
I should be lost. Dear Heaven, take my part!'

102

Now waxen-pale her once so shining face,
Wasted her limbs, as one who day by day
Stood, when she dared, to gaze upon the place
Where she was born, where she had longed to stay,
All the night long in tears, alas, she lay;
Thus she despaired of comfort or relief,
And led her life, a creature full of grief.

103

Many a time she sighed in her distress,
In her imagination picturing
Her Troilus in all his worthiness,
And all his golden words remembering,
From when her love had first begun to spring;
And so she set her woeful heart on fire
By the remembrance of her lost desire.

104

In all the world there is no heart so cruel,
Had it but heard her thus lament her sorrow,
But would have also wept at the renewal
Of tender tears; she wept both eve and morrow;
Many her tears; she had no need to borrow.
And yet, sharper than any grief beside,
There was no soul in whom she dared confide.

105

How ruefully she stood and stared at Troy,
Saw the tall towers and the lofty hall,
'Alas,' she said, 'the happiness and joy,
That once I had beyond that very wall,
But now is turned to bitterness and gall!
Troilus! What are you doing now?' she cried,
'Lord! Do you still give thought to your Criseyde?

106

'Alas, had I but trusted your advice
And run away with you! If we had run,
I should not now be sighing bitter sighs.
And who is there could say that I had done
Amiss to steal away with such a one?
But all too late the medicine comes to save
The corpse that they are bearing to the grave.

107

'For it is now too late to speak of it;
Prudence, one of thine eyes – for thou hast three –
I ever lacked, as now I must admit;
Time past I safely stored in memory,
Time present also I had eyes to see;
Time future, till it caught me in the snare,
I could not see, and thence has come my care.

108

'Nevertheless, betide what may betide,
Tomorrow night, be it by east or west,
I'll steal away, on one or other side,
And go wherever Troilus thinks best,
And in this firm intention I will rest.
Who cares what scandal wicked tongues uncover?
Wretches are always envious of a lover.

109

'He who takes heed of every uttered word,
Or will be ruled by others, in the end
Will never come to good, so I have heard.
For there are things which some will reprehend
That many other people will commend;
And various as may their reasons be,
My own felicity suffices me.

110

'So, without any further argument,
I'll make for Troy; let me conclude it thus.'
And yet, God knows, two whole months came and went
And still her purposes were dubious.
For both the town of Troy and Troilus
Shall knotless slide away out of her heart;
She never will take purpose to depart.

111

This Diomede of whom I have made mention
Now went about imagining a way,
With all the cunning of a swift invention,
How to enmesh Criseyde with least delay
And bring her heart into his net; by day
And night he worked, perfecting his design
For fishing her; he laid out hook and line.

112

Nevertheless he had the secret thought
That she was not without a love in Troy;
For never, since the moment he had brought
Her thence had he beheld her laugh for joy;
He knew not what might prove the subtlest ploy
To coax her heart, 'But trying will be fun,'
He said, 'nothing attempted, nothing won.'

113

And yet he argued with himself one night
'Now am I not a fool, well knowing how
Her grief is for another, to invite
Her fancies my way, and attempt her now?
It may not do me good, I must allow;
And grave authorities have held the view
"A time of woe is not a time to woo."

114

'Yet, if a man should win so sweet a flower
From him for whom she mourns so constantly,
Might he not say he was a man of power?'
So, ever bold, he thought 'Well, as for me,
Happen what may, I'll try, and we shall see;
If I'm to die for it, I'll try to reach
Her heart; I shall lose nothing but my speech.'

115

This Diomede, or so the books declare,
To serve his needs, kept ever in good fettle;
His voice was stern, his mighty limbs were square;
Chivalrous, hardy, headstrong, quick to settle
For action – of his father Tideus' mettle.
He was a boaster, so the stories run,
And heir to Argos and to Caledon.

116

Criseyde herself was of a modest stature,
And as to shapeliness, and face, and air,
There never can have been a fairer creature;
Often enough it was her way to wear
The heavy tresses of her shining hair
Over her collar, down her back, behind.
These with a thread of gold she used to bind.

117

Save for the fact her eyebrows joined together,
There was no fault that I can recognize;
Her eyes, they say, were clear as summer weather,
For everyone who saw her testifies
That paradise was seated in her eyes;
Her love and her rich beauty ever strove
Which was the greater – beauty in her, or love.

118

She was discreet and simple and demure,
And the most kindly-nurtured there could be;
And she was pleasant-spoken, to be sure,
Stately and generous and joyous; she
Had a free nature, having the quality
Of pity; but she had a sliding heart.
I cannot tell her age, I lack the art.

119

Troilus was well-grown, for he was tall,
Shapely, and in proportion strong and fleet;
Nature could not have bettered it at all.
Young, fresh, a lion-hardy man to meet,
He was as true as steel from head to feet,
Dowered with excellence of such a cast
As none will equal while the world will last.

120

And certainly historians have reckoned
That, in his time, no other was in sight
To whom he could have been considered second
In daring deeds, such as become a knight.
Although a giant may have greater might,
His heart, among the first, among the best,
Stood equal in its daring and in zest.

121

But, to go back again to Diomede,
It happened afterwards, on the tenth day
After she left the city as agreed,
That Diomede, as fresh as a branch in May,
Came visiting the tent where Calkas lay;
On a pretence of business in he went,
But I shall tell you of his true intent.

122

Now, to be brief, Criseyde on this occasion
Gave him a welcome and sat down beside him,
Nor did it seem he needed much persuasion
To make him stay; and presently she plied him
With wine and spices, seeking to provide him
Some entertainment with a dish or two,
And so they fell in speech, as old friends do.

123

And then he started speaking of the war
Between his people and the folk of Troy,
And he discussed the siege and begged her for
Her own opinion, which he would enjoy;
Descending thence, he then began to toy
With whether she had found the Grecian style
Of doing things quite foreign for a while,

124

And why her father had delayed so long
In marrying her off to a leading light.
Criseyde, who felt her suffering grow strong
For love of Troilus, her chosen knight,
Summoned her sorrowing thoughts as best she might,
And gave some answer; as to his intent,
She seemed to have no notion what he meant.

125

Nevertheless this fellow Diomede
Began to feel assured, and he replied
'If my impressions are not wrong, indeed,
It seems to me, dear lady, dear Criseyde,
That since I took your bridle on our ride
From Troy – do you recall that happy morrow? –
I never yet have seen you but in sorrow.

126

'I cannot guess at what the cause may be,
Unless it is the love of someone dear
To you in Troy; it would much trouble me
Were you to spill so much as half a tear
For any fancied Trojan cavalier.
Do not deceive yourself; it's not the style;
You may be sure it isn't worth your while.

127

'The Trojans, one and all, are, so to speak,
In prison; if you think, you must agree;
Not one among them shall escape the Greek
For all the gold between the sun and sea;
And you can count on that, believe you me.
No mercy will be shown, not one shall live,
Though he had twice five conquered worlds to give.

128

'Such vengeance will be taken by our legions
For Helen's ravishing before we go
That all the gods of the infernal regions
Will stand aghast, outdone by such a show,
And men on earth, to the world's end, will know
The bitter cost of ravishing a Queen,
So cruel the revenge that will be seen.

129

'Unless your father's doubling on his traces,
Using equivocations and those sly
Words that are sometimes said to have two faces,
You will discover that I do not lie,
Yes, you will see it with your very eye,
And soon enough; you won't believe the speed
At which it all will happen, so take heed.

130

'What! Do you think your reverend father could
Have given Ántenor to ransom you,
Unless he knew full well the city would
Be utterly destroyed? Why, no! He knew,
And knew for certain, no one would come through
Who was a Trojan; having that to fear,
He dared not leave you there, so brought you here.

131

'What would you have, my loveliest of creatures?
Let Troy and Trojan in your heart give place;
Drive out that bitter hope and cheer those features,
Call back the beauty to that saddened face,
On which salt tears have left so deep a trace.
Troy is in jeopardy and Troy will bow;
There is no remedy to save it now.

132

'Among the Greeks, believe me, you may find
A love more perfect, ere the fall of night,
Than any Trojan love, and one more kind,
Ready to serve you with a better might;
And if you would vouchsafe it, lady bright,
I would be happier to be your lover
Than to be King of Argos twelve times over.'

133

And on the word he turned a little red,
And in his speech his voice a little shook,
A little to one side he cast his head,
Then he fell silent. Presently he took
A glance at her and said, with sober look,
'I am – although it be to you no joy –
As nobly born as any man in Troy.

134

'For if my father Tideus had not died,
I should by now be King of many a city
In Caledon, and Argos too, Criseyde!
Indeed I hope to be so yet, my pretty;
But he was killed at Thebes, and, more's the pity,
So Polynices was, and many more,
Too soon, unhappily. It was the war.

135

'But, sweetheart, since I am to be your man,
And since you are the very first to whom
I ever knelt, to serve as best I can,
And ever shall, whatever be my doom,
Let me have leave, before I quit the room,
To visit you tomorrow in this fashion,
And, at more leisure, to reveal my passion.'

136

Why should I tell you all the things he said?
He spoke enough, at least for the first day.
It proved successful, for Criseyde was led
To grant him his petition and to say
That she would see him, if he kept away
From certain subjects, which, as she made clear,
He must not touch, speaking, as you shall hear,

137

Like one whose heart was set on Troilus
As firmly as upon its very base;
She gave a distant answer, saying thus
To him 'O Diomed, I love the place
Where I was born. Ah, Jove, in heavenly grace,
Soon, soon, dear Lord, deliver it from care,
For Thy great glory, keep it strong and fair!

138

'I know the Greeks would like to have their way
And wreak their wrath on Troy, our citadel;
But yet it will not happen as you say,
God willing; and I know my father well;
He's wise and has his plans; if, as you tell,
He bought me dearly, let me argue rather
That I'm the more beholden to my father.

139

'And that the Greeks are men of high condition
I'm well aware; but certainly they'll find
Young men in Troy as worthy of position,
As able and as perfect and as kind,
As, East or West, a man may call to mind.
That you could serve your lady, I believe you,
To earn the thanks with which she would receive you.

140

'But – if we are to speak of love – ' she said,
'I had a wedded lord, to whom, I mean,
My heart was wholly given; he is dead.
No other love, so help me Heaven's Queen,
Was ever in my heart, nor since has been.
That you are noble, and of high descent,
I've often heard, and it is evident.

141

'And so it seems an even greater wonder
That one like you should scorn a woman so.
God knows that love and I are far asunder;
I am the more disposed, as you should know,
To grieve until my death and live in woe.
What I shall later do I cannot say;
As yet I have no fancy for such play.

142

'I am in tribulation and cast down;
You are in arms, busy day in day out.
Hereafter, should you ever win the town,
Then, peradventure, it may come about
That when I see what never was seen, no doubt
I then may do what I have never done;
And that should be enough for anyone.

143

'I'll talk to you tomorrow if it's plain
That you are not to speak of this affair.
And, when you care to, you may come again;
This much, before you go, I will declare,
As help me Pallas of the Golden Hair,
If ever I took pity on a Greek,
It would be you, and it's the truth I speak.

144

'I am not saying I will be your love,
Nor am I saying no; but, in conclusion,
I mean well, by the Lord that sits above.'
Then she let fall her eyelids in confusion,
And sighed 'O God, let it be no illusion
That I shall see Troy quiet and at rest,
And if I see it not, then burst my breast!'

145

But in effect – let it be briefly spoken –
This Diomede, with freshened appetite,
Pressed on and begged her mercy, asked a token,
And after that, to tell the story right,
He took her glove, which gave him great delight.
And when the day was over and night fell,
He rose and took his leave, for all was well.

146

Bright Venus, following her heavenly courses,
Showed the way down for Phoebus to alight,
And Cynthia laid about her chariot-horses
To whirl her out of Leo, if they might;
The candles of the Zodiac shone bright,
And to her bed Criseyde that evening went,
Within her father's shapely, shining tent,

147

Ever in soul revolving up and down
The sayings of this sudden Diomede,
His high position and the sinking town,
Her loneliness, the greatness of her need
Of friends and helpers; thus began to breed
The reason why – and I must make it plain –
She made it her intention to remain.

148

In sober truth, when morning came in glory,
This Diomede returned to see Criseyde,
And, shortly, lest you interrupt my story,
He spoke so ably and he justified
Himself so well that she no longer sighed;
At last, to tell the truth, I must confess
He took from her the weight of her distress.

149

And then – so it is handed down to us –
She made him present of the fine bay steed
Which he had taken once from Troilus,
Also a brooch – what can have been the need? –
That had been his, she gave to Diomede
And, to console his passion, they believe
She made him wear a pennon of her sleeve.

150

From other histories it would appear
That once, when Troilus gave Diomede
A body-thrust that hurt him, many a tear
She wept upon his wound, to see it bleed,
And nursed him carefully with tender heed,
And, in the end, to ease the bitter smart,
They say – I know not – that she gave her heart.

151

But we have this assurance given us
That never woman was in greater woe
Than she, when she was false to Troilus;
'Alas!' she said 'that I must now forgo
My name for truth in love, for ever! Oh,
I have betrayed the gentlest and the best
That ever was, finest and worthiest.

152

'No good, alas, of me, to the world's end,
Will ever now be written, said, or sung.
Not one fair word! No book will be my friend,
I shall be rolled about on many a tongue;
Throughout the world my bell, and knell, is rung;
And womenfolk will hate me most of all;
Alas, that I should suffer such a fall!

153

'And they will say "As far as she was able,
She has dishonoured us." Alas the day!
Though I am not the first to be unstable,
What help is that to take my shame away?
Since there is nothing better I can say,
And grieving comes too late, what shall I do?
To Diomede at least I will be true!

154

'Since I can do no better, Troilus,
And since for ever you and I have parted,
Still I shall pray God's blessing on you, thus,
As the most truly noble, faithful-hearted
Of all I ever saw, since first we started,
That ever had lady's honour in his keeping!'
And having spoken thus, she burst out weeping.

155

'Certainly I shall never hate you, never!
But a friend's love, that you shall have of me;
I'll speak your praise, though I should live for ever;
And O believe how sorry I should be
If I should see you in adversity.
And you are guiltless, as I well believe;
But all shall pass, and so I take my leave.'

156

But honestly, how long it was between
Forsaking him and taking Diomede
I cannot say; no author I have seen
Has told us; take the volumes down and read,
You'll find no dates, for none are given indeed.
Though he was quick to woo, before he won
He found there was still more that must be done.

157

I cannot find it in my heart to chide
This hapless woman, more than the story will;
Her name, alas, is punished far and wide,
And that should be sufficient for the ill
She did; I would excuse her for it still,
She was so sorry for her great untruth;
Indeed I would excuse her yet, for ruth.

158

This Troilus, as I've already told,
Went driving on and on, as best he might,
And many a time his heart went hot and cold,
And more especially upon the night
– The ninth – before the day he had the right
To hope for her – she had her word to keep.
That night he had no rest, nor thought of sleep.

159

Now laurel-crowned Apollo, with his heat,
Began his course and up the sky he went
To warm the eastern waves, on which he beat
In brilliance; and the lark with fresh intent
Began to rise and sing. And Troilus sent
For Pandar, and they walked the city wall
Seeking Criseyde, or sign of her at all.

160

Till it was noon, they stood about to see
Any who came; whenever one appeared
From far away, they said that it was she,
Until a little later when he neared;
And now his heart was dull, and now it cleared,
Mocked at so often, they stood staring thus
At nothing, Troilus and Pandarus.

161

Then Troilus said to Pandar with a frown,
'For all I know, it will be noon for sure
Before Criseyde will come into the town;
She has enough to do and to endure
To win her father over, nothing truer.
For the old man will force her to have dinner
Before she goes – God torture the old sinner!'

162

Said Pandar 'That may be, indeed, it's plain;
And therefore let us have our dinner too,
And after dinner you can come again.'
So they went homeward without more to-do
And then returned. But long will they pursue
Before they find the thing they're gaping after;
Fortune had planned to dupe them, for her laughter.

163

Said Troilus: 'I now can see she might
Be forced to stay with Calkas very late;
Before she comes it may be nearly night;
Come on! I'm going down to watch the gate.
These stupid porters get in such a state.
Make them keep open till she comes along;
I'll pass it off as if there's nothing wrong.'

164

Day dwindled fast, night fell, and the moon hove
Into the sky. Still there was no Criseyde.
Troilus peered at hedge and tree and grove,
He craned his head over the wall, he spied;
And in the end he turned about and cried
'By God, I get her meaning! It's quite plain.
Why, I was nearly in despair again.

165

'She knows what's good for her, and what she's at!
She means to ride back secretly, of course;
And I commend her wisdom too; my hat!
She can't have people gathered in a force
To stare at her! She'll quietly take horse
When it is dark. Then she can reach the gate.
Patience, dear friend; it can't be long to wait.

166

'We've nothing else to do, and anyhow –
Look! There she is, I see her! Yes, it's she!
O Pandarus, will you believe me now?
Heave up your eyes, look there, man! Can't you see?'
Pandar replied: 'It's not like that to me.
All wrong again. You gave me such a start;
The thing I see there is a travelling cart.'

167

'Alas, you're right again!' said Troilus,
'Yet it is not for nothing, certainly,
That I should feel my heart rejoicing thus;
My thought holds presage of some good to me;
I don't know how, but all my life,' said he
'I've never felt such comfort, such delight;
My life upon it, she will come tonight.'

168

Pandar replied 'It may be, like enough,'
Agreeing with his friend in all he said,
But, laughing softly at his foolish stuff,
He kept this sober thought inside his head
'It is as likely Robin Hood will tread
The path to Troy as she you wait for here;
Ah me! Farewell the snows of yester-year.'

169

The Warden of the Gates began to call
To those outside the city, left and right,
Bidding them drive their cattle, one and all,
Inside, or stay without till morning light.
With many a tear, far on into the night,
Troilus turned his horse; he understood,
And home he rode; waiting would do no good.

170

Nevertheless he cheered himself along,
Thinking he had miscounted to the day;
He said 'I must have understood it wrong,
For, on the very night when last I lay
With her, she promised "Sweetheart, if I may,
I shall be here with you as now I am
Before the moon has passed out of the Ram."

171

'She still may keep her promise; she knows best.'
Early next day he went back to the gate
And up and down he wandered, east and west
Upon the walls with many a weary wait,
But all for nothing – he was blind to fate,
Blinded by hope; and sighing as before,
He went back home, for there was nothing more.

172

And clean out of his heart all hope had fled;
Nothing was left for him to hang upon;
Pain throbbed within his heart as if it bled
In sharp and violent throes – for she was gone.
And when he saw that she stayed on and on,
He could not judge of what it might betoken,
Since she had given her word and it was broken.

173

The third, the fourth, the fifth, the sixth ensued
After those ten long days of which I told;
His heart, between his fears and hope renewed,
Half trusted to her promises of old;
But when at last he saw they would not hold
And there was nothing left for him to try,
He knew he must prepare himself to die.

174

Then came that wicked spirit that we know
(God save us all!) as manic jealousy
And crept into his heart of heavy woe;
Because of which, since dead he wished to be,
He neither ate nor drank for misery,
And from all human company he fled;
During this time, that was the life he led.

175

For so defeated and so woebegone
He was, that those with whom he came in touch
Could scarcely know him; he was lean and wan,
As feeble as a beggar on a crutch,
His jealousy had punished him so much;
To those who asked him where he felt the smart
He said he had a pain about his heart.

176

Priam his father, and his Mother too,
His brothers and his sisters, asked in vain
Why he looked sorrowful, to what was due
So much unhappiness, what caused his pain?
But all for nothing, he would not explain,
But that his heart was injured by a blow
And if death came he would be glad to go.

177

And then, one evening, he lay down to sleep;
It happened so that in his sleep he thought
He had gone out into the woods to weep
For her and for the grief that she had brought,
And up and down the forest as he sought
His way, he came upon a tusky boar
Asleep upon the sunny forest floor.

178

And close beside it, with her arms enfolding,
And ever kissing it, he saw Criseyde;
The grief he suffered as he stood beholding
Burst all the bonds of sleep, and at a stride
He was awake and in despair, and cried
'O Pandar, now I know it through and through,
I am but dead, there is no more to do.

179

'She has betrayed me, has not played me fair,
She that I trusted more than all creation,
For she has left me, given her heart elsewhere;
The blessed gods have made their revelation,
I saw it in a dream, a divination;
It was Criseyde, and I beheld her thus!'
He told the whole of it to Pandarus.

180

'O my Criseyde, alas, what subtle word,
What new desire, what beauty, or what art,
What anger justly caused, by me incurred,
What fell experience, what guilt of heart
Has torn me from you, set us far apart?
O trust, O faith, assurance deeply tried!
Who has bereft me of my joy, Criseyde?'

181

'Why did I let you leave me, when the pain
Of parting nearly drove me off my head?
O who will ever trust an oath again?
God knows, my brightest lady, I was led
To take for gospel every word you said!
But who is better able to deceive
Than one in whom we hunger to believe?

182

'What shall I do, my Pandarus? Alas!
So sharp, so new, so desperate the ache!
No remedy for what has come to pass!
Were it not better with these hands to take
My life than thus to suffer for her sake?
For death would end my grief and set me free,
While every day I live disgraces me.'

183

Pandarus answered him 'Alas the day
That I was born! have I not said ere this
Dreams can deceive a man in many a way?
Why? Their interpretation goes amiss.
How dare you speak so to her prejudice,
Calling her false because you dreamt of her
And are afraid? You're no interpreter!

184

'Perhaps this boar that figures in your story
(It well may be) is there to signify
Her father Calkas who is old and hoary;
He struggles out into the sun to die
And she in grief begins to weep and cry
And kiss him, as he wallows there confounded.
That is the way your dream should be expounded.'

185

'But what am I to do,' said Troilus,
'To know for certain, how am I to tell?'
'Ah, now you're talking!' answered Pandarus,
'Here's my advice; since you can write so well,
Sit down and write to her, and you can spell,
Or at least try to spell her answer out,
And know the truth where you are now in doubt.

186

'And now, see why; for this I dare maintain,
Supposing she is faithless; if she be,
I cannot think she will write back again,
And if she writes, you very soon will see,
If she has any sort of liberty
To come back here; some phrase of hers will show
Why she's prevented. She will let you know.

187

'You haven't written to her since she went.
Nor she to you; and I will take my oath
She may have reasons that would win consent
Even from you (though now you may be loth)
To say it would be better for you both
For her to stay; so make her write to you;
Feel for the truth, that's all there is to do.'

188

And so it was they came to a conclusion,
These same two lords, and that without delay;
And Troilus in haste and some confusion
Of heart sat down, revolving what to say
And how to tell her of his disarray
And misery; so to his lady dear,
His own Criseyde, he wrote as you shall hear:

189

Troilus' Letter

'Freshest of flowers, whose I am for ever,
Have been, and shall be, elsewhere never swerving,
Body and soul, life, thought, desire, endeavour
All being yours, in humble undeserving
More than my tongue can tell of, since, in serving,
My service fills my being, as matter space,
I recommend me to your noble grace.

190

'Please you, my love, to think; have you reflected
How long a time it is – ah, well you know! –
Since you departed, leaving me dejected
In bitter grief; and nothing yet to show
By way of remedy, but greater woe
From day to day? And so I must remain,
While it shall please my well of joy and pain.

191

'Humbly, and from a heart that's torn in pieces,
(As write he must when sorrow drives a man)
I write my grief, that every hour increases,
With such complaining as I dare, or can
Make in a letter, wet with tears that ran
Like rain, as you can see; and they would speak
Remonstrance, were there language on a cheek.

192

'First I beseech it of your clear, sweet eyes
Not to consider what is fouled in it;
But more than this, dear love, not to despise
But read it well; and if it be unfit,
Cold care in me, alas, has killed my wit;
And so if a wrong thought should seem to start
Out of my head, forgive me, sweetest heart.

193

'Could any lover dare, or have the right
To make a sad remonstrance, at the last,
Against his lady, it is I who might,
Considering this, that for these two months past
You have delayed, whereas you promised fast
Only to stay ten days among the Greeks;
Yet you have not returned, after eight weeks.

194

'But inasmuch as I must needs assent
To all that pleases you, I will complain
No more, but will sigh out my discontent
Humbly, and write to you in restless pain;
Day in, day out, and over and again
I long to hear from you and how you fare
And all that you have done since you were there,

195

'Whose happiness and welfare God increase
In honour; so that upward it may go
Ever and always; may it never cease;
And as your heart would have it, may it grow
And prosper; I pray God it may be so.
And grant that you may soon have pity on me
As I am true to you and true shall be.

196

'And if it please you hear of how I fare
Whose sorrow there is no one could contrive
To paint, I am a garner stored with care,
And, when I wrote this letter, was alive,
But hold my soul in readiness to drive
It sorrowing forth; I hold it in delay
In hope your messenger is on the way.

197

'And these two eyes, with which I see in vain,
Are turned by tears into a double well,
My song into adversity and pain,
My good to grief, my ease of heart to hell,
My joy to woe; what more is there to tell?
And every joy – curse on my life for it! –
And every ease are now their opposite.

198

'Which with your coming back again to Troy
You can redress, and, more than ever I had
A thousand times, you can increase my joy;
For there was never yet a heart so glad
As mine will then be; if you are not sad
To think of me, and feel no kind of ruth
At what I suffer, think of keeping truth.

199

'If, for some fault of mine, I have deserved
To die, or if you care no more for me,
Still, to repay me, in that I have served
You faithfully, I beg of you be free
And generous, and write immediately;
Write, for God's love, my lode-star in the night,
That death may make an end of my long fight.

200

'If any other reason makes you stay,
Write to console and bring me some relief;
Though it be Hell for me with you away,
I will be patient and endure my grief;
Of all my hopes a letter is the chief;
Now, sweetheart, write, don't leave me to complain;
With hope, or death, deliver me from pain.

[292]

201

'Indeed, indeed, my own dear heart and true,
I cannot think, when next you see my face,
Since I have lost all health and colour too,
Criseyde will know me, such is now my case.
My heart's dear daylight, lady full of grace,
The thirst to see your beauty, like a knife,
Cuts at my heart; I scarce hold on to life.

202

'I say no more, although I have to say
Many more things than I have power to tell;
Whether you give me life, or do away
My life, God give you many a happy spell!
My beautiful, my fresh-as-May, farewell!
You that alone command my life or death;
I count upon your truth at every breath.

203

'I wish you that well-being which, unless
You wish it me, I shall have none. You gave
It once, and now it lies in you no less
To name the day to clothe me in my grave.
In you my life; in you the power to save
Me from all misery, all pain, all smart!
And now farewell, my own, my sweetest heart!
                                    Your T.'

204

This letter was delivered to Criseyde
And in effect she answered as she should;
She wrote with greatest pity, and replied
That she would come as soon as ever she could
To mend what was amiss and make all good,
And so she finished it, but added then
That she would come for sure, but knew not when.

205

Her letter fawned on him and sang his praises
She swore she loved him best; but, to be brief,
He could find nothing there but empty phrases.
Now, Troilus, away and pipe your grief,
Be it east or west, upon an ivy leaf!
Thus goes the world; God shield us from mischance,
And all that mean true dealing, God advance!

206

So misery increased by night and day
For Troilus, his hopes began to sink,
His strength to lessen at her long delay;
He took to bed, but could not sleep a wink,
He did not speak, he did not eat or drink,
Imagining that she had proved unkind,
A thought that drove him almost out of his mind.

207

This dream of his I spoke about before
Haunted his soul, he could not drive it thence;
He felt for certain she was his no more,
And Jove, of his eternal providence,
Had shown him, sleeping, the significance,
Of her untruth and of his own sad story,
And that the boar contained an allegory.

208

And so to fetch his sister then he sent,
A Sibyl, called Cassandra[5] round about,
Told her his dream and asked her what it meant,
And he implored her to resolve his doubt
About this boar with tusks so strong and stout;
And finally, after a little while,
Cassandra gave her answer with a smile,

209

Saying, as she expounded, 'Brother dear,
If it's the truth of this you wish to know,
There are a few old tales you'll have to hear,
Concerning Fortune and her overthrow
Of certain lords of old, and they will show
At once what boar this is, and whence he took
His origin; it's written in the book.[6]

210

'Diana being angry – and her ire
Turned on the Greeks who would not sacrifice
To her, or at her altar set the fire
To the incense – had recourse to this device
For her revenge; they paid a cruel price;
She sent a boar, large as an ox in stall,
To root their crops up, corn and vines and all.

211

'To kill this boar the countryside was raised;
Now, among those who came to see it slain,
There was a maiden, one of the best praised;
And Meleager, King of that domain,
Fell so in love with her he swore again
To show his manhood; so he plied the spur,
And killed the boar and sent the head to her.

212

'And out of this, as ancient books record,
Envy arose and the dispute ran high;
Tideus is descended from this lord
Directly, or those ancient volumes lie;
But how this Meleager came to die
(It was his mother's fault, she did the wrong)
I will not tell you; it would take too long.'

213

But of Tideus (ere she made an end)
She did not spare to tell, and how he came
To claim the city of Thebes and help his friend
Called Polynices; by a wrongful claim
It was defended in his brother's name,
Eteocles, who held the place in strength.
All this Cassandra told him at great length.

214

And how Haemonides had had the art
To get away when fifty knights were slain
By fierce Tideus; prophecies by heart
She told, of seven kings and all their train
That had encircled Thebes in this campaign,
And of the holy serpent, and the well,
And of the Furies; she went on to tell

215

Of Archemorus and his funeral game
And of Amphiaraüs swallowed down
Into the earth: the death that overcame
Tideus: how Hippomedon came to drown:
Parthenopaeus dead of wounds: renown
All shorn from Campaneus, called the Proud,
Slain by a thunderbolt; he cried aloud.

216

She told him how Eteocles, the brother
Of Polynices (celebrated pair)
Met in a skirmish and they slew each other,
And how the Greeks had wept in their despair,
And how the town was burnt and looted there.
So she descended from the days of old
To Diomed; and this is what she told:

217

'Now this same boar betokens Diomede,
Tideus' son, descended as he is
From Meleager, who had made it bleed;
Your lady, wheresoever now she is,
Diomede has her heart and she has his;
Weep if you will, or not, for out of doubt
This Diomede is in, and you are out.'

218

'You're telling lies,' he said 'you sorceress,
You and your spirit of false prophecy!
You hope to be a famous prophetess;
Just look at her, this fool of fantasy!
One who takes pains in her malignity
To slander ladies! Off with you! God's sorrow
Light upon you! I'll prove you false tomorrow!

219

'You might as well lay slanders on Alceste,
Who, of all creatures – if it be no lie –
That ever lived was kindliest and best;
She, when her husband was condemned to die
Unless she took his place, immediately
Made choice to die for him and go to Hell;
And die she did, as all the stories tell.'

220

Cassandra left; his rage at what she'd said
Made him forget the grief he had endured;
And suddenly he started out of bed
As though some doctor had completely cured
His illness; day by day, to be assured,
He sought to find the truth with all his force,
And thus endured his doomed adventure's course.

221

Fortune, to whom belongs the permutation
Of things under the moon, to her committed
By Jove's high foresight and adjudication,
When nations pass and kingdoms are uncitied
And peoples perish sullied and unpitied,
Fortune, I say, began despoiling Troy
Of her bright feathers, till she was bare of joy.

222

And, among all these things, the end and goal
Of Hector's life was now approaching fast,
When Fate, after unbodying his soul,
Would find a means to drive it forth at last;
And who can strive with Fate? His lot was cast.
So, going into battle, he was caught,
And death came down upon him as he fought.

223

It therefore seems to me that it is right
For all who follow arms and soldiering
To mourn the death of such a noble knight;
For, as he dragged the helmet from a king,
Achilles with an unexpected swing
Shore through his armour, and his body then;
And thus was killed the worthiest of men.

224

For whom, so it is handed down to us,
The general grief was more than tongue can tell,
And above all the grief of Troilus,
Who, next to him, was deemed to be the well
Of honour; so it was his spirit fell
What with his love, his sorrow and unrest;
He wished the heart would burst within his breast.

225

And yet, although beginning to despair,
And dreading that his lady was untrue,
His heart returned to her and lingered there,
As hearts of lovers will, and sought anew
To get her back, Criseyde the bright of hue.
And in his heart he would excuse her, saying
That Calkas was the cause of her delaying.

226

Many a time he planned for them to meet
By wearing pilgrim kit for his disguise
And visiting her, but could not counterfeit
So well as to conceal him from sharp eyes;
Moreover, what excuse could he devise
Supposing he were recognized and caught?
Many a tear he shed as thus he thought.

227

Many a time he wrote to her anew
And piteously – he showed no sign of sloth –
Beseeching her that, since he had been true,
She would return again and keep her oath;
And so, one day, in pity (I am loth
To take it otherwise) she took her pen
And – you shall hear it all – wrote back again:

228

Criseyde's Letter

'Dear son of Cupid, mirror of perfection,
O sword of knighthood, fount of nobleness,
How may a soul in terror and dejection
Send word of joy when she is comfortless?
I heartbroken, I sick, I in distress;
Since neither with the other may have dealing
I cannot send you either heart or healing.

229

'Your long, complaining letter has acquainted
My pitying heart with all your misery,
And I have noted, too, that tears have painted
Your papers, and that you require of me
To come to you; as yet that cannot be.
Lest it be intercepted, it is better
Not to say why, in writing you this letter.

230

'Grievous to me, God knows, is your unrest,
Your urgent haste; you should observe more measure.
It seems you have not taken for the best
What Heaven has ordained, and what you treasure
Most in your memory is your own pleasure.
Do not be angry, please, or out of humour;
What keeps me waiting here is wicked rumour.

231

'For I have heard far more than I expected
Of how things stand between us; I am staying
In order that report may be corrected
By my dissimulation; and they're saying
(Now, don't be angry) you were only playing
With me; no matter for that! In you I see
Nothing but truth and pure nobility.

232

'Come back I will; but in the disarray
In which I stand just now, what day or year
This is to happen, I can hardly say.
Yet, in effect, I beg you persevere
In your affection, speak me well, my dear,
For truly, and as long as life may last,
You may be sure my friendship will hold fast.

233

'Again I beg you not to take it ill
If what I write is short; for things are such
Where now I am, I dare not write; but still
Letters are things for which I have no touch.
Moreover one short sentence can say much.
The intention is what counts and not the length.
And now, farewell; God give you grace and strength!
Your C.'

234

Poor Troilus thought this letter very strange
When he had read it, and was sadly stirred;
He sighed; it seemed the calends of a change.
But finally, for all that had occurred,
He could not think she would not keep her word;
And easier for those who love so well
It is to trust, though trusting be a Hell.

235

Nevertheless they say that at long last
In spite of all, a man will finally
Perceive the truth; this happened, and quite fast,
To Troilus; she was – he came to see –
Less kindly-natured than she ought to be;
And in the end he knew beyond all doubt
That all was lost which he had been about.

236

Standing one day in melancholy mood,
With his suspicions clouded in a frown
Thinking of her, he heard a multitude
Of Trojans clamouring about the town,
Bearing, as was their fashion, up and down
A fine piece of coat armour (says my story)
Before Deiphebus, to show his glory.

237

This coat, as says my author, Lollius,
Deiphebus had rent from Diomede
That very day, and when this Troilus
Beheld it there, he gave it sudden heed
– The length – the breadth – the pattern in the bead
And all the worked embroidery in gold –
And suddenly he felt his heart turn cold.

238

There, on the collar, could he not perceive
The brooch he'd given her when they had to sever,
Yes on the very day she took her leave,
In memory of his grief and him for ever?
Had she not pledged her faith that she would never
Part with that brooch? But that was long before;
He knew he could not trust her any more.

239

Homewards he took himself and soon he sent
For Pandarus, and told him from the start
About the brooch and of this new event,
Clamoured against her variable heart,
Mourned his long love, his truth to her, the smart
Of this new anguish, cried for the release
Of death without delay, to bring him peace.

240

And thus he spoke: 'O lady bright, Criseyde,
Where is your faith to me? And where your vow?
Where is your love? Where is your truth?' he cried,
'And is it Diomede you are feasting now?
Alas, I would have thought that, anyhow,
Had you intended not to stand upon
Your truth to me, you'd not have led me on.

241

'Who now will trust an oath? Ah, let them go!
Alas, I never would have thought ere this
That you, my own Criseyde, could alter so!
Nay, were I guilty, had I done amiss,
Could there have been the cruel artifice
In you to slay me thus? And your good name
Is now destroyed; there lies my grief and shame.

242

'Was there no other brooch you had in keeping
To fee some newer lover with?' said he,
'Except the brooch I gave you, wet with weeping,
For you to wear in memory of me?
There was no reason why this had to be,
Unless it were for spite and that you meant
To make an open show of your intent.

243

'Cast from your mind, I see I have no part
In you, and yet I neither can, nor may,
For all the world, find it within my heart
To un-love you a quarter of a day!
Born in an evil hour, still I say
That you, for all the grief that you are giving,
I still love best of any creature living.'

244

And then 'O God Almighty, send me grace
That I may meet again with Diomede!
For truly, if I have the fighting-space
And power, I shall hope to make him bleed!
O God,' he said, 'that shouldest take good heed
To foster truth, and make wrong pay the price,
Why wilt thou not do vengeance on this vice?

245

'O Pandarus, so ready to upbraid me,
Who mocked me for believing in a dream,
See for yourself! Has not your niece betrayed me?
How stands the bright Criseyde in your esteem?
And many are the ways, or so I deem,
In which the gods reveal our joy and woe
In sleep; my dream has proved that it is so.

246

'Certainly now, without more waste of breath,
Henceforward and as truly as I may,
I will bear arms and I will seek my death;
Little I care how soon will be the day.
Truly, Criseyde my sweetest, let me say
To you, whom I have wholly loved and served,
What you have done to me was not deserved.'

247

This Pandarus, who stood the while and heard,
Knew it was true, and he had known it long;
He made no answer to him, not a word,
Sad for his friend and for a grief so strong,
And shamed because his niece had done a wrong.
Stunned by these things, he stood in deep dismay,
Still as a stone, without a word to say.

248

But at the last he spoke, and thus he cried:
'O my dear brother, I can do no more;
What should I say to you? I hate Criseyde;
God knows that I shall hate her evermore!
As for the thing which you besought me for,
Having no true regard to my own honour
Or peace of mind, I worked your will upon her.

249

'If I did anything that gave you pleasure
I am glad of it; as for this treason now,
God knows that I am sorry beyond measure!
Would I could ease your heart of it; I vow
I would most gladly do so, knew I how;
Almighty God, deliver her, I pray,
Out of this world; there's no more I can say.'

250

Great was the grief and plaint of Troilus;
But on her course went Fortune, as of old.
Criseyde consoles the son of Tideus,
And Troilus may weep in care and cold.
Such is the world for those who can behold
The way it goes; there's little of heart's rest;
God grant we learn to take it for the best.

251

The knighthood and the prowess, do not doubt it,
Of Troilus, this very gallant knight
– As you can read in all the books about it –
Were plain to see in many a cruel fight;
And certainly his anger, day and night,
Fell savagely upon the Greeks, I read;
And most of all he sought out Diomede.

252

And many a time, my author says, they met
With bloody strokes, and mighty words were said;
The spears that they had taken care to whet
They tried on one another, fought and bled,
And Troilus rained down blows upon his head.
In vain, however; Fortune had not planned
That either perish at the other's hand.

253

And had I undertaken to relate
The feats in arms of this distinguished man,
It is his battles I would celebrate;
Seeing, however, that I first began
To tell his love, I've done the best I can.
As for his deeds, let those who would recall
Them, read in Dares, he can tell them all.

254

Beseeching every lady bright of hue
And gentle woman whosoe'er she be,
That though, alas, Criseyde was proved untrue,
She be not angry for her guilt with me;
Her guilt is there in other books to see,
And I will gladlier write, to please you best,
Of true Penelope and good Alceste.[7]

255

Nor am I only speaking for these men,
But most of all for women so betrayed
By treacherous folk – God give them sorrow, Amen!
Who by their subtlety and wit have played
On your affections in their faithless trade,
Which moves me to speak out; be careful, then,
Listen to what I say: beware of men.

256

Go little book, go little tragedy,
Where God may send thy maker, ere he die,
The power to make a work of comedy;
But, little book, it's not for thee to vie
With others, but be subject, as am I,
To poesy itself, and kiss the gracious
Footsteps of Homer, Virgil, Ovid, Statius.

257

And since there is such great diversity
In English, and our writing is so young,
I pray to God that none may mangle thee,
Or wrench thy metre by default of tongue;
And wheresoever thou be read, or sung,
I beg of God that thou be understood!
And now to close my story as I should.

258

The wrath of Troilus, I began to say,
Was cruel, and the Grecians bought it dear,
For there were thousands that he made away,
Who, in his time, had never any peer
Except his brother Hector, so I hear.
But O alas, except that God so willed,
He met with fierce Achilles and was killed.

259

And, having fallen to Achilles' spear,
His light soul rose and rapturously went
Towards the concavity of the eighth sphere,[8]
Leaving conversely every element,
And, as he passed, he saw with wonderment
The wandering stars and heard their harmony,
Whose sound is full of heavenly melody.

260

As he looked down, there came before his eyes
This little spot of earth, that with the sea
Lies all embraced, and found he could despise
This wretched world, and hold it vanity,
Measured against the full felicity
That is in Heaven above; and, at the last,
To where he had been slain his look he cast,

261

And laughed within him at the woe of those
Who wept his death so busily and fast,
Condemning everything we do that flows
From blind desire, which can never last,
When all our thought on Heaven should be cast;
And forth he went, not to be long in telling,
Where Mercury appointed him his dwelling.

262

Lo, such an end had Troilus for love!
Lo, such an end his valour, his prowess!
Lo, such an end his royal state above,
Such end his lust, such end his nobleness!
And such an end this false world's brittleness!
And thus began his loving of Criseyde
As I have told it you, and thus he died.

263

Oh all you fresh young people, he or she,
In whom love grows and ripens year by year,
Come home, come home from worldly vanity!
Cast the heart's countenance in love and fear
Upwards to God, who in His image here
Has made you; think this world is but a fair
Passing as soon as flower-scent in air.

264

And give your love to Him who, for pure love,
Upon a cross first died that He might pay
Our debt, and rose, and sits in Heaven above;
He will be false to no one that will lay
His heart wholly on Him, I dare to say.
Since He is best to love, and the most meek,
What need is there a feigning love to seek?

265

Behold these old accursèd pagan rites!
Behold how much their gods are worth to you!
Behold these wretched worldly appetites!
Behold your labour's end and guerdon due
From Jove, Apollo and Mars, that rascal crew!
Behold the form in which the ancients speak
Their poetry, if you should care to seek.

266

O moral Gower, I dedicate this book
To you, and you, my philosophical Strode,[9]
In your benignity and zeal to look,
To warrant, and, where need is, to make good;
And to that truthfast Christ who died on rood,
With all my heart for mercy ever I pray,
And to the Lord right thus I speak and say:

267[10]

Thou One and Two and Three and Never-ending,
That reignest ever in Three and Two and One,
Incomprehensible, all-comprehending,
From visible foes, and the invisible one,
Defend us all! And Jesu, Mary's Son,
Make us in mercy worthy to be thine,
For love of her, mother and maid benign!

Amen.

NOTES

BOOK I

1. (p. 3)   *Tisiphone.* One of the three Furies, known also as the
Eumenides, daughters of Night, here invoked by
Chaucer to act as his Muse, because of her tormented
and tormenting nature. She is again invoked, together
with her sister-furies, at Book IV, line 24. They set the
tone for suffering with which he wishes both Books to
open.

2. (p. 8)   *Dictys* and *Dares.* Supposed eye-witnesses of the Trojan
War; Dares was a Phrygian in Troy at the time and
was believed to have written a work called *De Excidio
Trojae Historia* (The story of the Fall of Troy)
which comes to us in a late (sixth century) Latin text;
Dictys was a Cretan believed to have written the
Ephemeris Belli Trojani (Diary of the Trojan War)
which comes to us in a fourth century text, said to be
a translation made from his original into Latin in the
fourth century. These documents are the basis of the
medieval legend of Troy.

3. (p. 8)   *Palladion.* A sacred image of Pallas, supposed to preserve
Troy from capture.

4. (p. 9)   *Just as an A now heads our alphabet.* See Introduction
page xv.

5. (p. 10)   *Dobbin.* I do not know if this generic name for a cart-
horse is still current, as it was in my childhood. Its
last recorded use in literature is in 1871 (see *Oxford
English Dictionary*). The name in Chaucer's poem is
Bayard; I have changed it to *Dobbin* to avoid confusing
the reader, whose associations with the name *Bayard*
might lead him to think of a more recent and more
famous character, Pierre du Terrail, Chevalier de
Bayard (1476–1524), 'sans peur et sans reproche'.

6. (p. 11)   *And no one can undo the law of Nature.* This means far
more than simply that it is natural to fall in love and
that nobody can set himself up against it. Chaucer,
following his beloved Boethius, regards Love as the
supreme creative principle ('God is love') that keeps

[311]

all things in harmonious being; it is 'the holy bond of things' (Book III, stanza 181), its law 'is set upon the universe' (Book III, stanza 6). There is a more detailed passage in *The Knight's Tale* affirming the same position:

> *The Firste Moevere of the cause above,*
> *Whan he first made the faire cheyne of love,*
> *Greet wan th'effect, and heigh was his entente.*
> *Wel wiste he why, and what thereof he mente;*
> *For with that faire cheyne of love he bond*
> *The fyr, the eyr, the water, and the lond*
> *In certeyn boundes, that they may nat flee.*
> (lines 2987–93)

The very elements obey love. Throughout the whole poem, Chaucer most markedly makes use of the ambivalence of love, natural and supernatural, pagan and Christian; it is a part of that widening of the context of the significances of love which reaches its climax in the 'palinode', at the end of Book V.

7. (p. 14) *an Order*. Troilus is mockingly comparing the strict rules and rituals of lovers committed to the conventions of 'courtly love', with the rules of poverty, chastity and obedience to which the monastic Orders were bound by oath.

8. (p. 17) *Lollius*. No such author is known to have existed. Chaucer's 'author' was, or course, Boccaccio, as has been explained; but he never mentions him by name. Why he thought, or pretended to think, that he was translating from a Latin original (See Book II, stanza 2, last line) by the unknown 'Lollius' has never been fully explained; but it has been suggested that he got the notion from the opening lines of the Second Epistle of the First Book of Horace:

> *Troiani belli scriptorem, Maxime Lolli,*
> *Dum tu declamas Romae, Praeneste relegi*

A very careless glance at this might have given Chaucer the notion that it was to be translated 'O Maximus Lollius, writer on the Trojan War, while you are declaiming in Rome, I re-read you at Praeneste.' Alternatively, it may be supposed that the manuscript of Horace was corrupt, and had *scriptor* for *scriptorem*.

The lines in Horace mean 'I was reading the author of the Trojan War (i.e. Homer) at Praeneste, O Maximus Lollius, while you were declaiming at Rome.'

9. (p. 17) *The Song of Troilus*. These stanzas are taken by Chaucer from the 88th sonnet of Petrarch.

10. (p. 19) *Polyxena*. One of the daughters of King Priam and Queen Hecuba, and sister of Troilus.

11. (p. 31) *Tityus*. A giant, son of Terra by Jupiter, sent to Hell, to be devoured by vultures, for offering violence to Latona, beloved of Jupiter. Described in Boethius Book III, metre 12, line 28.

12. (p. 33) *Fortune's Wheel*. See Introduction, page xviii.

13. (p. 35) *Took on about the cold*. The colloquialism is much the same in the original:

> *And some of hem toke on hem, for the colde*

The image is one of shivering – the hot-and-cold shiver of fever (see the last line of Book I, Stanza 60); Pandarus urges Troilus later on (Book II, Stanza 217–18) to feign that he has a fever (to delude his brother Deiphebus). Troilus replies (219) he has no need to feign, for he is sick in truth, that is, love-sick.

14. (p. 37) *Celestial or natural love*. Chaucer is thinking in terms of the Christian distinction between the love of God (for which those in Holy or monastic Orders undertook the celibate life of priest, monk, Friar or nun, under vow of chastity) and the love of man and woman; Pandarus is of the opinion that everyone feels either one or the other kind of love. See Introduction page xx.

BOOK II

1. (p. 45) *O lady mine, Clio*. Clio, the first of the Muses, of whom there were nine, all daughters of Jupiter and Mnemosyne; they presided over the liberal arts. Clio was the Muse of History.

2. (p. 45) *Latin*. Chaucer was translating from Italian, but may have intended Latin to include it. See note[8] to Book I, above, and Introduction pp. xvi.

NOTES

3. (p. 47)   *Progne.* Progne, daughter of King Pandion of Athens,
was the wife of Tereus; her sister Philomela
was raped by him, and had her tongue torn out by him to
prevent her from accusing him. Her sister Progne, to
revenge herself on Tereus slew, cooked and made him
eat his son Itys. When he knew what he had done,
Tereus pursued Progne and Philomela with a sword,
but as he caught up with them, they were super-
naturally delivered from him by being turned into
birds, Progne into a swallow, Philomela into a
nightingale. Ovid, *Metamorphoses*, VI.

4. (p. 48)   *The Siege of Thebes.* They were listening to a reading
from the *Thebaid* of the Roman poet Statius (A.D.
49–96), an epic in twelve Books, that tells the fatal
tale of the sons of Oedipus, Eteocles and Polynices,
who were to reign in Thebes alternately, year in, year
out. Eteocles refused to let Polynices have his rightful
turn, and Polynices allying with Adrastus, King of
Argos, collected a force, headed by seven champions,
against him. In the end it was agreed to end the matter
by a straight fight between the two brothers in single
combat. In this fight, each killed the other.

5. (p. 48)   *Amphiaraüs.* A prophet, son in law to Adrastus (see
previous note), who foresaw that he would perish in
the expedition against Thebes. He tried to hide, but
was betrayed by his wife, and had to go. He attempted
to flee from the field of battle, but the earth opened and
he was swallowed down alive into Hell.

6. (p. 57)   *Woe to the gem that has no native force!* Precious stones
were supposed to have inherent magical powers or
virtues.

7. (p. 68)   *O who has given me drink?* The original ('*who yaf me
drynke?*') may either mean, as Skeat thinks, 'Who
has given me a love-potion?' or more simply 'Who
can it be that has made me drunk?' She can think of no
other way to account for the intoxicating shock
Criseyde feels on seeing Troilus for the first time
since she knew of his feelings for her.

8. (p. 69)   *Venus in her seventh house.* According to W. W. Skeat,
the celestial sphere was divided into twelve equal
parts, each termed a 'house' by Astrologers, through

[314]

which the planets passed every twenty-four hours. The first and seventh were considered very fortunate; the seventh was just below (but R. K. Root says just above) the Western horizon; Venus, a planet of good will, beneficent to lovers, was in her luckiest position at the moment when Criseyde first saw Troilus after Pandarus' revelation of his feeling towards her.

9. (p. 73) *But violent delights have violent ends*. The original reads *Ful sharp bygynnynge breketh ofte at ende*. As Shakespeare seems to have borrowed this idea from Chaucer for use in *Romeo and Juliet*, I have borrowed this line from Shakespeare to repay Chaucer.

10. (p. 74) *Flexippe, Tarba and Antigone*. The first two names are inventions of Chaucer's (he spells Tarba *Tarbe*, a two-syllable word). Antigone was the name of one of the daughters of Oedipus, and appears in the *Thebaid*. Chaucer borrowed it for the occasion.

BOOK III

1. (p. 111) *Over all Third Heaven*. Each of the seven planets moved in its own sphere or 'heaven'; that of Venus is the third counting from the central, stationary Earth: Moon, Mercury, Venus, Sun, Mars, Jupiter, Saturn. After these came the sphere of the fixed stars, the eighth sphere, up to and beyond which the soul of Troilus ascends in Book V, stanza 259.

2. (p. 112) *that makes them tick*. See Appendix 4.

3. (p. 137) *Hersé* and *Aglauros*. Mercury fell in love with Hersé, and asked her sister, Aglaurus, to help him to her; she agreed to for a great weight in gold. This angered Minerva (Pallas); the story is told by Ovid, *Metamorphoses* II, 711–832.

4. (p. 139) *Horaste*. This is Chaucer's variant for the name Orestes, which he has borrowed for the occasion; this whole episode is Chaucer's free invention, not in his source.

5, 6 (p. 144) *Dilemma* and *The Donkeys' Bridge*. The original text runs:

But whether that ye dwelle or for hym go,
I am, til god me bettre mynde sende,
At Dulcarnon, right at my wittes ende.'

Quod Pandarus: 'ye, nece, wol ye here?
Dulcarnon called is "flemyng of wrecches."
It semeth hard, for wrecches wol nat lere

Dulcarnon is the corruption of an Arabic word *du'lqarnayn*, meaning *two-horned*, a name given in the Middle Ages to the forty-seventh Proposition of the First Book of Euclid, which has two prongs, and I have translated it here as *dilemma*. Pandarus scornfully (perhaps intentionally?) confuses this Proposition with another, the fifth of the First Book, known in the Middle Ages as *flemyng of wrecches* (the putter of wretches to rout), which is known nowadays as the *Pons Asinorum* and which I have rendered *The Donkeys' Bridge*.

7. (p. 158) *The numbering of the stanzas.* Scholars distinguish three groups of manuscripts, α, β, γ. I am here following the order as given in the β group. The order as given in the α γ groups is indicated in brackets.

8, 9. (p. 160) *Midas* and *Crassus*. Midas, King of Phrygia, prayed that all he touched might turn to gold; his prayer was granted; much to his frustration, all that he thereafter attempted to eat or drink turned to gold as he touched it. Even his daughter did when he touched her.

Crassus, a man of enormous wealth, was killed in a Roman war against the Parthians in 53 B.C. Orodes, the Parthian King, to show his contempt for millionaires, had molten gold poured into his dead mouth.

10. (p. 161) *Fortuna Major.* The planet Jupiter, so called because it was believed to be benign and was greater than the planet Venus (also called the Morning Star and Lucifer, the light-bringer). Venus was also benign, but being smaller, was called *Fortuna Minor.*

11. (p. 167) *God let him off his death, and so did she.* In the original the second and third lines of this stanza read:

What! *god foryaf his deth*, and she also
Foryaf, and with hire uncle gan to pleye,

Skeat and some other learned scholars with whom I hate to disagree think this means 'Christ forgave his foes, and she did too', and they base their view on the

NOTES

fact that it is a proverbial phrase, and quote it from
Morawski, *Proverbes Français*, '*Dieu pardonna sa mort*'
in support of this view.

God knows – none better – that Chaucer was a
writer who delighted in proverbs. But here, I think,
this knowledge leads us astray from the real meaning
of the passage, which is to be found in the previous
stanza (225) in which Pandarus mischievously asks
Criseyde how she feels after her night with Troilus,
which he had engineered, and offers her his sword to
'chop off his head' by way of a jesting punishment for
his share in the night's doings. But God did not in fact
exact this forfeit, nor did Criseyde, and in a moment
they are at one with each other in the matter, 'laughing
happily and playing' (Stanza 226). Nothing so heavy
as a reference to Luke 23, 34 is called for.

12. (p. 171) *Pyrois*. One of the four horses of the sun; the others,
according to Ovid, *Metamorphoses* II, 153-4, were
Eous, Aethon and Phlegon.

13. (p. 173) *Love that is ruler over earth and sea*. Troilus' beautiful
hymn is a free rendering into rhyme royal of Boethius'
Consolation of Philosophy, Book II, metre 8.

14, 15, 16, *Dioné's daughter*. i.e. Venus who was the daughter of
17. (p. 175) Jupiter and Dioné; the *Nine* (line 3) are the Nine
Muses, daughters of Jupiter and Mnemosyne. *Helicon*
(line 3) was a mountain in Boeotia from which flowed
the stream of the fountain Hippocrene. *Parnassus*,
sacred to the Muses, is a mountain in Phocis.

BOOK IV

1. (p. 180) *Phebuseo* is Chaucer's not very happy invention to save
his rhyme-scheme. The other names are taken from
Boccaccio.

2. (p. 183) *Phoebus* and *Neptune*. Neptune and Apollo were said to
have built the walls of Troy. Priam's father, King
Laomedon, refused to pay their wages at the end of
the year, so they were angry against the city.

3. (p. 186) *O Juvenal!* The reference is to Juvenal's Satires X,
2-4.

NOTES

pauci dignoscere possunt
Vera bona atque illis multum diversa, remota
Erroris nebula . . .
[Few can discriminate and catalogue
Their own true good from Error's distant fog.]

4. (p. 193) *Zeuxis*. Chaucer calls him *Zansis*, but he means Zeuxis, the famous painter of antiquity who lived in Sicily and flourished towards 468 B.C. His paintings were so realistic that birds were said to have pecked at the fruit in one. The remark attributed to him by Chaucer really comes from Ovid's *Remedia Amoris* (462), but Chaucer did not verify his references.

5. Stanzas 138–54 (pp. 213–17) They are for the most part a close verse rendering of Boethius' *Consolation* Book V, prose 3, in which Boethius runs over the difficulties of the head-on collision between Free Will and Predestination, before proposing his solution to them; see Introduction, page xx. Awkward and repetitive as it is, it is the philosophic core of Troilus' position, and this passage in soliloquy is his 'To be, or not to be'; he comes back and back to the idea that his sufferings were pre-destined by the cruelty of Fortune. This view of his position has its consolations, for if Troilus is right nothing is his fault.

6. (p. 219) *Myrrha*. Myrrha was the daughter of Cinyras, King of Cyprus; enamoured of her father, she went by stealth into his bed and led him into incest. When the king realized what had happened he attempted to kill her, and, afterwards himself. She fled into Arabia and was there turned into a tree, called myrrh, which split open when she was delivered of her child, Adonis.

7. (p. 221) *Minos*. Son of Jupiter and Europa and King of Crete, whose justice on earth was so famous that after death it was decided that he should be the absolute and supreme Judge in the Infernal regions.

8. (p. 222) *Atropos*. One of the three *Parcae*, powerful goddesses. Clotho held the distaff with the wool of human life on it, about to be spun into thread; Lachesis spun the thread itself; Atropos cut it with a pair of scissors.

9. (p. 229) *Delphi*. Calkas had been sent to Delphi (according to Benoît) to find out for the Trojans what their fate in the war would be; there he learnt that Troy would

[318]

fall, and so he deserted to the Greeks. Benoît gives
Delfos, but he meant Delphi in the Gulf of Corinth,
famous for its oracles. Delphos seems to be a confusion
between Delos and Delphi. Apollo was born on the
island of Delos and this island was often referred to as
Delfos or Delphos, right up to the seventeenth
century. Shakespeare uses the form in *The Winter's
Tale* II. 3, 195.

10. (p. 231) *Argus*. Argus had a hundred eyes, of which not more
than two were ever asleep at any one time.

11. (p. 233) *Athamas*. King of Thebes, driven mad by Juno, who
sent the Fury Tisiphone to haunt him.

12. (p. 235) *The Ram*. The moon is now in the Ram; Criseyde
promises to return when the moon has passed through
Taurus, Gemini and Cancer to the end of Leo, which
would take ten days.

BOOK V

1. (p. 254) *Escaphilo*. Chaucer's name for Ascalaphus, a young man
changed by the Queen of Erebus into a bird of ill
omen for tale-bearing. See Ovid *Metamorphoses*,
V, 539–50.

2. (p. 259) *A helmet made of glass*. The original reads: *Fortune his
howve entended bet to glaze*, meaning literally 'Fortune
intended to give him a better glass hood'; this is a pro-
verbial phrase, also used in *Piers Plowman*, and is
thought to suggest 'a delusive protection' – for glass
is brittle.

3. (p. 265) *Charybdis*. The dangerous whirlpool on the coast of
Sicily, that swallowed a part of the fleet of Ulysses.

4. (p. 266) *Phaeton*. Son of Phoebus, demanded of his father the
loan of his chariot (the chariot of the sun) for a day; his
father gave him full instructions how to manage the
horses, but he was inattentive, showed his incom-
petence, and the horses went off at a gallop on
devious courses. Jupiter, seeing what was going on,
threw a thunderbolt and slew him; he fell from heaven
into the river Po.

5. (p. 294) *Cassandra*. A daughter of Priam and Hecuba who was
beloved of Apollo. In return for her favours she
demanded the gift of prophecy; this was accorded to

her by the god. She then went back on her promise
and refused him his rights; so he wetted her lips with
his tongue, by which he ensured that however true her
prophecies were, no one would ever believe her.

6. (p. 295) *It's written in the book*, in Chaucer's words '*as men in
bokes fynde*'. i.e. in the *Thebais* and in the *Meta-
morphoses*, already mentioned.

7. (p. 306) *Of true Penelope and good Alceste*. Penelope was the
faithful wife of Ulysses, who held her many suitors at
bay until his return from the Trojan War, when he
slaughtered them. Alcestis was the wife of Admetus
who laid down her life for her husband. Some
authorities say that Hercules brought her back from
Hades, restored to life. Penelope and Alcestis are
types therefore of faithful lovers (as opposed to
Criseyde) and Chaucer says he would more gladly
have written of them; he was given the opportunity to
do so in his next poem *The Legend of Good Women*,
which the Queen is said to have commanded him to
undertake, as a penance for having spoken ill of women
in the person of Criseyde. Alcestis appears in it but
not Penelope.

8. (p. 307) *The eighth sphere etc.* (lines 3–7). The visual image in-
tended by Chaucer is not absolutely clear and can be
variously interpreted; the note in R. K. Root's
edition is very helpful. The way I understand and
have rendered it is, however, slightly different from
his.

We are (I think) asked to imagine the soul of
Troilus taking flight vertically from 'this little spot
of earth' (Stanza 260) towards 'the full felicity that
is in Heaven above'.

Surrounding the earth, which was at the motionless
centre of things in medieval astronomy, there were
eight '*spheres*' or rings, each in succession outside the
one before, in the first seven of which each of the
planets – which were also sometimes called *elements* –
moved in orbit, and made heavenly music as they did
so. Thus, leaving earth, Troilus' soul would suc-
cessively mount through the spheres of the moon,
Mercury, Venus, the sun, Mars, Jupiter and Saturn.
On leaving the sphere of Saturn he would have the

vast bowl of the fixed stars above him, in its huge concavity. This Chaucer tries to present in his phrase '*Up to the holughnesse of the eighte spere*'. He is here following word for word a passage from the *Teseida* that describes the death of Arcite, which he borrowed for Troilus. Boccaccio's word for '*holughnesse*' is '*concavita*' which I have adopted as more intelligible than 'hollowness' even if less picturesque, for a modern reader.

Looking up, then, Troilus sees the concave of the sphere of the fixed stars *above* him; *conversely* he sees the *convexity* of the spheres through which he has just passed *below* him. Boccaccio's word for this is *convessi*, which Chaucer renders '*in convers*'. I have tried to use Chaucer's word with Boccaccio's meaning in rendering the former's phrase '*In convers letyng everich element*' by '*Leaving conversely every element*' meaning *element* in the sense of *planet*. The *wandering stars* is another phrase for the planets.

9. (p. 309) *Moral Gower* and *Philosophical Strode*. John Gower the poet was a close friend of Chaucer's; Gower had looked after Chaucer's affairs at home for him while Chaucer was away in Italy in 1378, so he had well earned the dedication of this poem imported from Italy. Later Gower returned the compliment by a fine passage of greeting to Chaucer as the poet and disciple of Venus at the end of his own poem the *Confessio Amantis*. Gower was older than Chaucer and survived him by eight years (c. 1325-1408).

Philosophical Strode is thought to be Ralph Strode, onetime Fellow of Merton College, Oxford, who was the author of some writings on logic and philosophy, and is probably to be identified with a Ralph Strode who died in London, in Aldersgate, not far from where Chaucer lived, in 1387.

10. (p. 309) lines 1-3 are directly translated by Chaucer from Dante's *Paradiso* XIV, 28-30,

> *Quell' uno e due e tre che sempre vive,*
> *e regna sempre in tre e due e uno*
> *non circonscritto, e tutto circonscrive*

SELECTED READING LIST

The texts on which this version is based are in the editions of W. W. Skeat (1900), R. K. Root (1926) and F. N. Robinson (1957).

Those interested in medieval thought and feeling about love *par amour* may find an early allegorical vision of what it is like to fall in love, in the *Roman de la Rose*, particularly in the earlier part of the poem, by Guillaume de Lorris (*c.* 1237). This was beautifully translated into English in the fourteenth century and a large part of this translation has been attributed to Chaucer; it is usually published in modern editions of his work. Another early work is the *De Amore Libri Tres* of Andreas Capellanus (*c.* 1186) translated, under the title of *The Art of Courtly Love*, by John Jay Parry (Columbia University Press, 1941); a third and more pleasing source is in the work of Chrétien de Troyes (*c.* 1175) whose romances have been well translated into modern English by W. W. Comfort and are published in the Everyman series.

For a masterly presentation of the whole subject there is the already-mentioned *Allegory of Love* by C. S. Lewis, first published in 1936. Although some of his views have been qualified by subsequent scholarship, it remains the most absorbing book in this field. It is however a widening field, and there have been many new contributions, such as Peter Dronke's *Mediaeval Latin and the Rise of European Love-Lyric* (1965), and many shorter articles such as are the essays by various hands in Professor John Lawlor's *Patterns of Love and Courtesy* (1966), Professor T. P. Dunning's *God and Man in Troilus and Criseyde*, printed in *English and Mediaeval Studies Presented to J. R. R. Tolkien* by Professors Norman Davis and C. L. Wrenn; *Troilus on Predestination*, by Howard Rollin Patch, in *The Journal of English and Germanic Philology*, XVII (1918), reprinted in Edward Wagenknecht's *Chaucer, Modern Essays in Criticism* (Galaxy Books, 1959), in which will also be found other relevant essays. See also Muriel Bowden's *Reader's Guide to Geoffrey Chaucer* (1964) and John Lawlor's *Geoffrey Chaucer* (1969).

FOUR BRIEF APPENDIXES

1. *The Proper Names in the Poem*

I HAVE sometimes followed Chaucer and sometimes conventional usage in the spelling and accentuation of the proper names in the poem. I have, for instance, kept Chaucer's *Agámenoun* for Agamemnon, for my own convenience, since it affords a necessary rhyme, and Chaucer's *Horaste* for the character invented by Pandarus in Book III stanza 114, instead of *Orestes*, the classical form of the name, for the convenience of the reader, who might wonder what Orestes was doing in the story of Troy. So too I have followed Chaucer in stressing the name Antenor as he stressed it (*Ántenor*) and not in the classical way (Anténor). On the other hand I have used the classical form Amphiaraüs for Chaucer's Amphiorax, Progne for his Proigne, Oedipus for his Edippus, Homer for his Omer, and so on.

Chaucer's heroine appears either as Criseyde or as Criseyda in his poem, but I have only used the form Criseyde, which I rhyme with *pride* (not with *prayed*) to suit my convenience. The exact value of the vowel sound in the second syllable of her name in Chaucer's time is in dispute; but I had to make a firm choice.

2. *Early Versions of Troilus and Criseyde*

The translation of Chaucer began early in the seventeenth century with two uncompleted versions of our poem. The first to appear was by Sir Francis Kynaston, in 1635. It consisted of the first two Books only, rendered into Latin, in rhyme-royal stanzas, the metre of the original. The opening stanza will supply a fair sample of the author's dexterity:

> *Dolorem TROILI duplicem narrare,*
> *Qui Priami Regis Trojae fuit gratus,*

Vt primum illi contigit amare
Vt miser, felix & infortunatus
Erat, decessum ante sum conatus.
Tisiphone fer opem recensere
Hos versus, qui, dum scribo, visi flere.

Kynaston's friends rallied round with sets of commendatory verses, mostly also in Latin, congratulating him on having made Chaucer intelligible to his fellow-countrymen.

Meanwhile another, more sensitive hand was at work on *Troilus and Criseyde*; there is a manuscript in the British Museum of a version of the first three Books, attributed to 'J. S. Gent'. This is believed, with good reason, to stand for Jonathan Sidnam, a translator of experience and repute, at work in the 1630s, who had also rendered *Il Pastor Fido* of Guarini and the *Filli di Sciro* of Bonarelli into English. The manuscript of Sidnam's version of Chaucer's poem has recently been edited by Mr Herbert G. Wright and published as one of *The Cooper Monographs* by the Francke Verlag, Berne (1960).

Sidnam gives us a fresh and moving poem, as far as his version goes, as wonderfully close to Chaucer as his airy Cavalier manner and vocabulary permit; two stanzas will illustrate the high quality of his work; I have modernized their spelling and rather odd punctuation:

Upon a cedar sat a nightingale
Under her chamber window where she lay,
And to the pale-faced moon so told her tale
In her bird's language, as perhaps we may
Believe she sang of love a roundelay;
Fair Cressida gave ear to her so long
Till sleep at last deprived her of her song.

And as she slept she dreaméd that she saw
A brave well-feathered eagle, white as snow,
Who underneath her breast did fix his claw
And out her heart he rent, yet left not so,
But made his heart into her breast to go;
All which was done without or pain or smart,
And forth he flies with heart exchanged for heart.

(Book II, stanzas 132-3)

If Sidnam could have brought himself to complete his version, it would rank among the most charming translations of a long poem in our language; unhappily, when he came to that part of the story which tells the infidelity of Criseyde, his disgust at her behaviour overcame him and he concluded his work at the end of Book III with a stanza all his own:

> But yet let him that list go on to tell
> The wanton slips of this deceitful dame,
> And what misfortunes afterwards befell
> Poor Troilus, who underwent the shame
> Of her misdeeds, though he deserved no blame;
> For I am loath to do true love that wrong,
> To make her fall the subject of my song.

Sidnam wrote no Preface or Dedication for his work, but contented himself with a rather haughty title-page:

A
Paraphrase
upon
The three first Bookes of
CHAUCERS
TROILUS AND CRESIDA
Translated into our Moderne English
For the satisfaction of those
Who either cannot, or will not, take ye paines to understand
The Excellent Authors
Farr more Exquisite, and significant Expressions
Though now growen obsolete, and
out of use.
By
J:S:

Semel insaniuimus omnes.
Quas habeat Meretrix merie-tricks, ediscere Noli
Namque mere trux est, cum meretrice jocus.[1]

1.   *I would not learn what merry tricks*
            Are practised by a meretrix,
            For it is barbarous at best
            With prostitutes to sport and jest.

Sidnam, it seems to me, is a little peremptory in tone where he speaks of *'those who either cannot, or will not, take the paines'* to understand Chaucer in the original; it rings a little like a Mosaic reprimand: *Hear now, ye rebels; must we bring you water out of this rock?* In the seventeenth century the texts, glossaries and notes available were few and unreliable; there was plenty of excuse for finding Chaucer difficult. In our own days the case is altered. Chaucer's text, skilfully edited with all the apparatus required for understanding it, is easily available in a variety of editions, and all who wish to read him in the original may do so at the expense of a little time and trouble. The first reading of Chaucer's poem in this way is one of the greatest experiences in the whole range of English reading.

But because in our time there are many more fine things to read and many more necessary subjects of study than there were in Sidnam's day, there may still be some 'who cannot or will not' find the time or energy to attempt Chaucer in the original, and it seems fair to offer them an easier alternative. In the version here offered the main loss is the incomparable music of his language. There is no way in which this loss can be supplied. Our tongue has simply lost that kind of music. But in all other respects I have been as exactly faithful to the imagery, meaning and feeling of the poem as I could – that is, in so far as I have been able to discern and express them in modern English. Here and there I have lost a thought in Chaucer, here and there I have added one; these departures however are few and slight, and were occasioned by the difficulty of the stanza form.

3. The Problem of Tone

The most difficult problem was that of *tone*. There are many tones of voice in the plentiful conversations and soliloquies of the poem, and these are often shot through with ironies, sometimes consciously – that is, the speaker is well aware of his double meanings – and sometimes unconsciously – that is, when the speaker means one thing, but Chaucer intends the reader to understand another; for instance, Criseyde calculates her love in a way in which Troilus never does; yet she does not think of herself as less in love than he is, though the male reader may think her so; the way her mind works is different, and the tone of her talk is different in consequence; not that she uses a different vocabulary, but that she has a cautious femininity of approach, never heard in Troilus, who is a great self-dramatist in the romantic style and an utter innocent at the same time; one might say of him his poses are spontaneous and sincere, however foolish or theatrical; and they are masculine, if emotional, and in accordance with his code. But of course Chaucer is holding up the code itself for judgement. Criseyde, however, has devious depths.

Pandarus offers other difficulties to the translator; it is a great temptation, and all too easy, to exaggerate his mannerisms and moods, volatile as he is. He has a comic zest that lends itself to double rhymes, and these, though they help (if not too frequently used) to make up for the loss of feminine endings that grace so many of Chaucer's rhyme-words, can sometimes suggest Victorian pantomime effects, which I have studied to avoid; yet I have taken some risks in trying to recreate the tone and taste of his ever-varied moods.

All these individual voices have to be subordinated to the tone of the poem as a whole, and to the supreme voice which is Chaucer's again, a many-mooded thing, pregnant with irony and with sympathy too. These are the things I have found most difficult and I am aware that in so long and subtle and lovely a poem I cannot always have succeeded, even to the limited degree within which success is possible. There is, however, one respect in which I must attempt to forestall criticism, and I have separated it into an Appendix of its own, on slang.

4. Slang and Colloquial Expressions

Readers will be struck by modernisms which they will perhaps attribute to an effort on my part to persuade readers that Chaucer was more 'modern' than he is. But I must assure them that the modernisms I have used are either Chaucer's exact phrases, or

very close renderings of them; here are a few, with the parallel
expressions in Chaucer:

BOOK I

13, 7 Skin and bones – *fel and bones*
89, 7 How the devil can you – *How devel maistow*
113, 2 As Tityus does – the fellow down in Hell – *he Ticius in
Helle*
119, 7 Drag me in pieces, hang me on a tree – *To pieces do me
drawe, and sithen honge*

BOOK II

13, 3 'Ey, uncle, – *Ey, uncle,*
44, 3 The worst is over – *the werste of this is do*
45, 2 Come off it, tell me what it's all about – *Come of, and
telle me what it is*
135, 2 And said 'Who's this that's taken such a beating? – *And
seyde thus: 'who hath ben wel ibete*
137, 2 It's all arranged; you can put on your hat – *And don
thyn hood; thy nedes spedde be.*
154, 6 And lied like thunder – *and leigh ful loude*
159, 1 I hop along behind – *I hoppe alwey byhynde.*

BOOK III

28, 1 But ho! No more of this – *But ho, no more as now*
46, 5 And knew no more of them than my old hat – *Ne knewe
hem more than myn olde hat*
70, 4 So on he shoved – *He shof ay on*
122, 7 Delays aren't worth a blackberry anyway – *Nay, swich
abodes ben nat worth an hawe*
158, 7 And stop this fuss – *and stynt al this fare*
167, 5 Not worth a bean – *nat worth a beene*

BOOK V

15, 3 If I should speak of love, or make it tough – *If that I
speke of love, or make it tough*

Examples of these modernisms can easily be multiplied. The most interesting and intriguing of them all occurs in the serious and beautiful hymn that opens Book III. After a celebration of how Love, in Heaven, in Hell, in earth and the salt sea, makes its power felt, Chaucer goes on to praise Love's power of keeping realms and homes at unity, and speaks of it as knowing the secret natures – 'thilke covered qualitee' – of things, that make men wonder why people fall in love; what is it that makes them do so? Why does this fish come to the weir and not another? Here is Chaucer's stanza at this point in the hymn, and I have put the phrase I wish to discuss into italics:

> Ye holden regne and hous in unitee;
> Ye sothfast cause of frendship ben also;
> Ye knowe al thilke covered qualitee
> Of thynges, which that folk on wondren so,
> *Whan they kan nought construe how it may jo*
> She loveth hym, or whi he loveth here,
> As whi this fissh, and naught that, comth to were.

There is no parallel for the phrase *how it may jo*, either in Chaucer or in any other writer; *jo* is what is called 'a nonce word' that occurs nowhere else. The *Oxford English Dictionary* does not quote this passage, but quotes two late sixteenth-century uses of a word *jo* – a noun, not a verb – which clearly means *pleasure* – as follows:

> 1560   Hir court hes jo, quhair evir they go
> 1567   Now lat vs sing with myrth and jo

Skeat thinks there is a connexion between these uses of the word and Chaucer's; he derives it from Old French *joer* to play, hence to play a game, hence to make a move, hence to come about, or happen. This would be a strange shift of meaning, but it would give what seems a reasonable interpretation of Chaucer's word.

On the other hand R. K. Root would like to connect it with American *gee*, in current colloquial use (as he asserts) meaning 'fit, suit, or agree'. Like Skeat's, this interpretation seems to hover near the meaning embedded in Chaucer's phrase, which also seems very colloquial; I ventured to render the passage:

Thou knowest all that covered quality
Of things, that makes us wonder what or who
It is that *makes them tick*; where is the clue
Why she loves him, or he loves there or here,
And why this fish, not that, comes to the weir.

but having done so I felt qualms about this commonplace metaphor from a clock, at present in slang use, at least in England. I wrote therefore to Professors Kurath and Kuhn at Ann Arbor who are engaged in compiling a Middle English Dictionary that aims at completeness and accuracy, but which (when I wrote) had not reached the letter J, and I asked their opinion. Professor Kuhn most kindly replied, confirming the derivation from Old French *joer*, repeating that Chaucer's word was a nonce word, and making the interesting suggestion that, whether it was to be regarded as slang or not, it was perhaps a word confined to the Chaucer set. He was kind enough to add that he thought 'makes them tick' reflected Chaucer's intention admirably; so I have dared to retain it, aware that some will find it shocking; but it fits into the colloquial tone from which Chaucer seldom strays very far, since he writes his best poetry as if he were addressing an audience of princely friends in person.

Chaucer

THE CANTERBURY TALES

Translated by Nevill Coghill

The Canterbury Tales stands conspicuous among the great
literary achievements of the Middle Ages. Told by a jovial
procession of pilgrims – knight, priest, yeoman, miller, or
cook – as they ride towards the shrine of Thomas à Becket,
they present a picture of a nation taking shape. The tone of
this never-resting comedy is, by turns, learned, fantastic,
lewd, pious, and ludicrous. 'Here,' as John Dryden said,
'is God's plenty!'

Geoffrey Chaucer began his great task in about 1386. This
version in modern English, by Nevill Coghill, preserves the
freshness and racy vitality of Chaucer's narrative.

CLASSICS IN TRANSLATION
IN PENGUINS

☐ *Remembrance of Things Past* **Marcel Proust**
☐ Volume One: *Swann's Way, Within a Budding Grove*
☐ Volume Two: *The Guermantes Way, Cities of the Plain*
☐ Volume Three: *The Captive, The Fugitive, Time Regained*

Terence Kilmartin's acclaimed revised version of C. K. Scott Moncrieff's original translation, published in paperback for the first time.

☐ *The Canterbury Tales* **Geoffrey Chaucer**

'Every age is a Canterbury Pilgrimage . . . nor can a child be born who is not one of these characters of Chaucer' – William Blake

☐ *Gargantua & Pantagruel* **Rabelais**

The fantastic adventures of two giants through which Rabelais (1495–1553) caricatured his life and times in a masterpiece of exuberance and glorious exaggeration.

☐ *The Brothers Karamazov* **Fyodor Dostoevsky**

A detective story on many levels, profoundly involving the question of the existence of God, Dostoevsky's great drama of parricide and fraternal jealousy triumphantly fulfilled his aim: 'to find the man in man . . . [to] depict all the depths of the human soul.'

☐ *Fables of Aesop*

This translation recovers all the old magic of fables in which, too often, the fox steps forward as the cynical hero and a lamb is an ass to lie down with a lion.

☐ *The Three Theban Plays* **Sophocles**

A new translation, by Robert Fagles, of *Antigone, Oedipus the King* and *Oedipus at Colonus*, plays all based on the legend of the royal house of Thebes.

CLASSICS IN TRANSLATION
IN PENGUINS

☐ *The Treasure of the City of Ladies*
   Christine de Pisan

This practical survival handbook for women (whether royal courtiers or prostitutes) paints a vivid picture of their lives and preoccupations in France, *c.* 1405. First English translation.

☐ *La Regenta* **Leopoldo Alas**

This first English translation of this Spanish masterpiece has been acclaimed as 'a major literary event' – *Observer*. 'Among the select band of "world novels" . . . outstandingly well translated' – John Bayley in the *Listener*

☐ *Metamorphoses* **Ovid**

The whole of Western literature has found inspiration in Ovid's poem, a golden treasury of myths and legends that are linked by the theme of transformation.

☐ *Darkness at Noon* **Arthur Koestler**

'Koestler approaches the problem of ends and means, of love and truth and social organization, through the thoughts of an Old Bolshevik, Rubashov, as he awaits death in a G.P.U. prison' – *New Statesman*

☐ *War and Peace* **Leo Tolstoy**

'A complete picture of human life;' wrote one critic, 'a complete picture of the Russia of that day; a complete picture of everything in which people place their happiness and greatness, their grief and humiliation.'

☐ *The Divine Comedy: 1 Hell* **Dante**

A new translation by Mark Musa, in which the poet is conducted by the spirit of Virgil down through the twenty-four closely described circles of hell.

ENGLISH AND AMERICAN LITERATURE IN PENGUINS

☐ *Emma* **Jane Austen**

'I am going to take a heroine whom no one but myself will much like,'
declared Jane Austen of Emma, her most spirited and controversial
heroine in a comedy of self-deceit and self-discovery.

☐ *Tender is the Night* **F. Scott Fitzgerald**

Fitzgerald worked on seventeen different versions of this novel, and
its obsessions – idealism, beauty, dissipation, alcohol and insanity –
were those that consumed his own marriage and his life.

☐ *The Life of Johnson* **James Boswell**

Full of gusto, imagination, conversation and wit, Boswell's immortal
portrait of Johnson is as near a novel as a true biography can be, and
still regarded by many as the finest 'life' ever written. This shortened
version is based on the 1799 edition.

☐ *A House and its Head* **Ivy Compton-Burnett**

In a novel 'as trim and tidy as a hand-grenade' (as Pamela Hansford
Johnson put it), Ivy Compton-Burnett penetrates the facade of a
conventional, upper-class Victorian family to uncover a chasm of
violent emotions – jealousy, pain, frustration and sexual passion.

☐ *The Trumpet Major* **Thomas Hardy**

Although a vein of unhappy unrequited love runs through this novel,
Hardy also draws on his warmest sense of humour to portray
Wessex village life at the time of the Napoleonic wars.

☐ *The Complete Poems of Hugh MacDiarmid*

☐ Volume One
☐ Volume Two

The definitive edition of work by the greatest Scottish poet since
Robert Burns, edited by his son Michael Grieve, and W. R. Aitken.